Nom de Plume

An Extraordinary Life—Vol 1

Also by Djuna Shellam

The Em Suite Series

**The Incredible Transformations of
Alice Hollywood**—*Book One*

Mackenna on the Edge—*Book Two*

Prairie Fire—*Book Three*

Dot in the Weeds—*Book Four*

For information, please contact:

Magnhild Press PO Box 414, Coeur d'Alene, ID 83816

Interior and Cover Design by JL Magnhild

Portrait by Kristina Kauffman

First Magnhild Press Edition: 2020

Baskerville Typeface 11.5 pt

Paperback ISBN: 978:1-953819-00-0

Digital   ISBN: 978:1-953819-01-7

Acknowledgements

If I could, I'd personally thank every single person I know, and everyone who's been in or passed through my life, as you all have, in some measure, contributed to my work. Consciously or unconsciously, you have given me a mannerism, a word, a look, a way of speaking… ah, the list is endless. Thank you. My characters live because of parts of you.

Many thanks to my dear, long-time friend, Kristina Kauffman, a talented artist.

Loads of appreciation to T.M. who has been an unwavering fan and constant patron of this writer. I'm humbled by your generosity.

Shout outs and heaps of gratitude to Jarrick, Cryssida, X and Barrister… your time, input and encouragement for this book mean so much to me.

Whoever invented the internet, I thank you! It is the greatest creative writing tool ever invented. Without it, this would be a far different book —if even a book. You, dear internet, have saved me thousands of dollars and endless flight hours (and since flying is not my thing), my gratitude is… well, unending.

Finally, to my true blue friends who have always allowed me to wax on about my current work in progress without complaint, I thank you. I know my projects can seem like my whole life while I'm in the middle of them, and they're all I think or talk about, so your loving patience is so very much appreciated. Without you, I expect I'd already have gone mad without the opportunities you've given me to share what's knocking around in my head.

Nom de Plume

An Extraordinary Life—Vol 1

A Novel by

Djuna Shellam

Magnhild Press

Dedication

This book could not have happened without my loving mom "by my side." Though she's been physically gone from this earth for half a decade now, she is with me always, whispering encouragement and praise, particularly as I write.

She always believed in me; and, not only knew I could do this, but she expected it. Without her boundless love and unwavering faith instilled in me, my books would forever remain nothing but ideas and unrealized dreams.

As always, Mommy, I dedicate this book to you.

Nom de Plume

An Extraordinary Life—Vol 1

In loving Memory of Djuna Moon, and B. & L.

Preface

My name is Djuna Shellam. Rather, Djuna Shellam is the name of my nom de plume. Nom de plume is an assumed name much like nom de guerre; though, *de plume* relates specifically to one who writes. Simply put, it's a pen name. My actual name is… well, let's just say it's not for public consumption. There's so little privacy left in this modern, tech-connected world, I'm determined to cling to whatever semblance of it I can, thus the nom de plume.

As the moniker implies, I'm a writer, mostly writing about the human condition. I'm an explorer, of sorts, in that I explore the complex realm of human nature. I consider myself a private person, but since publishing my novels, too frequently, I'm asked about myself and my life. My life is uneventful and, dare I say, mediocre. But, Djuna Shellam's? Ah well, now that's another kettle of fish as she's had quite a life. She's travelled extensively, knocking around this planet, fictionally, for six and a half decades. As such, she has a story or several to tell. Djuna's own story is fantastic and heartbreaking, but more than anything, it's quite extraordinary.

As my nom de plume's story is not ordinary by any measure, it's rather difficult to tell in snippets and soundbites. After much deliberation, it seemed rather fitting I should share her life and adventures in a book—or several. Perhaps in doing so, it'll answer persistent queries about the writer, Djuna Shellam.

You should know straight away, however, what I have to tell you is not for the faint of heart. Djuna's story involves instances of unspeakable violence, despicable and abhorrent acts, heartbreak and tragedy. If you believe any of the aforementioned might upset you, or trigger some visceral reaction, you'd best avoid the story altogether. I hope you don't, but I feel it's important to give full disclosure up front. I'll also leave it to you to decide what of Djuna's story belongs to her, and what is mine. We are, after all, one in the same, yes? If you pay close attention, you might find inspirations for Djuna's novels.

As this volume is set in Australia and Ireland, throughout Djuna's story, should you run into words, phrases or terms of which you are unfamiliar or are unsure how to pronounce, I've included a translations page at the end of the story.

Part One

Nom de Plume

∞ ∞ ∞ ∞ ∞

Until my early twenties, Siobhán Aoife O'Shea was my name. Throughout the years I've adopted several names for as many reasons; but today, I am the writer known as Djuna Shellam. Why Djuna Shellam? I'll just say it *might* be an anagram—then again… it might not. As my Da used to say to me, and always with a mischievous chuckle, his eyes twinkling, "Don't ever let people know ya, Siobhán. Change your name like your knickers, girl—*at least* twice a year!" Rest assured, dear readers, my knickers are fresh every day. My identity, however, hasn't changed near as often as twice a year, but unusual circumstances in my life have led me to take the gist of my da's suggestion to heart.

Fairly certain I was born in Australia, for a long time, I had no idea when I was born or even how old I was. My parents had raised me in the Australian countryside, but beyond that, I knew nothing until after I left our farm for good. I was about sixteen when I took off. Up to that point, though I was unaware of it, I'd lived quite an extraordinary and secluded existence. As a wee child, the O'Sheas, who I knew only as Mam and Da, often told me how I was born in our barn, delivered from Mam's belly, and by Da's own hands.

Oh, it was a fine story. I loved hearing it, and never tired of it. You'll soon discover, as I eventually did, their story of my birth, and most else in my young life, was a monumental tale. The tallest of tall tales, in fact, and an earth-shaking discovery for me when I realised it. It took many, many years for me to overcome the shock and disbelief of it. Ultimately I did, leaving it all behind me. Until now, I've not really looked back. As I tell my story, I'll attempt to reference my age, or what I think it might have been, or the approximate year; understanding in most cases they'll both be guesses or suppositions.

∞ ∞ ∞ ∞ ∞

My mam and da, were slight, wiry people. Da had black hair and dark eyes. Mam's hair was a light brown that lightened in the summer, but her eyes were blue. Sometimes, amid a story or conversation, Da would roar with laughter and proclaim we were Black Irish. Mam would say, no Da was the Black Irish, and he would say since Mam married him she got Black and because I was theirs, I was Black, too. Though I was never sure what they meant by it, that the very idea of it filled them with such mirth, I concluded it was a pretty fine thing that's what we were.

My da was taller than mam, but not by much; and he wore a considerable moustache he'd shape with some waxy muck, twirling the ends until they pointed out as if magnificent wings. Sometimes, for a laugh, he'd let me twirl them, which, I have to say, was quite entertaining for me. Whenever I think of him now, along with his spectacular facial hair, what stands out most vividly were his hairy arms and bushy eyebrows, which fascinated me to no end. Straight and shiny hair fell over his shoulders, though mostly Da kept it tied into a ponytail with a piece of tanned leather. It was black and lightly peppered with grey.

His eyes were deep grey, that would sometimes go almost black, depending upon the light or his mood. A pronounced extension of his forehead, Da's nose was slightly crooked with a distinct, jagged scar across the bridge. I'd ask him if his nose was always that way? With a wink and a touch of pride, he'd remind me it was from an accident while building our house, "*With me own bare hands, lass.*"

I especially favoured Da's smooth cheeks and chin in the mornings, right after he shaved. With a straight-razor sharpened with a thick leather strop, he'd quickly drag the blade to his right, then left across the leather several times back, then forth, slow and sure as part of his morning ritual. To this very day, all I have to do is close my eyes and I can hear the blade pulled against the strop, as if he were standing right next to me. I so loved watching Da shave his tan, weathered face. He could make his bone-handled razor do his bidding without ever drawing a single drop of blood, not even once. I'd watch him, spellbound.

The scent of his shaving soap, another part of his morning habit, also remains with me after all these many years. As the earthy aroma filled the room, I'd experience such a great and overwhelming sense of love and contentment. Late in the afternoons, his beard would rebel against the elapsing day. I didn't care one bit for his sharp and scratchy whiskers against my tender young skin. He knew it, too, teasing me mercilessly as he'd chase me, threatening to rub his scruffy face against mine as I squealed.

My da wasn't a substantial man, considering the back-breaking work he often did around the farm. His muscles were of the long, sinewy type and strong. Not a tall man, with somewhat narrow shoulders that slouched, it was almost as if my da's worn leather suspenders pulled him right over, making him seem even shorter.

I cherished everything about my da, but I loved his hands the most. Large for his body, at least I always thought as much, they were a right obsession for me. Powerful, and rough from working around the farm they were; yet deft, graceful and fast as lightning, in particular when he'd show me his endless and magical collection of card tricks. Though his skin seemed coarse to me, Da's hands could be like giant, gentle and loving mittens. My hand in my da's was heaven to me, leaving me feeling safe.

If I got hurt, needing his comfort, he'd quickly gather me up with his big mitts and hold me right close to him, stroking my skin to soothe me. Truth be told, Da was always the one I wanted when I'd fall and scrape a knee, get a scratch, or any of the other myriad childhood injuries or illnesses for what one might want comfort.

Far less compassionate than my da, my mam would look at my injury, scoffing, "You're not gonna die today, Siobhán. No need for tears now. Wash yourself and get back to yer work." But, my da? Oh, he'd pick me up, cuddle me close to him, with the faint odor of tobacco, and say, *"You'll be just fine, wee girl. Wait 'n see. Hmmm…? Have I ever lied t'ya?"* His soft, yet deep timbre voice could soothe me like no other. From the moment Da spoke, comforting me in an instant, my condition always improved.

When I think of how he must have been off the farm, the one thing about him that stood out was his large and inviting smile, and hearty laugh. Both were likely winning attributes to strangers. When he laughed, Da's large, crooked and pale yellow teeth would show from behind his whiskers. His chest puffed with pride, he'd often brag about how he still had all of his teeth. I always thought it was a right peculiar thing for him to say. Why would anyone *not* have all of their teeth, I wondered? I never asked, but I found it a puzzling concept until I found myself in the outside world with other people. Soon enough, exposed to all levels of dental neglect, decay and toothlessness, I understood his pride.

A hand-rolled cigarette, or sometimes a small brown cigar, were as a part of Da as any physical characteristic. One or the other was ever-present, clenched between his teeth at the corner of his mouth. It amazed me that Da's smoking devices never got in his way, no matter the task at hand, managed with a skill I found unduly impressive. In my entire life, I've never seen such clean and artful management of a habit that, for most who smoke, can be a dirty and dangerous one, with dropped ashes and burn holes evidence of such.

More than any descriptive I have for him, Da was a nice, loving man. I was glad he was my da and no one else's.

Beautiful and sweet, my mam had a personality and physicality both similar and dissimilar to Da's. Though petite, I suppose you could call her body average. Despite her size, she was a hearty woman in every way. It was a rare occurrence for her to ask Da or me for assistance.

In warmer weather, Mam's daily attire was a simple cotton shift dress, sleeveless with a length just below her knees. In colder seasons, she'd wear dungarees and a wool jumper. In the house, no matter the season, she wore moccasin loafers. For working outside, she'd put on a pair of well-worn desert boots.

Unless plaited into a single braid, or wrapped into a neatly braided bun on the top of her head, Mam's slightly wavy and shiny hair hung down just past the small of her back. A shock of white hair about two-and-a-half centimetres went from above her left eye to halfway down her back. Her eyes were a brilliant pale blue that could flash crystal with her mood. Dark eyebrows framed her eyes like arches and almost, but not quite, joined over the bridge of a nose I considered strong, dignified. Not pert, but also not too large, Mam's nose fit her face perfectly.

Like my da, Mam enjoyed a good laugh, hers being hearty and boisterous. She'd often play tricks on Da just to give herself a piece of fun. They always had a magnificent time together. Not once did

I ever hear or see them argue or even use cruel or disrespectful language with each other.

Mam also had a great and captivating smile, accentuated by a fairly decent gap between her two front teeth. Some might say her teeth were a flaw in her beauty, but I thought the gap made her even more beautiful. Although, once I entered the real world as I call it, based on other people's definition of beauty, I realised some might consider my parents homely or even unattractive, particularly by those who didn't know them, judging them by looks alone. But, where Mam and Da lacked conventional popular looks, they made up for it with an overabundance of charm.

Indeed, my mam and da were quite a charming pair. In fact, I believe they charmed me into proper behavior. Not only did they not use unseemly or unkind words with each other, but I heard nothing but kindness from either of them, even when I fully expected otherwise because of my misbehaviour. Oh, to be sure, me being a child prone to do childish things, they'd get cross with me. I'd get a good chewing out and sometimes extra chores, but that was the worst I'd *ever* experience from them.

As I mentioned, Mam and Da would often tell me how much I favoured them, though at some point, I towered over them by a head. Mam always kept my hair short, quickly snatching up remains from the floor when she'd give me a haircut, mumbling something about spells being cast. When I'd try to glimpse my clippings, Mam would swiftly admonish me.

"Siobhán! Don't look! D'spirits'll catch ya! Ya don't want none of dat, girl," she'd warn.

Because I didn't know any different, I thought my parents were normal, as was *my* life. That the books I read about other people and families were pure fiction, the oddity, not the norm. Mam and Da were always kind to me. They also took great care to educate me in all areas of life, whether it was outside around the farm, or learning about the world from our expansive library. Their own competencies and education limited, they still taught me everything, including how to read.

Early in my education, especially once I began reading on my own, I soon surpassed their meager abilities. Particularly when they needed information from one of the more advanced books in the library, I became *their* teacher! I often wondered if their interest in teaching me might have been less about educating me and more about improving themselves.

Once I began reading, I started noticing the way we spoke didn't match how some of the words were spelled. Obviously, the English language is fraught with inconsistencies and confusing spelling and pronounciations, but I was particularly curious about 'th' words, or 'ing' words where we dropped our gs. I once ask Mam about it, how to say th words, and why there was a *g* on *ing* words, but we didn't say it that way, but… she didn't know. Actually, she didn't seem to fully comprehend the question.

Later, of course, I learned that think is not tink, or that, they, them, etcetera, is not dat, dey and dem. Eventually, I learned the h and ing gs are silent in the Irish dialect of my parents'. It took me a while after I entered the real world to adjust my speaking. It wasn't that I wanted to erase my history, but that I had a strong desire to speak as correctly as possible, and not be identified or judged by some dialectic region. I wanted to blend in, not stand out.

Since before I can even remember, I helped Da on the outside and Mam on the inside in every way needed to maintain our farm. I was both their daughter, and the son they never had. Da taught me to care for the animals, the machinery, the house; how to hunt and butcher, build things, and everything else you can imagine one would need to know to operate a farm.

From Mam I learned how to take care of the inside of the house; doing the wash, cleaning, canning, cooking, sewing and various other necessary homesteading skills. By the age of ten years old, there wasn't much I couldn't do around the farm by myself.

From an early age, they had already begun leaving me to care of our property on my own—sometimes for weeks when they'd leave to "get supplies."

Beyond the meager information my parents meted out, I had very little understanding of who they were. From time to time, they'd mention Ireland and their families, but without further elaboration. If I dared inquire, they'd change the subject. I didn't learn their given names until after they'd passed, as they only ever referred to each other as Mam and Da, or Mammy and Dada. I couldn't say how old they were, if they had siblings, or how they even met. Remember, I didn't even how old *I* was!

They never celebrated their own birthdays or mine, though sometimes they'd allude to me being certain ages. Because I learned about the world from reading, I was well aware of the concept of birthdays, so I'd pester them about when I was born.

"How old am I, Mammy? When was I born, Dada? Shouldn't I have a birtday?" I'd ask too often to count, with always the same reply from both: "You're here, ain't ya. Dere's plenty time t'worry about all dat. 'n who gives a monkey's, anyway? Birtdays? Rubbish. Mebbe someday…"

I knew our last name as they would often address me using my entire name: Siobhán Aoife O'Shea in conversation. "Siobhán Aoife O'Shea… it's time t'milk d'goats. Best get t'bed naw, Siobhán Aoife O'Shea. Siobhán Aoife O'Shea, go fetch yer Da for supper," etcetera. Once they passed on, I ultimately learned the answers to certain questions I either didn't think to ask, or dared not ask.

Homestead

∞ ∞ ∞ ∞ ∞

Our farm was located in the countryside of Victoria, Australia, and covered a tremendous expanse of land. Right in the middle of it stood our substantial and beautiful three-storey house, ruggedly built in the popular Arts and Crafts style of the early Twentieth century. An abundance of wood beams and trim—all hand-hewn, allegedly by Da, who claimed to be a trained architect and builder —and a plethora of built-in cabinets throughout made our home warm and inviting. Absent, however, were modern conveniences such as indoor plumbing or electricity.

If not for our library books, I'd never have known such things even existed until forced to venture out into the world on my own. I cannot imagine how shocked I might have been when I entered the actual world had I not gained knowledge from our significant collection of books.

The library, stocked floor to ceiling with every sort of book you can imagine, took up half the house and dominated my isolated world. French doors with decorative stained glass closed off the space to the rest of the home. With its ceiling taller than most of the rest of the house, the library didn't have a proper second story. A catwalk above what would have been the second floor wrapped around the entire perimeter of the room, allowing for even more books reaching midway up to what would have been the top of a third floor. Above those books were large paintings from what appeared to be late 1800s and early 1900s by unknown artists.

A wooden ladder reaching almost to the underneath of the catwalk to access first and second floor books, and a short stepladder were used to reach books on the catwalk. My favourite place on the entire farm was that room. It's where I learned about other people, the world, history, art and all else I couldn't learn from my parents.

We stored home-canned goods, root vegetables, and dry goods in our cellar. On the first level our kitchen opened to an enormous living area filled with over-stuffed furniture, hand-built tables and stained glass oil lamps. The centrepiece of the room was a floor to ceiling rock fireplace large enough to cook in if we chose to do so, though we used it to heat the house in winter.

A cast iron, wood-burning cookstove, and an enormous claw-foot bathtub stood near the kitchen side door. We didn't have running water or indoor plumbing, so the tub sat in the kitchen where we'd more easily heat water for our routine weekly baths. A wood screen maintained our privacy on bath day. We might have to take more than one bath in a week, depending on what kind of mess we'd been in around the farm, but mostly it was a weekly event. The toilet, or what we called the Jacks, resided outside in its own small structure—what Americans call an outhouse—and sat less than a hundred metres from the house.

Our stove, a Homewood Matriarch model from New Zealand was over a metre and a half wide. It required a certain finesse with which to cook and bake, but it also served double duty. It cooked our food, including Mam's canning. If we ever needed to, it could feed an army, but it was only ever the three of us. Also, in the winter, we kept it fired up constantly, mostly to keep us warm once the fire in the hearth extinguished for the evening. Just before sunrise, we'd fire up the stove again.

On the second floor, there were three rooms. Two were about the same size. The third was more than twice the size of the other two combined. That's where my parents slept. I slept in the room furthest from theirs. Mam's sewing took up the room between us. Above the second floor was The Attic. They told me they kept old furniture and other uninteresting things there. They kept The Attic locked up tight, or so they told me, expressly forbidding me to go near it, let alone enter it. So dire was their warning, I always kept my distance from the stairs leading to The Attic .

Evening lighting for us consisted of candles, the fireplace, and kerosene lamps. By sundown, we were likely in bed already, and up with or before the sun rose again. Sometimes, though, once in my room and in bed, I'd read by the dim, flickering light of a candle. True enough, I'd pay dearly the next day from lack of sleep as I've always been the type who latches onto a book and reads it straight through, even if it means reading through the night. I'm sure reading by candlelight wasn't fantastic for my eyes as I definitely felt the body fatigue and eye strain the following day. It's funny how some things never change—I was that way then, and after all these many years hence, am still that way now.

We kept track of time by an antique oak grandfather clock in the living area. It had a calendar and the moon phases. It was a beautiful masterpiece of craftsmanship, made by a watchmaker named Nicolas Blondel. Its majestic bell chiming every hour and half hour of my life was a constant reminder of the steady pace of time. Each morning, without fail, Da would wind the key to ensure our timekeeper kept on track. Whatever year we were in remained a mystery to me until I first ventured off the farm.

Our farm was perfect for our needs, with a dozen chickens we called chooks or chookies and their rooster, several ducks, two geese, a dairy cow, a small herd of cattle twenty to thirty, two mischievous milk goats, a billy goat, six pigs, six sheep, and our horses. We had both working horses and riding horses. Our property was quite expansive, so the only way to properly access the land was by horseback. Da once told me our property covered over four thousand hectares of countryside, which, he explained, might be as big as the earth.

I wasn't sure exactly what a hectare was, but Da convinced me what we owned was substantial. In fact, it's fifteen square miles, or almost forty square kilometres. Though some refer to our Australian countryside as the Outback; in fact, in Victoria, the part of Australia where we lived, it's more farmland than wilderness. Though some would argue otherwise, we considered the Outback far less inhabitable than where we resided. The remote location of our land seemed a reasonable explanation for our lack of visitors—we were too difficult to find in the countryside's vastness.

Not quite ninety metres from the house, a water pump provided us with ample water for our needs—drinking, bathing, growing and cooking. We also had an underground catch water system where rainwater collected from the house gutters. A large above-ground tank in the back of the house was where we'd collect rainfall for our garden and watering the livestock.

We only had one motorized vehicle on the property—a dulled Kelly green behemoth 1952 Austin K4 Loadstar truck with a flat bed, dual rear tyres and a loud, strong diesel engine. In its former life it'd been a commercial truck. Mam and Da would drive it on their many excursions to parts unknown—at least unknown to me. Other than it, our only other means of travel were a rickety wheat wagon from the 1920s, and a creaky two-seater horse carriage.

Prior to losing my parents, I'd actually never travelled off our property, though from time to time, Da would give me rides on the carriage or the wagon around our land. Those times were thrilling for me. Once I could properly reach the pedals, he taught me to drive the Loadstar. It was a right hard thing to learn, but Da was a good and patient teacher. Soon after I began driving lessons, I could drive the truck as if I'd been born to it.

My Tree

∞ ∞ ∞ ∞ ∞

Not more than fifty or sixty metres from our house stood an enormous tree, easily twice as tall as our multistorey home. It had a significant canopy, providing delicious shade from the Australian summer sun. I can say with confidence it was an old tree, perhaps even ancient. When I wasn't helping Mam inside the house, or working outside with Da, I'd sit for hours staring up at that gigantic tree, all the while fantasizing about climbing to the top. This fixation of mine began at a young age, four, maybe younger, perhaps older. I'm just not sure when it started; nonetheless, I remember being utterly preoccupied by that bloody tree. *My* tree.

While staring at it, I'd calculate how I might get up to the first foothold, which for me was quite high. Because this preoccupation began when I was still wee, I had no means or mental acuity to figure out how to get myself into it. When exactly it finally came to me, I'm not sure, but one day I had one of those delightful "Aha!" moments. On that day, I finally got to climb my tree.

I'd left Mam busily putting up a sizeable crop of green beans, when for some inexplicable reason, she told me to get out of her hair and go occupy myself. Mam enjoyed the canning process and preferred to do it herself, which was fine by me. She knew I didn't care for it. Early on I found canning boring, and dare I say, right *tedious*. Da was somewhere out in the countryside searching for a lost calf, leaving me completely to my own devices.

Typically, Da was fastidious about his tools, but the day before, the ladder he'd used to get up onto the roof got left behind. As often happened, Mam must have called him into the house, distracting him. To my utter delight, I found it on the ground as if lying in wait just for me.

I was still a small child, so moving the long, heavy wooden ladder proved a bit of a challenge for me. Still, single-minded in my desire, I pulled, pushed and dragged that unwieldy thing over to my tree. I had a devil of a time propping it up, but once I figured out how to do it and set it in place, I wasted no time climbing up to the first branch. Unluckily, in my elated state, as I stepped from the ladder onto the branch, I inadvertently kicked the ladder away from the tree. With a sickening thud, it fell into the foot high grass, effectively hiding itself.

I might have been only three metres from the ground then, though when you're barely over a metre tall yourself, it can seem many times that. I only wasted a moment worrying about the ladder, as my sole intent was to climb to the absolute tippy top of my tree. As I climbed up, up and up, I had many branches from which to choose. I continued climbing with focused determination, my only aim being to get to the top. I never looked down, not even once. I don't recall being scared in the slightest going up, because I had a goal, and I meant to reach it!

It might have taken all of thirty minutes to an hour to make it as far as possible; but at a certain point, I realised I could go no further as the branches were far too thin to support my weight. From my vantage point, which would actually be an exaggeration as branches and leaves still surrounded me, blocking most of my view, I could see well across our property, and maybe even beyond. I can't say for sure as I didn't know where our farm actually began or ended.

The foliage hid our house from me, but through it I could still see farther than I had ever physically been. It was exhilarating! I could see in every direction, nothing but green, empty land dotted with trees and some hills here and there. We really were the only ones in the world! I'd never seen another human besides my parents in my life, so it seemed reasonable to me we would be the only people on earth. For a long while, I swayed gently in the breeze, clinging to a rather thin branch, reveling in my accomplishment. Satisfied with my achievement, I decided to climb back down. At that very moment, regret set in with a vengeance.

As I started down, I realised what a frightful folly it would be to even try. Looking down to find my footing, well, as soon as I saw how far up I'd gotten, that was it for me. Petrified, I could do nothing but cling to my spindly branch. I held on with every ounce of strength I had to keep from falling to my certain death as the realization of what I'd done overwhelmed me. I wanted to scream, but I knew it would be futile. Mam was busy in the kitchen and wouldn't hear me, and Da was likely somewhere far away. He wouldn't hear me, either.

With my feet perched on a branch just strong enough to hold me, I had wrapped my arms around an offshoot branch from that foothold. I waited and waited for them to miss me, to wonder where I was, to call out, anything... but I heard nothing. From time to time I'd whimper, berating myself for doing such a stupid thing and not telling Mam or Da what I planned to do. Well, naturally I didn't tell them of my plans as they would have quashed them immediately. So there I stood, stuck in my tree, hour after hour after hour, with nary a call out of my name from my parents.

Convinced I would die, either from a terrible fall when I got too tired to hang on, or from starvation and exposure, a sense of hopelessness began creeping in, permeating my entire being. When the sunset began, the temperature plummeted. Stuck up there for the better part of the day, I became drowsy and terribly cold. I am loath to admit; I wet my pants. Holding my water for as long as I could, I had no choice when it finally let go. Yet another blow to my ego, it only added to my extreme physical discomfort.

Soon, my feet and legs numbed, heightening my angst even more. Naturally, I worried if I fell asleep or lost all feeling in my legs, I would no doubt fall to earth, hitting each and every branch on the way down—indeed, a painful way to go.

Thankfully, shortly after sunset, my parents must have realised something was amiss when I didn't show up for supper. They came out to the area surrounding our house and immediately began calling for me. I could tell in their voices they feared dingoes had gotten me.

"Siobhán! Siobhán Aoife O'Shea! Where've ya got to, child? SIOBHÁN!"

My joy at hearing my name called was short-lived once they discovered me stranded somewhere near the top of the tree. They couldn't see me, nor I them, but once they found the ladder hidden in the tall grass and heard my distant whimpers from above, it confirmed their fears.

Da was none too happy having to climb the giant tree in the dark; and Mam, well, she was hopping mad, mostly, I suspect, because she was about scared to death. The difficulty, as Da quickly realised, was that he could not reach me to bring me down because the branches past a certain point could not bear *his* weight. To my misfortune, that point was far from me. Once that realization became clear to Da, words came out of his mouth I'd never heard before.

When he realised he could climb no higher, it was up to me to climb down to him, all the while trying not to plunge to the ground. I was so frightened I would fall, I wept like the wee girl I was. Wailing is probably a more apt description for what I did. At that point, I could not imagine why reaching the top had been so bloody important to me, and wished with every part of me I could go back in time and undo my spectacular mess. Fear and remorse overwhelmed me. If it was frightening during the day when I realised I couldn't go down, you can just imagine how terrifying it was in the pitch dark of the countryside, stuck at the top of a four-storey tree.

With continuous coaxing from both Da and Mam hollering from below, over the course of an hour, I somehow wriggled my way down to Da. It seemed like an eternity to me. Once I reached Da, he grabbed me ever so gruffly and hugged me so tight with one arm I could barely breathe. But I was glad, because I was finally in my da's protective arms. For the first time since I realised I'd become stranded atop my tree, I knew with certainty I would not die that day. Da had me climb onto his back where I clung to him, wrapping my arms around his neck in what I can only describe as a death grip, while he carefully brought us back down.

Thankfully, my parents were never physical with me with punishment. Nor did they yell at me. I got an earful of passionate scolding, for sure, but I was thankful I was still alive to hear it. They ran me ragged for the next month with extra chores piled on to even more chores. I never knew there was so much to do around the farm. In time it became quite apparent they'd put extra energy into finding unpleasant tasks for me, never letting me rest from the time I awoke, until I finally laid my head on my pillow at the end of each day.

From the day I conquered my tree and every day after, I never quite looked at it with the same fondness as I had prior to my misadventure. If I'm being completely honest, that harrowing experience produced more than a few nightmares for me. Despite my aversion to it, I will never forget that magnificent view—even through the leaves and branches—as far as my eyes could see, from my perch high atop my tree.

4

Pippa

∞ ∞ ∞ ∞ ∞

One day my da brought home a Blue Heeler/Border Collie mix puppy. By my calculations, I might have been ten years old. He said the pup would help him with the cattle when she grew up. The second I saw her, I fell in love. Oh, what a beautiful little ball of fur! She was mostly white with bluish freckles under her coat, a black mask and ears, and a fluffy tail. On the top of her head she had a bluish mark in the shape of a V. Her eyes were light blue, almost like Mam's, but not nearly as pale. At only a month old, she was such a wee little babe, and the runt of the litter. Da said the owner planned to put her down, thinking her too weak, but Da convinced him to let him take her instead. The thought of that precious little beauty being put down ran shivers down my spine.

Fortunately for me, Da made the fatal mistake of putting her into my eager arms. To hold her was thrilling! Oh, she was so soft and adorable, I almost couldn't contain my excitement. Her fur felt like heaven. She cuddled right into my body, laying her head in the crook of my arm, and fell right to sleep. Da kept calling her a wee pipsqueak and wanted to call her that, but I begged him not to. It wasn't a dignified name for such a sweet little being, though I wasn't exactly sure at the time why I objected so.

I held her in my arms, staring at her with wonder, trying to think of the perfect name for her. The name Pipsqueak got me to thinking of the Pippi Longstocking book we had in the library, but the tiny creature in my arms didn't seem like a Pippi. Then it came to me—*the* perfect name.

"What about Pippa, Dada?" I asked, excited by my idea. "She looks like a Pippa, doesn't she? Heya, Pippa," I said in a high-pitched voice.

The little puppy opened her blue eyes, lifted her head and licked my arm as her fluffy tail wagged.

Da smiled and proclaimed, "Well, lass... seems she likes it. Ah... Pippa she is!"

Almost from our first day together, Pippa never left my side other than to go outside to do her business. No matter what I was doing, she was right with me. I never had to train her to stay by my side, she just did. If I told her to stay put, she'd do it until I called to her. It was uncanny how she listened to me, right from the start, almost as if she were human.

The closer we got, the more stern Da's warnings became.

"Naw," he'd say, with an unnerving seriousness, "dunna go gettin' too attached t'her Siobhán. When she's old enough, she'll be workin' wit me. She ain't a pet, lass. She's a workin' dog."

I'd nod as if I completely understood and accepted Pippa's future, even though the idea of her not being with me every second of the day and night filled me with a sense of dread I'd not yet experienced in my young life.

In the following weeks, Pippa's colouring changed, ever so subtly. Except for her chest and paws, everywhere her coat had been white eventually turned into a bluish silver. Her fluffy white tail turned into a striped raccoon tail. She was my little blue, black and white pup. And that's what I'd call her: my little Pippa BlueBlack'nWhite O'Shea. She loved her name. I'm sure of it.

Through the next months her black floppy ears made a few valiant attempts to stand up, showing the pink of the hidden side of her ears. Poor Pippa could never maintain them upright for more than a minute. Each time one would flip up only to flop back down, I'd laugh and laugh, making Pippa laugh, too. She'd dance around and yip at me, showing her pretty white teeth. That was how she laughed. Pippa had a lovely sense of humour. She knew I never meant to make fun of her. Don't ask me how I knew, I could just tell.

True to his word, six months after her arrival, Da took Pippa with him out to tend to his small herd of cattle. The first chance she got, Pippa ran away and came back to me. He tried again and again with the same result. Da would tie her to a lead when he'd go out on horseback, but she'd fight him the entire time until she'd slip the lead and run back home. If he took her in the Loadstar or on the wheat wagon, at the first opportunity she'd jump down and hightail it right back to me.

Mam thought it was the funniest thing she'd ever seen. The second Pippa showed up, and sat at my feet, Mam would howl with laughter. Da was none too pleased about the situation. He'd storm back to the house and give Pippa a right stern piece of his mind, but to no avail. He was not about to change her mind and keep her away from me. She was mine, and I was hers. Period.

After more than a dozen futile attempts, Da gave up. Several days after his last attempt, he took the Loadstar and left the farm by himself. A week later he returned with another pup—an eight-week-old full-blooded Blue Heeler. Da named him Dudley. I hated the name straight away because it didn't fit him. Da said the pup reminded him of a lad he knew in Ireland, so Dudley it was. Naturally I wondered how a dog could possibly remind one of a person, but I didn't question my da. It was his dog to name as he pleased. I'm only thankful *I* never reminded Da of anyone.

When he arrived, Dudley's colours had already changed, leaving him mostly blue with black and tan markings. Even at eight weeks old, it was abundantly clear he would also be a much bigger dog than Pippa. She wasn't even two Stones, closer to one and a half, in fact. Da's boy dog ended up being nearly twice her size. He was a right smart little chap with golden brown eyes, and sturdy, pointy ears. Sadly, he didn't have the raccoon tail like Pippa's as his had been docked shortly after birth. I felt terrible sorry for him not having a tail, though I never let him see it in my eyes. I always made it a point to tell him how handsome he was.

Every day, Da would scold me good-naturedly, "Y'keep your lil' pipsqueak away from m'boy Dudley, Siobhán. I'll not have d'likes of dat lil' mutt ruinin' an actual workin' dog!"

Learning from my experience with Pippa, Da kept Dudley by his side at all times. Like Pippa, Dudley immediately bonded with Da and became the working dog Da envisioned Pippa would be. I was concerned we'd have trouble between Pippa and Dudley, but the two dogs seemed oblivious to one another, never socialising or even fighting.

I worried some that Dudley, being a bigger dog, might hurt her. But I needn't have fretted. It was as if neither pup existed in the other's world. Although, early on, I will say that when he was still a puppy, Dudley would approach Pippa, but she never acknowledged him or his presence. I swear, it almost seemed she made a concerted effort to ignore him. You could tell he wanted her attention so much, but she wouldn't give it. Truth be told, I think Pippa thought she was a person and had nothing in common with Dudley the dog.

In time, smart as he was, Dudley stopped coming around. That Da neutered him early on might have had something to do with Dudley's disinterest. Three years later, though, when an angry bull kicked Dudley in the head, killing him instantly, Pippa went into what I would describe as a state of mourning. She behaved differently, acting listless and almost melancholy for nearly two weeks after. At first I worried she might be sick, but I soon realised she was grieving, which made me adore her even more.

I have so many stories I'd love to tell about my best friend, Pippa. But, then I'd be like the parent who goes on and on about their amazing, one in a million child. Not that I ever thought of Pippa as my child or my baby. No, she was my friend, companion; dare I say, my soulmate. Still, I try not to be that person who drones on and on about their pet. Instead, I'll tell you one of the more delightful stories I have that may give you a better idea about my Pippa's precious and funny personality.

Years before Pippa, Mam had made a cloth dolly for me. She thought I might like a baby to play with and to keep me company. She handed it to me, a gingerbread shaped thing made from burlap and wool, with button eyes, yarn for its hair and mouth. It even had a little pink dress on it. It was the ugliest thing I'd ever seen, but Mam seemed pleased by it.

I studied her when she gave it to me and asked, "What's dis yoke, Mammy?"

"'s a dolly, Siobhán."

"A dolly?" I held it away from my body as if it were contagious. "What…? What do I do wit it?"

Mam looked at me like I was strange. "Why, y'play wit it, lass. Like… y'know, like it's yer babby."

Now I looked at her and wrinkled my nose with disdain. "My… babby? But… I don't wanna babby."

With a scoff, Mam shook her head and went back to her work in the kitchen. "Do wit it what y'will, lass. I canna teach you what y'ought t'know yerself."

Once again, I examined the dolly in my hand, shrugged, then took it up to my room and threw it on my bureau where it stayed, untouched, for the next several years. Obviously, I didn't love it. I didn't hate it, either. I just didn't care.

Soon after Pippa arrived, she began biting me incessantly. Da said she was teething and needed something to chew on. Her sharp little teeth hurt me, so after too many puppy bites, out of frustration, I finally gave her Mam's dolly for my own relief.

"Here, Pippa. Bite Dolly!"

Thankfully, Pippa took the dolly from me, appearing relieved to have something in her mouth. Shortly after, Pippa and I came downstairs, Pippa with Dolly still in her mouth.

Upon seeing us, Mam said straight away, not happy to see the doll she'd made was in Pippa's mouth, "What d'devil, Siobhán Aoife O'Shea? You know dat pup's gonna tear yer dolly t'pieces— dat I took t'make for ya?"

Pippa sat down next to me, holding the dolly, mouthing her, but not tearing it in the least. "Look, Mammy. She's only holding it. She won't hurt it. I tink it makes her teet feel better."

"Oh, yeah, yeah. Famous last words, naw. Ya'll see soon enough when y'find yer dolly torn t'bits 'n pieces on d'floor."

Every day after that Dolly remained intact, Mam groused that soon... *soon* I'd see she got it right. She didn't. Pippa loved her dolly and took her everywhere. On our walks it was Pippa, Dolly and me, always. If I wanted to play with Pippa, she would put Dolly down, play with me, and when we quit playing, she'd run and gently pick Dolly up. If I tried playfully taking Dolly from her, Pippa would softly growl as her tail wagged. But if there was ever a danger of her harming Dolly by holding onto her too tightly, Pippa would relent and let go. Still, she wouldn't take her eyes off Dolly until Dolly was safely back in her mouth. When it was time to eat, Pippa would drop Dolly right by her bowl, eat her food, then pick Dolly up again when she finished.

Right from the start, Pippa slept next to my bed every night. For some strange reason, she wouldn't come up on the bed. She steadfastly refused. Even if I'd put her up there with me, she'd last not even a minute before she'd leap off and curl up on the floor beside my bed. Except for the time I fell ill and almost died. Then she jumped onto the bed on her own and didn't leave it for days and days until I finally got up.

Each morning we'd greet each other upon waking, me saying, "Good mornin', Pippa BlueBlack'nWhite O'Shea! Good mornin', Dolly Doll!" and Pippa, holding Dolly with her mouth, would push Dolly against me as she made little soft barks, wagging not just her tail, but her entire body.

That's just one example of the funny things about Pippa, and why I adored her so completely. Throughout her life, though Pippa was especially gentle with her, each year Dolly would need a bit of tending to in the way of cleaning and small repairs. Those times were hard on Pippa as she would pace back and forth, her watchful eyes never leaving her dolly until I finished. When I'd finally return Dolly to her, Pippa could not have been happier, running around and jumping in the air with her beloved dolly in her mouth.

Education

∞ ∞ ∞ ∞ ∞

Not too long before Mam and Da left me on my own for the first time, I got my first lesson in self-defence. One morning after breakfast, Da got up from the table and grabbed his rifle from where it stood, propped up by the back door.

Da said to me, "Lass, it's time y'got a gun in yer hands." He reached up atop the dish cupboard for a hand gun he kept there, also bringing down two small boxes he stuffed into his jacket pockets. "C'mon, den," he said, then exited the house.

Excited beyond measure and ready to bolt to follow Da in an instant, I looked to Mam for her approval. With a grin, she gave me a nod. I let out a gleeful yelp and leapt from my chair. I pulled my jacket off the hook by the door as I hollered, "Da! Wait for me!" and in a flash, I was out the door and at my da's heels.

Da's guns had forever fascinated me. I'd been pestering him as far back as I could remember to let me shoot them. He'd always reply it was too dangerous. I was too wee to handle them properly. I never thought so; but, of course, I was. Despite my powerful desire to shoot Da's guns, I never laid hands on them. I knew where they were, and they were completely accessible to me, but it never crossed my mind to touch them without permission.

Years before, when I was perhaps only four years old, Da first showed me the power and capable destruction guns possessed. Though I was little, I still had my jobs to do on the farm. The most important one, and one I enjoyed, was tending to our barn livestock. I fed and watered the milk cow, the goats, the pigs and the horses. At that time, Mam still milked the cow and the goats, and Da mucked the stalls. I wouldn't take on those duties until I got older. I loved spending time with and tending to the animals.

It was no secret how much I loved our livestock. I named each and every one, and never complained about caring for them. In fact, I couldn't wait for when it was time to tend to them. I loved stroking them, talking to them and hugging them. After I finished my chores, I'd hang out in the barn, having long, one-sided conversations with them. They were my only friends. My parents warned me continuously not to get too chummy with the animals because they'd be our food someday. Naturally, at my age, I wasn't able to comprehend the strange concept of our animals as food, so I continued to love on them without restraint.

One morning, right before daylight, Da took me out to the barn with him.

"Naw, wee lass," he said as I followed him, "yer gonna see where our supper comes from."

I had no trepidation at all as we walked all the way around to back of our main out building.

"Wait here, darlin'," Da said, almost as an aside as he left me waiting for him.

He returned only minutes later with Elmer, our enormous hog, on a rope lead. The moment Elmer got to me, I hugged him around his neck. He grunted, but not with the normal sense of glee he'd typically express when he'd greet me. There was something different about him. I was too young to comprehend; but in reflection, I now understand he likely had a sense of foreboding.

"Naw, darlin'," Da said, tenderly, "I dunna mean t'hurt ya, lass; but y'need t'learn, 'n I know no better way dan t'show y'right here 'n naw."

Da pulled a revolver from his waistband. I'd see it many times before—a blued Smith & Wesson.

"Y'see dis, lass?"

I nodded.

"Dis ain't no toy, Siobhán. It's a weapon. It protects us from wild boars, 'n dingoes, 'n anytin' else—animal or man—dat wants t'hurt us or take what's ours. 'n… it kills tings, darlin' girl. Animals. People. Yeah?" He looked at me, waiting for a response.

I nodded, though perplexed.

"Naw…" Da looked down and said nothing for a long time. I waited, unsure what was happening. "Elmer here," he continued, finally, "he's food, Siobhán."

Confused, I wrinkled my forehead.

"I know y'love 'im, but we raised him up from a lil' piglet to… well, t'feed us…. for monts 'n monts. D'meat we been eatin' up t'naw? Dat… well, naw, dat were Elmer's da. 'member 'im?"

My eyes opened wide as the picture Da painted for me emerged. "Douglas?"

"Aye, Douglas. 'N weren't our Elmer's dada good meat to eat? Eh, Siobhán?"

I nodded hesitantly, not quite sure what I was agreeing to as I attempted to process the new information.

"Well, lass, dis mornin' we enjoyed d'last bit of Elmer's da. If we want t'eat tonight, or… tomorrow…"

The horror of what he was saying finally registered in my small brain. "*NO! Dada, nooooo!*" I wailed as I grabbed Elmer by the neck, hugging him tightly.

"*Siobhán!*" Da barked, stopping my wail in that instant. "Let 'im go! Yer makin' dis harder on dis animal, lass." Da squatted down to my level, taking me by my shoulders and looked directly into my eyes. His voice softened.

"Darlin'… we all got a purpose in life, 'n dis aul hog has one purpose—t'fill our bellies. Mebbe he dunna know it, but…" My da shrugged. "… dat's what 'e is, love. Y'know we've told ya… He's not our pet."

My tears fell from my eyes like a waterfall as I stifled sobs boiling up from the deepest part of my body.

"Naw, naw… we warned y'bout gettin' too close t'the livestock, wee girl. Dis is why."

I sniveled, "But, Da…"

"No buts, Siobhán. We've fed dis hog for a year. Food we'll never get back if we let 'im live. 'n he'll eat even more food. For what? So y'can hug 'im 'n pet 'im? 'n, we? We won't have our bacon, or chops, or… Y'understand? Hmmm…?"

My tears continued to flow as I nodded. Da pulled me to him and hugged me, holding me for a long while. "I'm sorry, lass. Y'understand, yeah?"

I bowed my head. I didn't want to, but, yes, I understood.

What happened next traumatized me for days. I couldn't eat, especially when I was well aware the meat on my plate used to be my friend. Da made me stand back and cover my ears with my hands as he placed the muzzle of the gun behind Elmer's ear, then calmly pulled the trigger. The sound of the .38 caliber gunshot blasting through my hands, immediately followed by the sickening thud of Elmer dropping to the ground shot straight through my body and deep into my heart.

I stared with disbelief at the lifeless animal, watching the blood trickle down his neck, feeling as if the bullet had gone through me first—and that I'd been trapped in a terrible nightmare. I couldn't move or breathe as I continued staring. Thankfully, Da sent me back inside to be with Mam while he butchered Elmer. In years to come, I also learned to butcher, but I was exceedingly grateful my da saved that lesson for a later date. It took years for me to come to terms with the concept that growing food wasn't limited to veggies.

When I got back inside with Mam, she held me to her while I bawled. As I did, she gently reminded me why we raised our livestock, and especially why I could not touch the guns until I had learned how to use them properly.

"Can y'see naw why we don't want y'touchin' 'em?"

"Aye," I whispered into the soaked fabric of her cotton dress.

The morning I finally learned to shoot, I'd followed Da to a spot far from the house. Before we even got there he'd set up some tin cans and a few pieces of wood as targets for me.

Da held his rifle out for me to see. "Dis, darlin' girl," he began, "'s a Marlin tree-tree-six. Dis rifle's older 'n y'are, darlin' girl—which ain't dat old," he laughed. "Y'see here, it's a lever-action," he continued as he quickly pushed the lever forwards, then pulled it back, ejecting a bullet. "Dat's 'ow y'cycle used rounds," he said, bending over to retrieve the ejected round. He held it up for me to examine. "Dis is a tirty-tirty caliber cartridge. It'll not knock y'down when y'fire it, but it'll damn sure give a wee ting like yerself a good knock." Da then pushed the bullet into an opening on the side of the rifle.

He then showed me how to hold the gun, first by holding it correctly himself, then handing it to me to try copying him. As I examined it and tried to mimic his stance, Da went through a list of rules for me to remember.

One: I wasn't to put my finger on the trigger unless I was ready to shoot. Two: I mustn't point any gun at anything or anyone I wasn't prepared or willing to kill. That rule shook me a bit, but it's the one that stuck with me most prominently. Three: A gun is always loaded he stressed—always.

"But… how could dat be, Da?" I asked.

"Y'just gotta tink ev'ry gun is loaded, lass, *always*, 'cause dat way," he explained, "y'ain't likely t'kill yerself or anyone else by accident. Accidents happen. Believe me."

Once Da properly explained the reasoning to me, it made sense. Finally, the fourth rule was I had to know what was behind my intended target to avoid accidentally killing anything I didn't intend to kill.

"Do people really get killed by accident, Dada?" I asked with great skepticism.

"Aye, dey do, lass. Aye, dey do. I could tell y'stories… 'n I will… someday. Naw, repeat d'rules, Siobhán."

Throughout the day he'd ask me to recite each rule and then tell him why it was a rule. Once Da believed I knew the rules proper, he taught me how to load and shoot both the rifle and the revolver—the same one he used to kill Elmer. I didn't want to touch it, knowing it had killed my friend, but Da urged me to despite my ill will towards it.

"Dis weapon may save your life someday, Siobhán," he urged. "Y'gotta learn t'shoot it, 'n ya canna do dat if yer afraid of it." He held out the gun grip for me to take, which I did, reluctantly.

For the next hour or so I shot at the targets using the rifle, then the revolver. The first many, many times I missed everything. Frustration took hold as I missed every target, big and small. I didn't understand it, nor did my da. The targets were in the sights perfectly, I thought, but then again, though I thought I'd gotten the gist of shooting guns, the truth of it was, I really didn't know what I was doing. I was left-handed, so naturally, Da had me try shooting that way.

When I couldn't hit a target to save my life, frustrated, Da suggested I try with my right hand because I might have an odd shooting eye. I shrugged, not truly understanding what that meant. I tried again with the rifle propped against my right shoulder, where I have to admit, it felt more natural. Straightaway I hit first one target, then the next and again until I'd shot them all. Both Da and I were so excited. We set the targets up again so I could try firing the revolver using my stronger hand. The same thing happened. I shot every target with the first shot for each.

"Ah, naw… looks like we got ourselves a sharpshooter in d'family," Da boasted. "Good on ya, Siobhán. Yer mammy'll be right proud of ya. Just like me," he said, beaming.

From that day on, Da brought me along whenever he hunted. We went after fox, boar, rabbit, and even the odd kangaroo. Da wanted to teach me how to butcher meat, but given how shaken I'd been over Elmer, he thought it might be best I first learned to kill and butcher meat we'd hunted. As always, he was right. I won't say killing and then butchering wild animals was easy, but it was far easier than killing livestock I'd fed and come to know and love.

∞   ∞   ∞   ∞   ∞

Daily chores and learning filled my life on the farm. Depending upon the time of year, from the time we awoke, at or before dawn, we didn't stop until we went to bed. During the day I had my own chores to do; then between chores, Mam or Da would either need my help, or they'd teach me something I needed to know to help run the farm. Some nights after supper we'd sit by the fireplace, and in the flickering light of the fire, they'd tell me a fun story or fairytale before bed.

We were always working. As soon as we got up in the morning, we each had a mental list of chores to finish before breakfast. Then, after breakfast, there were more tasks to tend to until the next meal, followed by even more. After supper, Da or Mam would sit with me for my studies. We'd work on some problem that needed solving, or investigate history or geography, or whatever struck our fancy on that day. Da, I realised later, was better at bluffing his way through my lessons than he was at actually teaching the subjects at hand. Mam knew more than Da, but not too much more.

My overall education lacked any semblance of structure aside from when our lessons would occur. Mam and Da felt if I learned something new each day, I was doing all right. At some point, once I began reading proficiently, I delved far beyond our after-supper lessons. As my reading time increased, naturally, my time for chores decreased. It never failed that before supper I would get a holler from my parents reminding me to get back to my work, or that they needed my help. Likely as not I'd gotten lost in some fascinating book and lost track of time.

I loved reading and learning. I could have easily stayed in the library every hour of every single day and been a content child. By the time I left home, I'd read every single book in the library more than once, if not three times. My thirst for knowledge has never ebbed since, and thankfully continues to this day.

For my entire life, I believed my da and mam built our house and our farm because that's what they always told me. I had no reason to doubt them, and the farm was our home. Once I learned how to read, I began questioning whether we were the only people in the world, because I had seen no other humans but my parents. They assured me the reason no one ever visited is we lived so far away no one cared to make the trip. Couldn't we travel to them, I would ask? Oh, no, no, they would scoff—such a far, far distance would be too much for a wee girl such as myself, and where other people were was *quite* far away.

Because I didn't know any better, it seemed a reasonable explanation. I'd never been off the farm, so I hadn't any idea what might lie beyond our borders. It might have been a kilometre, a thousand, or a million. I had no clue, so I trusted and believed them with little reservation. Some nights I'd lie on our grass and stare at the blanket of stars above me, wondering if the closest star was how far civilization was from us.

Before they began making provisions trips together, Mam stayed behind with me while Da left to go wherever he was going. Once they felt they could leave me on my own, they did, travelling together on their excursions, sometimes for weeks at a time. As I made my way through our extensive library, whenever I came across a world map, I'd ask Mam or Da to show me where we lived and where they travelled when they left me. I needed some visual reference, a way to understand my place on the planet and where they might be while I was alone. Yet, no matter which continent I showed them, we seemed to live somewhere in the middle of it. As a result, I became more and more confused in my quest to pinpoint where we were. I couldn't figure out if my parents were purposefully trying to keep me in the dark, or if they actually didn't know where on the planet we were located—at least where we might be on a map. Perhaps both were true.

From a very young age, I always experienced a conflicting undercurrent of longing—wanting to understand where I was and also yearning to go some other place. Not because I didn't love the farm, because I did with all my heart, but because I seemed to have been born with a wanderlust that would rise more often than not. Limited physically to our property, I'd satisfy my craving to explore the world by travelling via the books in our library, an array of beautiful world atlases, and my vivid imagination.

I learned to read early in my life. Though my parents had no formal schooling, Mam taught me my alphabets and how to recognize certain words. She used books I can only assume were school books on reading, writing and maths. In a short while, all I wanted was to read and learn new words, which I did with each new book. I couldn't quite understand everything I read, but I would read aloud to both Mam and Da, and they'd explain what I'd just read to them—when they could. Sometimes, I could tell when they didn't truly understand because their explanation seemed more fantastical than it should. As they'd craft their tale, I could see in their exchange of glances they had no idea.

Fortunately for me, my mam and da were brilliant storytellers. As I look back on my education, I can say with conviction, it was a most interesting version of home schooling, and I wouldn't have it any other way.

For me, learning to write was more of a challenge than learning to read. I'm left-handed, or ciotóg as Mam and Da called it. My early attempts to emulate her right-handed writing proved confusing and awkward, but Ma's steadfast patience never waivered as I struggled. When I look back at my mam's efforts in educating me, knowing now she'd only had limited, if any, formal education herself, I'm so grateful for her dedication and patience.

My da, though he participated in our nightly studies, never took part in any writing lessons. I also don't recall ever seeing him write or read anything. Mam, though, would write what I now know were letters to her kin in Ireland. I remember, so vividly, her sitting at the supper table, slowly printing on papers she would eventually fold and place in an envelope. I never saw what she wrote on the outside, and I never knew what she did with them until years later. Not knowing any better, I was so impressed and incredibly envious of her ability.

Given my parents' limitations, if not for our considerable library, and my own burning desire to learn as much as I could, I expect the level of my own education would have been similar to theirs. My burning desire to learn *everything* fuelled my continuing education. One day, as I searched the library for something new to read, I came upon a book called Cursive Basic Handwriting. At that point, I was able to print my letters and words, but I didn't realise there was yet another way to write. One quick glance through the book and I was hooked. The thing I called 'curly writing' intrigued me. In fact, I became obsessed with it.

When I'd finished my morning chores, some days I'd spend all my free time writing o's and l's and other similar letter exercises on a small chalkboard Mam and Da had brought back from one of their trips. I'd use my chalk until there was nothing left to hold. On subsequent trips, they'd bring me as much chalk as they thought I'd need until their next excursion. I'd fill my board until there wasn't a bit of space left, wipe it clean, and begin all over again. When I finally wrote my very first sentence, excited, I took my board straight away to my mam. I found her at the kitchen table snapping green beans into a large ceramic bowl she cradled on her lap. Fraught with a strange combination of doubt and pride, I presented my chalkboard to her.

"Mam! *Mammy!* Look what I did!" I exclaimed.

Mam's initial reaction took me by surprise.

"What den…?" she asked, puzzled. "What's dis?"

Her question convinced me I'd completely misunderstood the concept of handwriting. Until I showed Mam, I felt confident and proud I was spot on, that I had it right. In an instant, the expression on her face crushed me, making me doubt my accomplishment. When I could no longer hold in my intense disappointment, and tears spilled from my eyes and slipped down my face, Mam stopped snapping beans and looked at me with a look on her face I'd rarely seen. She put the bowl on the rough-hewn supper table and held her arm out for me to come to her.

"C'mere, darlin' girl," she soothed.

I bowed my head and went straight to her. Mind you, my mam was not a clucky mam, not affectionate or demonstrative in the least, so in addition to being devastated by my failure, her unusual behavior confused me.

She lifted my chin with her hand.

"Look at me, lass," she said, her voice soft.

I looked up and into her pale blue eyes. They were filled with kindness, but also with a hint of sadness, or something unfamiliar I couldn't quite recognize.

"Jus 'cause I dunna know what y've done," she explained with a gentleness in her voice I'd never heard before, "dunna mean y've done wrong. I only got a lil' learnin', darlin', 'n I've given ya ev'ryting I got." She looked gravely at my chalkboard. "Looks grand, it does," she declared, taking the chalkboard from me. "'s… lovely. What is it? Can y'tell me?"

I nodded.

"Well, c'mon, den," she said in a hushed voice, and a light squeeze. "Let's 'ear it."

"D-D-De sun… is…" I shook my head, nervous, then began again. "D-D-De s-s-un is…"

"'s all right, Siobhán," Mam soothed. "Try again, darlin' girl."

"Mmm… okay, erm…" I drew my breath in. "D-D-De sun is… yellow," I said, almost whispering, not sure that's what I'd written.

"Nah! *Really?*" Mam said, her surprise laced with pride.

I nodded.

"Brilliant," she said almost to herself, then hugged me tightly. I had no memory of Mam ever hugging me so tightly before. Suddenly, it was as if I owned the universe.

"What d'y'call dis ting y'done?" she asked.

"Oh, erm, i-i-it's h-h-handwritin', Mammy… c-c-ursive, but erm… I-I call it c-c-urly w-w-ritin'." I grinned self-consciously.

"Can y'show me how?" she asked with a vulnerability I'd never seen in her, touching me in a way I didn't understand.

I looked at the bowl of beans, knowing she always had ten more things to do than she had time to do every day.

"Ah," she scoffed. "Dey're not goin' nowhere. C'mon, den. How'd y'do dis curly writin'?"

Eventually Mam learned to write cursive, following me the entire way through my progress. Though her formal education was obviously limited, what Mam seemed to inherently understand was by having me show her everything I taught myself only reinforced it in me; and taught her along the way as well.

One of my greatest regrets in my ongoing education is that I've never been able to master a foreign language. Certainly not for lack of trying, but apparently I don't have the apptitude for it. Or the patience, more likely. Perhaps it's because my first attempt to learn was at an older age. In spite of my travels around the globe and my earnest attempts to learn every foreign language I've encountered, the reality is my language skills are, at best, wanting, and that's putting it kindly.

I've travelled quite extensively in English-speaking countries, but when frequenting countries where Romance languages such as French, Italian or Spanish; Germanic languages of Scandinavia and Germany, Slavic or Asian languages are spoken, I always find myself mostly befuddled. Inevitably, I become the source of great amusement to the locals. You've heard no one fully mangle a foreign language until you've experienced me try to speak anything but English, and given my "native" language combining Irish, Australian and American, even English can sometimes be a challenge—for others.

My native dialect is such a varied mess I know people must think I came from some strange country or even another planet sometimes. Now, after so many years in the U.S. and surrounded by Americans, it shocks people to learn I'm Australian by birth.

Mam and Da were Irish, and most likely were Irish Travelers, or some variation thereof. I can't say for sure how long they'd been in Australia before I came along, but their English was what I would consider a mashup of Irish and Australian, with Irish being, by far, the dominant of the two. Though, until I arrived in Big Smoke, or Melbourne, and began hearing the native Aussies speak, I didn't realise Mam and Da's dialects (or my own, for that matter) were unusual.

Sometimes Mam and Da spoke what I thought was a foreign language; but now that I've been around foreign language speakers, I now realise what they spoke sounded more like gibberish and not another language. My research into my parents' possible origins revealed they were likely speaking what's known as Gammon, The Cant or *aul ting*—a mixture of English and Gaelic Travelers used to hide their conversations from outsiders. Mam and Da never taught their strange language to me. Instead, they used it to speak openly between themselves whenever I was within earshot.

From my later discoveries, their language wasn't the only thing kept from me. There were things I couldn't know about them or me, but that is another part of my story. Nonetheless, I do envy people who have mastered several languages. It's the one aspect of my life about which I'm the most disappointed

Mourning Waits

∞ ∞ ∞ ∞ ∞

From time to time, my parents would leave me and the farm so they might purchase or trade for staple provisions such as flour, sugar, building supplies, fabric for Mam's sewing, chalk for me, and the like. Oftentimes they'd leave with livestock or return with new livestock. Each trip was unique. I might have been as young as eight years old when they began leaving me on my own—perhaps even younger. The first time, though it was only for a day, terrified me. I had a verbal list of chores to do, and instruction about what to do if *this* or *that* happened. They instructed me to carry the rifle and the revolver *everywhere*. I already knew everything I needed to do, as they'd taught me well; but, I was still only a wee child. Until then, I had depended upon them for everything.

Mam always told me *I* had it easy because by the time she was my age, she had six younger siblings to care for when her parents left them for work. Her mam and da would take the older children with them, leaving Mam alone with the younger ones, sometimes for months on end! And, when Da was my age, he was already mucking stalls to earn a wage, because he was also expected to contribute to the family income.

I know they meant me to feel fortunate for my own circumstances; but, that first time being left on my own, I didn't feel at all fortunate. As I watched the Loadstar drive away, I cried, and continued doing so well until they were out of sight. Upon their return, I was awash with relief when I heard the Loadstar approaching the house, though I made sure they were none the wiser about how frightened I'd been. Still, it seemed like the longest day I'd ever lived.

The next time they left me was for the better part of three days. The time after that, pulling a trailer of sheep, they might have been gone for a week. By what may have been my ninth or tenth year, they'd often leave me on my own for a month at a time. By then, I didn't mind their absence. With only me on the farm, I had far less work to do. I needed only to maintain our animals, tend the garden, feed and care for myself. The laying in of stores, repairs, and bigger jobs I left for my parents upon their return. When Mam and Da finally returned, they always came bearing several books to add to our library, and perhaps a sweet treat or two for me.

For the next six years or so, Mam and Da would go off on their adventures to do whatever it is they did—I never knew what—two, three, perhaps even four times a year, while I kept the farm running. I did my job, and I dare say, I did it well. Once Pippa came into my life, my parents being gone for interminable stretches affected me not at all. Strange noises at night no longer frightened me; and, I had a brilliant listener in Pippa to yack to.

While alone, I sometimes liked to imagine it was all mine, *everything*, and dreamed of what I might do to *my* farm if they never came back. Thankfully, they always came back. Not that I ever wished them ill will in thinking of the place as mine, or wanted them gone forever; rather, it was more that I enjoyed being on my own, doing my chores when *I* wanted, or reading without interruption if I chose. Still, though it was always quite an adjustment for me their first days back from a trip, when they were back home and in charge I couldn't be happier.

∞ ∞ ∞ ∞ ∞

Sometime around what I believe was my fourteenth year, in 1967, my parents left for supplies, right around the end of February—our hot season. Da needed lumber to rebuild the chicken coop and repair our covered porch. Mam said I had grown so much she needed material to make new clothes for me. I wasn't to expect them back for a month, perhaps even six weeks, they said. They also had other business to attend while in Melbourne. I had my nose in a book when they left, so as the truck drove away, without even looking up, I absent-mindedly waved goodbye. If they returned my anemic wave, I'll never know. I considered it just another trip. By that time they had left me on my own so many times their leaving was routine. They'd leave, I'd do my chores, eat, I'd read, play with my pup, I'd do more chores, eat again, and then I'd go to bed and read until my eyes ached. When the sun rose, we'd get up and do it all again—each day until their return.

Barely two weeks later, while cleaning out the henhouse in the back of our barn, I heard the telltale sounds of a motor engine pulling up in front of the house and the high-pitch of brakes as the vehicle came to a stop. Pip barked excitedly as she did whenever Mam and Da came home. I dropped my bucket, grabbing the rifle propped against the outbuilding as I ran to the sound. Though the engine sounded like the Loadstar, not expecting them back so soon, I half-hoped it might be a stranger coming to visit. Perhaps, I mused, someone had gotten lost and happened upon our farm. My heart full of promise as I rounded the building, it truly surprised me to see not a stranger, but my parents. Disappointed only for a fleeting second, I stopped right at the corner of the house, puzzled by their unexpected and early return.

Immediately, I noticed the bed of the truck was empty. Mam and Da also seemed off somehow. Normally full of energy and life upon their return, ordinarily they'd bound from the vehicle, often having a laugh as they disembarked. This time, leaving the engine running, both of my parents nearly crawled down from the truck, holding each other up as they weakly stumbled towards the front door. I called out as I ran to them, but they continued staggering to the door. They either ignored me, or didn't hear me, despite me being but not ten metres away.

I shut off the truck engine, and with my pup right with me, quickly followed them inside, interrogating them along the way. What's wrong? Did something happen? Were they hurt? Why were they home so soon? As I pelted them with question after question, I realised they were seriously ill. Pale, their skin moist and burning hot, they struggled for every breath as they dragged each other, step by agonizing step, upstairs to their room. The scene frightened me to my core.

For the next week I tended to Mam and Da as day by day, they failed to improve, becoming weaker. They said very little during that time other than mumbling there was some kind of illness going around where they'd been, which was killing people. Upon learning of it, they left, hoping to escape it; but on the road, a day from home, they both fell ill.

I didn't want them to die and did everything possible for them. I tried remembering how they had cared for me when I'd been feverish, but nothing I did for them helped. I couldn't begin to guess how high their fevers were just by touching their burning skin; but, instinctively I knew they were far too high.

On the seventh day after their return, barely able to secure one breath after another, Mam just stopped breathing and passed in her sleep. As I sat by her side, waiting for a last breath that never came, it seemed like an eternity. When the realization hit me she was gone and would breathe no more, I actually experienced no emotion—nothing. Likely because I was knackered to the centre of my bones. Da was so out of it by then, her passing didn't even register with him. I tried to think of what to do next, but my heart and my brain had all but shut down. How might I move her? What was I to do? I had so many questions running through my head, but I was helpless to process any of them on my own. I resolved to wait for Da to recover to help me, because he'd know exactly what to do.

Alas, on the morning of the eighth day, Da opened his glassy and lifeless eyes, gazed at me for what seemed a right long time, but might not have been more than a minute, wheezed deeply, and then, he, too, had gone. He continued staring at me with his grey, dead eyes, until, unable to bear it one more instant, I covered his face with the blanket.

Thoroughly numb, I didn't shed a single tear when Mam died. But when Da passed on, it was the final straw for me. I fell into hysterics. I wept on the floor beside his bed for such a long, long time with my sweet girl curled up next to me. I keened from the deepest part of me until my throat was raw. Several hours later, thoroughly spent, I finally dragged my body up from the floor. The household, in the meantime, had gone dark. Listless, I went downstairs to fix a cup of tea, still incapable of fathomimg what had happened to my parents. They were here, and then... they were gone—as was my young, idyllic life.

That night, I collapsed into my bed, and for the first time since Mam and Da's return, had no clue how to proceed. What should I do with my dead parents lying in their bed just down the hall from me? What *could* I do? How would I manage being absolutely and utterly alone? Yes, I still had my loyal companion, but my mam and da had gone forever. My Mammy. My Dada. I wept, sometimes wracked with deep, heartfelt sobs until finally, overcome with sheer exhaustion, I fell asleep.

On the ninth day after my parents' return, I awoke soaking wet and miserable with fever. I suspect it was a rather high fever as every part of my body ached like never before. I'd never known such pain and discomfort. The instant my eyes opened the next morning, there was no doubt I had contracted my parents' ailment. In that moment, I was certain that I, too, would be dead within a week. Before I fell asleep, I saw that Pip had come up onto my bed, lying next to me. That's when I knew for sure death's door had opened for me. Just before slipping into a near-comatose state, I heard the clock chime downstairs ring twice, indicating it was sometime on the hour. What hour exactly, I didn't know and didn't care. It was the last time I recall hearing it until a month or more later when I finally got it going again.

I cannot tell you precisely how many days I suffered, but in those lost days of delirium, alternating between burning up and freezing to my bones, I had an intimate introduction to Hell. I was unable to get out of bed to relieve myself—the gory details of such events I shall leave for the imagination—with no one left to clean up after me. Unable to care for myself, let alone deal with two bodies, still lying dead in the other room, it was a miracle I survived, left on my own, with no understanding of what was happening to me. The only thing that kept me going was my pup because I feared if I died, eventually she would, too. The thought of her dying alone was unbearable, so I fought. With every last bit of strength I had remaining, I battled my way back to life.

When able to finally function again, though only barely, I cleaned myself up as best as I could. Without the necessary strength to fill the bathtub which entailed pumping and then lugging water from outside, firing up the stove, heating up the water and then pouring it into the tub, I gathered clean clothes into my arms, and stumbled outside to the water pump. I stripped off my soiled clothing and slowly washed myself. Had I been of clearer mind and not so unbearably weak, I'd likely have disgusted myself. As it happens, I can barely remember doing it or even getting myself dressed.

Though all I wanted to do was to go back to bed, despite dreading it, I understood I had to do something about the bodies. I had no choice. Their decay now filled the air in the house. Once dressed, I somehow dragged myself out to the barn in search of a shovel. It took what seemed like forever for me to get there, having to stop and catch my breath every two or three steps.

The moment the livestock caught a glimpse of me they complained ferociously, setting up such a commotion, the disconsolate cacophony was unfathomable. Not knowing how long they'd been without food and water, I was forced to tend to the animals first. My parents' burials would have to wait. It was painfully obvious Pippa had not eaten either while I was ill—she was so thin!

After feeding and watering everyone, ensuring none of the livestock had perished in my absence, I finally returned to the house, so weak and dizzy, even putting one foot in front of the other was a terrific struggle. As I crossed over the threshold at the front door, a wave of stench hit me so intensely, it defies description. By then, so terribly debilitated, to even just lift my feet to cross through without falling to the floor was a monumental feat.

Fraught with hunger, thirst and being so incredibly frail, the ungodly stench of death overwhelmed me. I wobbled back out onto the porch, clapping my hands over my face, though too late to make even the slightest difference. In an instant, the foulness had permeated my respiratory membranes.

I dropped onto one of the wooden porch chairs built by Da. My girl and her friend Dolly sat at my feet. Pippa laid her head on my knee as I pondered a solution, but my mind could not latch onto a single clear thought. About to give up hope, as if by sheer inspiration, out of nowhere, it came to me what I needed to do.

I sat there, waiting for some strength to come back to me so I might return to the animals. Earlier, I had fed and watered them, but I'd also milked the goats, the cow, and collected eggs from the chooks. I didn't do it for my benefit, but for theirs. I'd given some milk and eggs to Pippa, leaving the rest there in the barn, with plans to retrieve it later. My mind had been on my mam and da, not food. At a certain point, once I determined I had the most strength I might have for a while, I got to work. I lifted myself out of the chair and hauled myself to the barn with my constant companions at my heels. My heart ached for Pippa as I could see she was so worried for me, sensing the gravity of our situation. I know she also feared losing me.

I'd seen my da eat raw eggs, but could never bring myself to do it myself, even though he'd offer them to me every time. Hungry, weak and desperate, I cracked one egg open and tried to dump it into my mouth like Da. I gagged it up promptly, spitting it onto the ground. Thankfully, ever the conservationist, Pippa made quick work of the discarded raw egg. I cried, thinking it might have been better if I had also died. My "poor pitiful me" jag lasted but a minute as I remembered Pippa. If I had died, I realised, all of our animals would eventually perish, including my beloved Pippa. Not of illness, but of starvation. Slow, painful, brutal deaths. That would not do. Because they depended upon me for their food and care, it was up to me to survive no matter what.

I decided some goat's milk would aid in lessening my hunger and hopefully increase my energy. Before I even got to the pail of milk, it occurred to me that if I put one or two eggs in some milk and stirred it up a bit, it would be easier for me to take; which is what I did. Two eggs and about a cup of milk quickly filled my stomach. Almost instantly I felt better. Oh, to be sure, I was still in awful shape, but dying no longer seemed a preferable solution.

That night, Pippa, Dolly and I slept in the barn. I could not bear to go back inside the house where my parents' decay had engulfed it. The following day, I had another dose of milk and raw eggs. I shared my eggs and milk with Pippa, tended to the animals, bathed again, then went about finding a final resting place for Mam and Da.

The very thought of it made me so sad when I remembered the last time I saw them healthy. When they left on their last trip, I'd been reading a book about the British Empire, and barely paid attention to them in their last days before leaving, or even the moment they drove away. I couldn't even pull myself from my book long enough to wave them off. I still regret my selfish single-mindedness. What precious moments of them did I miss by not being wholly present with them? I'll never know and will regret it until my last days.

I trudged through the dirt, pulling a shovel and a pickax behind me, one in each hand, to the shade under *my* tree. I determined it was where I would lay them to rest. I hoped if they could recognize where they were, it would suit them nicely. For me, it wasn't too terribly far away, considering I would have to get them from upstairs to the tree by myself. I still wasn't sure how I'd manage it, but I didn't have a choice. It had to get done, didn't it?

It took most of the rest of the day to excavate two graves. Bless her little heart, Pippa joined in to help me. Though quite the accomplished digger, Pippa's technique wasn't quite as focused as mine, but she was still helpful given the state of my health. As we dug, I became convinced we'd had a significant rainfall during my incapacitation, as the normally hard packed soil was easier than I ever imagined it would be to dig out. Difficult by any measure given my puny state, I was determined to bury my parents as soon as humanly possible. Given my limited strength, the moistened ground was a blessing and aided me greatly.

Before I sank into slumber that night, our second sleeping on straw, I plotted how I might manage the moving of my parents. No matter how I thought of it, I knew it would be gruesome, and it was. To this day, I still have nightmares about it.

With a plan formulated, in the morning, I pawed through Da's reject wood planks stacked behind the barn, looking for just the right ones, and spent most of the day fashioning a wooden stretcher. Beyond tending to the livestock, Pippa and myself, by day's end, it was all I could manage before I collapsed onto my bed of straw.

Right before dawn the next morning, I entered our home with some canvas, rope, and my crudely fashioned stretcher. I made Pippa stay outside. I didn't want her getting confused about my parents' current state. She didn't like it, but she obeyed.

Hoping to stave off the foul stench that filled the house, I used a piece of my shirt, torn into a strip, and fashioned it into a mask of sorts. I'd folded the material around crushed leaves of Mam's garden peppermint and rosemary, using it to cover my nose and mouth. I expected the inside of our home to be hot as an oven, but the cool temperature surprised. Another blessing. I did my best to keep my breathing shallow, knowing the slightest whiff of decay would end my resolve in an instant. When I opened the door of my parents' room, I expected the odor of rotting flesh to blow right through the protection of my mask, but thankfully, it didn't.

Mum and Da remained covered as I'd left them, so I couldn't see what lie in wait for me as I entered their room. My most pressing worry was how their present condition might be, having lain in an unkempt state for what could have been two weeks—or more. I'll tell you, I did not want to know. I wanted to avoid any visual contact at all costs. I knew myself well enough to know I'd have rather burned the entire house to a pile of ashes than see my parents' decayed bodies.

Armed with every bed sheet I could find, save two sets for my own use, I wrapped Mam, then Da in cocoons as quickly as I could. Sad to say, by the time I got to tending their bodies, they'd seriously decomposed; and, dare I say, were… falling apart? Yes, it was a wretched task, indeed. Though I didn't actually see them directly, I could feel the state of their bodies through the sheets.

Have I mentioned my vivid imagination? Twice I had to run from the bedroom to vomit, followed by a good measure of uncontrolled sobbing. Neither easy to do while trying not to inhale. Without the luxury of thinking about what the tragedy forced me to do as a young teen, all by myself, I didn't feel sorry for myself. I only knew I needed to start working and get the unholy task finished as soon as possible.

I began at dawn and proceeded until well after dark, moving each of my parents. Beginning from their second-floor bedroom, I needed to get their bodies down the stairs, through the house and then out to their burial plots. I brought my da down first, because I felt he would be the heavier of the two and I'd have more strength at the beginning to handle him. I hoped with all that I had I'd have enough energy to get them both down and out the same day. Better to finish my gruesome task with the lighter one, I thought. It didn't matter. Halfway to the plots with my da, it all proved too much for me. I passed out from my lingering infirmity and the crushing heat. How long I was out, I cannot say for sure, but when I finally regained consciousness, with Pippa licking my face, it felt as if it had been a long time.

After I rolled my da into his plot, I had to look after the animals and try to feed myself and Pippa. The livestock and Pippa had no trouble eating. I cannot say the same for myself. My skin, my clothes, my hair all smelled of putrid death, adversely affecting my appetite. Though I avoided the smell with my makeshift mask, once I took it off, the stench consumed me. The smell of death lingered on me for weeks after, despite several baths, clean clothes and vigorous scrubbing.

That awful night, somewhere near midnight, after I brought Mam down and buried her next to Da, Pippa and I lay on the ground between my parents. When I was finally able to stop and mourn my darling Mam, Da and my childhood, with my girl lying as near to me as possible, I sobbed through the night. The near unspoilt life I once knew was now dead and buried in the ground along with the only people on earth I'd ever known.

Part Two

The Attic

∞ ∞ ∞ ∞ ∞

Before losing my parents, there was one thing and one thing only I ever truly feared—*The Attic*. My earliest memory of *The Attic* is how vociferously Mum and Da warned me against it. I wasn't even to look at the staircase leading to it. Nor was I to stray anywhere near it. Otherwise, they warned terrible, *terrible* things would happen to me. *Terrible!*

"What terrible tings?" I'd ask.

"Ah, so terrible we canna say dem out loud, child," they'd warn. "*Dunna go near De Attic—ever!*"

Why, you can well imagine, as a wee child, with such emphasis attached to their warning, how terrified I must have been of those steps and the door just beyond them. As such, even when in the general vicinity, I gave the area a wide berth so as not to get inadvertently sucked upstairs and into it by some strange and evil alien force. When Mam and Da emphasized *terrible* in the way they did—being quite dramatic about it, I might add—believe me, I didn't doubt them.

About a month after Mam and Da passed, and after I'd mostly regained my health and strength, it almost seemed as if *The Attic* had begun to beckon me, or taunt me. I hadn't given it much thought in years, having made avoiding it part of my everyday routine. Yet, the longer I had only myself, Pippa, and the livestock for company, and as the daily routine of running the farm turned monotonous, the more that forbidden door and that beyond it intrigued me.

I cannot say what possessed me to do so, but one day, I found myself standing at the bottom of the stairs leading to the forbidden door, perhaps only five or ten metres from it. Still, even from that distance, the very idea of being that close to it gave me serious pause. Yet, for some strange reason, I couldn't make myself leave. I stood there, with Pippa patiently sitting next to me, staring at it for what had to be an hour or more. Like a loop, everything I ever heard my parents say about *The Attic* churned in my head, again and again and again. After a time, their words became ghostly and chant-like, almost frightening me. At one point, the chants grew louder and louder as I became convinced I'd become trapped in a frightful dream.

"Terrible tings'll 'appen… terrible tings'ill 'appen, lass… Dunna go near dat door… terrible tings'll 'appen… terrible tings'll 'appen…"

Throughout the incessant chanting, I tried reasoning with myself, conjuring numerous excuses why I should open the door— immediately countered by why I should walk away and forget about it. Just walk away, I commanded myself. I suppose my curiosity wielded far more power than Mam and Da's dire warnings, and even my own misgivings, because at a certain point, I threw caution away. I turned the doorknob, expecting it to be locked, but it wasn't. My curiosity piqued beyond reason, I slowly pushed open the unlocked door; then, without further thought, burst into the mysterious and forbidden room.

I stood inside the doorway for, well, I'm not sure how long, but a while. Oddly, Pippa remained sitting on the other side of it. It was almost as if she knew the inevitable terrible things were about to happen. I didn't move as I awaited the "terrible things." Though my body remained still, almost frozen in place, my eyes took in every detail of what appeared to be a room of significant size. I could barely see past the wood crates that mostly blocked the entryway, because dozens and dozens of them piled as many as six high, as well as furniture, paintings and other certain mysterious items covered with sheets obstructed my view. The entire scene felt strangely oppressive, and almost otherworldly. I considered the possibility I'd died upon opening the door, and that what I witnessed and felt might be the non-existent Hell Mam and Da used to go on about.

I took it all in, then shrugged. It wasn't so bad, I decided. Odd and strange, but… no, not dangerous. Convinced I wasn't dead or in Hell, and that nothing dreadful had gotten me, I allowed myself to creep further into the room. Two large crates at the entryway, however, prevented me from going much further. I considered my options, and concluded rather than climb over them, I would attempt to squeeze myself sideways through a narrow passageway between them. It was a narrow fit, but I somehow managed to get through to the other side. Though it was possible for her to slip through the slight space as well, Pippa chose to remain outside the room, softly whining at the doorway. I whispered and beckoned to her, urging her to follow me inside, but she remained steadfast where she sat. Disappointed, I continued on by myself.

Every cautious step I took in the attic made the wood floor creak and groan, running tiny quivers up my spine with each one. To that point, though nothing had yet struck me down, I dared not consider how long it might take for the fabled terrible things to happen to me. I worried should a daemon or worse jump out from behind a crate or covered thing, I might not have the ability to retreat fast enough. Would I even have time to run away? Would I cower, or would I fight back if the terrible meant to strike me down —or worse? I shivered as an icy tingle ran from the bottom of my feet to the top of my head. I drew a deep breath, attempting to calm myself.

Pushing my fear back down, I pressed on with extreme caution. Just past the crates, I came upon something taller than me, covered with a white cloth. I reached out to pull it off, but stopped short of the fabric. Everything seemed mysterious and held uncertain danger—I had to take care with every decision! I bent over to figure out what might be underneath the cloth covering. *Aha!* Furniture legs! I laughed aloud. Without hesitation, and with a swift yank, I removed the fabric. Gasping from shock as what was beneath it was revealed, I leapt back, crashing into another crate which caused me to tumble to the floor.

My heart pounded like it never had before as my mind reeled. I'd read about them, but I'd never seen one in our house. But the second I saw it, I knew exactly what it was. So often I'd asked both Mam and Da—too many times to count, "Mammy? Da…? What's a mirror? Do we 'ave one? Can y'really see yerself innit?" I'd inquire with intense curiosity.

Mam said no, never! They cast evil spells, she'd insisted. Da said they encouraged vanity. I didn't know if either was true, but the moment I saw another person in that reflective glass looking back at me—someone who wasn't Mam or Da—for the first time in my life, well, the image shocked me. No. Perhaps shocked is not the right word. Stunned? No. Frightened? No… *Gobsmacked!* Yes, that word is closer to what I experienced; but, to be honest, I suspect a word to describe how I felt in that instant has not yet been invented. Pippa finally entered the attic, coming to me where I still lay, sprawled out on the floor, my heart working to pound its way out of my chest.

"I'm alright, darlin' girl. I'm... alright..." I lied, whispering as Pip slathered me with frantic licks.

For a few bewildering moments, as I continued lying on the wood floor, I didn't know what to make of what I'd just seen. It didn't take long for me to conclude the face in the strange glass was my very own. All my life I'd had a vague idea of what I might look like based on how Mam and Da looked. They always said I favoured them, though I was significantly taller than either of them. They swore it was because of Da's great grandfather who was a real live giant is why I was so tall. *A giant?* Was I going to be a giant, I worried? I didn't want to be a giant. Mam and Da assured me that wouldn't happen, though I only half believed them, continuing to fret I might indeed be a giant someday.

I already suspected my hair was lighter than Da's and different than Mam's. After a haircut I'd caught glimpses of mine on the floor, right before Mam rapidly snatched up the evidence. And, my skin was fairer, too, but having never seen a clear image of myself, they left me to create my own self image. What I saw in my reflection, in that moment, was the antithesis of how I ever imagined myself. I looked nothing at all like either of my parents! Perhaps Mam was right and what I witnessed was The Terrible casting evil on me from the reflective glass. It had to be.

The thought of giving the mirror another chance to get me and my essence was untenable, so keeping out of sight of it, I crawled out of the attic, wriggling my way through the tight passageway with Pippa close behind. Once out the door, I pulled it shut behind us. My complete body shook as I leaned against the shut door, overcome with relief I wasn't dead. But... that mirror... the image inside it... Was that the something terrible? Had I been cursed so quickly?

"Pippa..." I said, my voice above a whisper, "... is dat...? Do I...? Is dat what I look like?"

She gazed at me with her frosty blue eyes, staring intently, as if attempting to send me messages telephathically, but always without an actual answer. Still, she was a terrific listener. I reached over to hug her and pulled her close to me. She snuggled into me, providing me the comfort I so thoroughly needed at that moment.

In the week after entering the attic, I searched through our vast library, seeking whatever information there might be about glass mirrors, curses and spells; but, aside from fairy tales, I found nothing sinister in regard to mirrors. The startling vision of myself, however brief it was, had gotten stuck in my head. What if that's what I actually looked like, I wondered? If it was, what could it mean? I was filled with questions.

Eight long, tense days after my harrowing experience, I once again stood in front of the forbidden door, determined to get some answers. With care, I opened the door, barely a crack. With the utmost caution, I peered inside. Nothing happened. Feeling bolder, ever so slowly I pushed the door a little more until it fully opened, the door creaking on its hinges as I did. Carefully, I stepped inside the room once again. There, beyond the wooden crates stood the dresser with an attached mirror. Though angled away from me, I could see other items in the room reflected in it.

After squeezing through the crates, I crouched down to my hands and knees to prevent it from seeing me. I looked at the mirror, then the reflected items. There was no distortion. It reflected all the items in the mirror just as they were; rather, exactly as I saw them. I drew in a deep breath, so deep it almost hurt my lungs; and as I held my breath, I crept ever so slowly towards the dresser. Just before I reached the edge, I exhaled soundlessly as if I thought it might hear me breathe. Convinced the mirror wasn't yet able to "see" me, I edged closer to it until I was right next to it, but out of sight of it. I held my hand up, wiggling my fingers. Still, not a hint of distortion.

Finally, I lifted myself until I saw only the edge of my reflection. Again, I gasped at the sight of myself, though not as dramatically as earlier. The face reflecting back to me shocked me.

It really did. Emboldened by the lack of terrible, before I knew it, I practically came nose-to-nose with myself, my heavy breathing instantly fogging my image. I stared as if entranced, intrigued and mystified by the reflection of my own strange and unfamiliar face.

For the next several days, I did little else but spend hours and hours studying myself in that mirror. The rest of the attic held no interest for me. I scrutinized every part of myself, wholly enamoured by my image. My face, my ears, nose, mouth… my smile, my teeth, my chin, my eyes… my body… all I'd been unable to see before was there for me to examine. Glimpses in window panes and water never prepared me for… well, me.

I was absolutely enthralled with how I looked. I had wavy auburn hair with a length to my jawline; fair skin, green eyes, refined features, white teeth with one upper tooth slightly crooked… I'd talk to myself in the mirror, completely amazed by my own likeness while marveling at how I looked. More than anything, I was struck by how unlike I was from Mam or Da. In fact, I looked *nothing* like them. The more I scrutinized my face, the less in common I had with either of them.

There were times I wondered if Mam and Da had both been right. Had the mirror cast a spell on me, making me obsessed with myself? A self that didn't exist? Or, did it? Just when I was about to decide they may have been right on the mark, I realised my entire life I'd no idea what I looked like. Didn't I deserve to make up for lost time getting to know myself? Truth be told, I found the reflection of myself captivating. Despite my devoted Pippa, I'd been so terribly lonely. From that day on, the mirror became my only human company—my mirror twin.

∞　∞　∞　∞　∞

Once my initial fascination with myself ebbed, my curiosity about the attic recaptured my attention. What about it made them so afraid? What didn't they want me to see? Did they fear I'd see or find some strange thing? Because that's what I worked out—there was some kind of terrible in *The Attic* they were desperate to keep from me. Was it my own face they were hiding? Would it betray what they tried to keep hidden? But, why? Reasonable questions, all, but despite the shocking discovery about myself, for the life of me, I didn't understand why I would look so completely unlike my own parents. I came to believe that because I loved them, trusted them, missed them beyond description, I'd insulated myself from the ability to see the truth. After they died, I realised I knew nothing about them—or myself. Nothing of import, anyway. Not their names, from what area in Ireland they came, little to nil about their families, how old they were, how they came to make the farm their home… nothing. As such, I concluded, I lacked even the most basic knowledge about myself and my life.

Over the next days, one by one, I began prying the lids off the wooden crates. Initially, what I found were liquor bottles of all sorts, with enough bottles to drink one a week for more than thirty years. Mam and Da always had a bottle of Irish whiskey in the cupboard for their nightly nip, as they called it, so I had some familiarity with the cargo. Wood crates dominated the space, each being approximately 43cm x 30cm x 23cm. After opening over fifty of them, all filled with liquor, I had nearly given up. What was the point of opening the remaining containers? The farther I got into the attic, all I discovered was more alcohol. Yet, something in me refused to stop. In spite of how exhausted I was from lifting and moving those heavy crates, I couldn't stop. It was almost as if an inner voice prodded me to keep prying lids open.

I kept going until there were only three more crates to go. They sat off by themselves, apart from the rest. Two were larger than all the others, by probably four times. The third was bigger still, taking a lot of the wall lengthwise. I pried the top from the third to the last one to find not more liquor bottles, but papers, books, photos and personal items of someone I didn't recognized. I took a cursory look, deciding to investigate further later on. I wanted to keep going and get the crate opening finished.

The second to last crate wasn't even nailed shut. It had a lid, or a cover I only had to lift off for access. In that crate were more personal items, which looked like they might be my mam's. The instant I pulled its cover off, Pippa whined as if she recognized it was Mam's. Even though Mam always groused about Pippa always being under foot (even though they were my feet), and would ruin the dolly she made for me (which Pippa never did), Pippa adored her. She'd always run up to Mam, pushing Dolly against her. It was Pippa's way of being affectionate and saying hello. She never behaved that way with Da. I suppose because of all the times he tried to kidnap her, but it was abundantly clear that after me, Mam was a favourite of Pippa's.

It was well into the evening by the time I got to Mam's crate and the light from the lone dormer window had faded considerably. I decided I'd wait until the morning to fully explore the last two mystery crates. The one I'd already opened looked like there was quite a lot to read and look through, and for that I'd need abundant light. Though I was dying to find out what it held, I would leave the final crate for later. It was easily two or three times larger than the last crates and sat pushed right up against the wall. It would be a week or more before I'd get to opening the remaining crate. It being the final crate was fitting, because, in a roundabout way it ended up being the grand finale.

Though my intention the next morning was to examine the crate with what appeared to be my mam's belongings, for some inexplicable reason I was drawn to and immediately absorbed by the stranger's crate. It was a treasure trove of information, filling in blanks while creating even more gaps and raising more questions about what I didn't know about my mam, my da and the farm. Before long, reading through his many and detailed diaries spanning several decades, I learned more about the mystery man than any other person in the world, including my parents.

Patrick Finley Mottorshaw

∞ ∞ ∞ ∞ ∞

His name was Patrick Finley Mottorshaw. According to his birth
certificate, he was born in London, England, January 17, 1901. As
best as I discerned, Patrick's family were wealthy and of the noble
class. Though he alluded throughout his early diaries to his family's
wealth and standing, there were no particulars. I had the distinct
impression he lacked any degree of fondness for his family.
Regretfully, when I left for parts unknown, I destroyed the diaries.

There were nearly sixty two leatherbound books with
approximately one hundred and fifty pages each. Some diaries
covered an entire year and part of another, some, only two months,
depending upon his mood or need to express himself, I suppose. I
worried they might hold incriminating or detrimental information

about my mam and da. I wanted to protect their memory. Why I thought anyone would care other than me, I cannot say, but I daren't take the chance that someone might.

Now, of course, I regret my decision more than I can express as I would have loved to have shared some of his writings verbatim. Patrick, as I was so pleased to discover, was a wonderful diarist—passionate, witty, circumspect, yet honest—with beautifully elegant penmanship that put my own to shame. Though, if I'm honest, my penmanship now owes at least some of its flourish to the influence of Mr. Patrick Finley Mottorshaw.

It's been many years since then, but I'll try to do my best to convey Patrick's story as accurately as possible—as I remember it, anyway. I use the familiar "Patrick" because, as I mentioned, by the time I'd finished reading his final entry, I felt I knew him better than the only other two people in my life. He became far more to me than Mr. Mottorshaw.

Educated at Cambridge University in England, Patrick trained as an architect with a London firm after graduation. He had a passion for it. He loved conceiving of something grand and spectacular, then building it. He seemed at odds with his da over his love of architecture, as his da wanted Patrick to choose another avocation. It's funny, but in the many times I read through his diaries, Patrick never said exactly what his da preferred him to do if not architecture. Patrick's focus in his diary entries was more how disappointed he was with his da who never seemed to understand him.

Patrick had three younger brothers and four older sisters who all seemed less bothered by their da than Patrick. His male siblings were highly successful men—a banker, an esquire, and a member of Parliament. The youngest of his sisters married a prince or some royal somebody from another country. The other three married well, improving their status considerably. Patrick regularly described his da as a tyrant, and his mam as weak and ineffectual, contributing, he supposed, to his da's incessant scorn. Nothing Patrick did ever made him happy—to the contrary.

In his thirtieth year, Patrick's favourite aunt, Vera Highcamp Beardsley from Australia, died, bequeathing much of her vast fortune to him. She was his mother's younger sister. In 1865, twenty-year-old Vera Highcamp had married her much older Australian husband, Talbot Evelyn Beardsley III, and emigrated from England. Talbot had recently struck gold in the Outback, allowing him to build a sizeable and diverse fortune. Part of that fortune included over four thousand hectares, the equivalent of ten thousand acres of countryside. That property ultimately became our farm.

Vera and Talbot visited London every few years during monsoon season until Talbot's death in 1880 or '81. Every other year until her own death, Vera made the treacherous trip to London and back by herself. As she was Patrick's favourite aunt, he was her favourite nephew. According to him, only his Auntie Vee understood him. Patrick stated in his diaries they corresponded regularly; but regretfully, I found no letters from her. She loved architecture, books and art, sharing her passion with Patrick. Her husband, apparently, cared for nothing but increasing his fortune. When Talbot died, Vera, a wealthy widow, had no interest in remarrying ever again, and never did. Not only did she become a patron to the arts, but with a head for business, though a woman living in a strong, patriarchal environment, she continued to increase her holdings.

Patrick's first memory of his Aunt was his tenth birthday when she took him to the British Library for the first time—just the two of them. He described it as a life-changing event. That memorable outing inspired his own library, the one that taught me almost everything I knew. Childless, Vera always considered Patrick her very own, and he, forever feeling like the odd man out in his own family, didn't mind her claim to him in the least.

When she passed, devastated at losing his beloved aunt, Patrick took advantage of his windfall inheritance and immigrated to Australia in 1933. Selling off other inherited assets to finance the farm structures, it took him five years to complete the house I grew up in, the same one my Da claimed *he* built with his own hands. Patrick is the one who built our house almost by himself, with occasional help from Aborigines living outside Adelaide.

During WWII, Patrick served as an Army officer for Australia. He didn't write much about what he did during his service, except to say his training in architecture proved helpful. Though much older than his peers, Patrick desperately wanted to serve. I wish he had written more on that subject, but during those years his entries were few. Part of the reason, I surmise, aside from the war was Jeanne Symonds. She was the sister to Patrick's commanding officer and ultimately became Patrick's wife. His entries were sparse during their courtship and subsequent marriage.

Despite the twenty years between them, it was obvious he'd been rightly smitten. That could be my interpretation, putting my own spin on his writings—the hopeless romantic in me, I suppose. Without a doubt, her dying in childbirth in 1948 left him bereft. Neither she nor their newborn son survived. At once I understood the abundant library selection of children's books and educational materials. Patrick had been prepared to thoroughly educate the children he obviously hoped for, but never had.

Following his wife and son's deaths, his diarying grew dark and morbid; and, in my mind, frightening. A man in pain for several years, Patrick relied upon his crated liquor to ease his agony. I'd love to say I could not relate to his anguish; but, alas, I could.

Two years later, Patrick first mentioned my parents in his writings. His description of them as the dark-featured little Gypsy and his fair-coloured no-nonsense wife from Ireland gave me a chuckle. His portrayal of them was spot on. He'd met them while on a supply run in Adelaide. They'd been looking for work, and though he claimed he didn't need farm hands, he brought them home, anyway. They never left. The man, Eoin, and his wife, Kellen, proved to be quite helpful to Patrick around the property. He also lamented how much he enjoyed their company.

I remember reading their names for the first time, shocked to learn they had names other than Mam and Da. Patrick seemed cautiously enamoured by them. Mam took over the care of the inside of the house: cooking, laundry, cleaning and such, while Da helped Patrick with projects on the farm. According to Patrick, he and Da built our barn together, and Da took on all the mechanical maintenance of which Patrick lacked anything more than basic skill. He mentioned trying to teach Da how to read and write, but Da was more interested in learning how to build things. Patrick thought Mam was a much better student, smart and eager to learn.

Early in 1953, though, something happened, affecting how Patrick felt about Mam and Da. He never wrote specifically what it could have been, but there was no doubt *something* happened between them. He'd become almost paranoid about my parents, often suggesting they might kill him someday for his money and his property. When I first read that entry, it was difficult to even consider Mam and Da might be capable of murder. Killers? *My Mam? My Da?* The sweetest and most gentle people who raised me? Well, to be fair, they were the *only* people I'd ever known, but I struggled even trying to imagine them as violent in any way. Even the suggestion of it troubled me greatly.

Then, best as I can recall, Patrick's final entry was mid-November of that year. It was brief, but ominous. He was certain he wouldn't survive another day, convinced Mam and Da were out to get him. He mentioned he'd heard them talking more and more in some strange language, but as soon as he would make his presence known, they would immediately switch to English, convincing him they were no doubt plotting his death.

As I devoured Patrick's entries just prior to his last, at times I almost felt like laughing aloud because his writing made him seem like a certified lunatic. And, then, I got to his final entry, and that, as they say, was that. It was only a half page more, and nothing after it. That was it, there was nothing. It stunned me. Truth is, the abruptness of the ending left me deeply disturbed. As the diary was but half-filled, I frantically pawed through the stack of thirteen blank diaries, as well as the rest of Patrick's belongings—photos, letters, newspaper clippings, business correspondence, and the like —desperately looking for another diary with entries, but found nothing. Why would he just end it like that?

I'd been reading his diaries, written from 1908 until November 15, 1953, for days and days, only stopping to eat, sleep, use the Jacks, and suddenly… no more? That was all? The end? What happened to him? Where did he go? Was it possible my mam and da had done him in?

What was I to think? Perhaps Patrick had lost his mind, did the unthinkable and killed himself. At times his writings did seem melancholy enough for him to take his own life. Or, maybe he died in an accident. He could have had a heart attack, a stroke, a fall… surely anything but to what he alluded. No, I refused to accept my parents might have anything to do with his eventual demise.

Undone

∞ ∞ ∞ ∞ ∞

The abrupt conclusion of Patrick's diaries affected me more than I'd have imagined possible when I first began reading about his life's journey. I'd come to know him, at least from what he wrote, and I liked him. I dare say I might even have loved him. His story was undone, which is much how it left me.

Unable to find any further writings, I decided my pup and I needed some sunshine and fresh air, having been cooped up in the stuffy attic for days. Other than quickly tending to the livestock each day, sleeping, eating and personal hygiene, I'd completely immersed myself into Patrick's story—his life. I felt terrible for neglecting Pippa all that time. Despite my inattention, she remained right there with me. With his diaries ending with more of a non-ending than anything else, I found myself in a somewhat agitated state. In fact, I felt right cheated.

With an urgent need to stretch my legs and get fresh air, I decided what we needed was a good walk. I went downstairs, my faithful companion, as always, closely following me. I filled a canteen for each of us with water, grabbed my straw hat, and tucked my revolver into my waistband. Slinging the rifle over my shoulder, I grabbed Da's walking stick on the way out the door. I had no agenda, no destination in mind, just the desire to put distance between Patrick's abrupt ending and me.

Mam and Da always limited where on the farm I could roam about. They were specific about how far I might venture, planting stakes marked with yellow paint to mark my boundaries. They warned if I ever ventured past the stakes, the dingoes might snatch me away, or a wild boar would eat me—either way, I'd be lost forever. Even after Pippa came into my life, they warned me. The dingoes or boars would get her, too, they stressed. I heeded their warnings and never passed beyond the stakes on my own. Anyplace I'd ever been beyond them were on my outings with Da.

As Pippa, Dolly and I walked, we came upon the first marked stake. Programmed as I was, I stopped, prepared to turn around, realising almost immediately I was free—I could go wherever I wanted. Armed and ready to defend our lives from predators, I took a step, then froze when all of Mam and Da's dire warnings rushed into my head. I shook it as if to scatter their words from my brain and into the air, proceeding with extreme caution past the stake. I strode a few steps before I stopped and waited. I looked around me, searching for any signs of feral dingoes or killer boars, then to Pip for any warnings, but there were none. She only looked to me for our next move. I shrugged, and we continued walking.

Our canteens were nearly empty when I thought we should turn around and head for home. I cannot say how long we'd walked, but by the sun, I figured perhaps two hours had passed since we first set out. I should have turned back sooner, but I had entered a sort of Zen state, losing track of time and space. About three-quarters from the house, I noticed something I'd missed on my way out—a small pathway marked by stones. I threw caution to the wind, in a manner of speaking since there wasn't even the hint of breeze, and took the path. The environment at that point was somewhat barren, with sparse grass and a few trees or bushes, but the path itself was distinct. My interest thoroughly piqued, I continued to follow it until I came to the end, about ten minutes from the entry. What I found stunned me.

There, in a fenced off area, with a lone tree shading it, were three wooden markers—headstones, if you will, but made from rough-hewn timber. The fencing itself comprised weathered wood pickets that had seen better days. I opened the rickety gate and entered the small graveyard. There were no markings on the headstones, but I could tell the near size of each resident by the stones piled atop each grave, meant to keep scavengers away. One was tiny, the other larger, and the third significantly larger still. I realised I'd likely found where Patrick, his wife Jeanne and their stillborn child Matthew Symonds Mottorshaw were buried. I fell to my knees, overcome with sadness. I wept into the earth for a man I'd never met, but loved. My girl leaned against me, pushing her dolly into my body to comfort me.

As the sun set, about to pierce the horizon, we left the graveyard and headed home. I was reluctant to leave, but I also wanted to avoid returning home in complete darkness. As it was, I had to step into top gear to beat the sunset. Swiftly hoofing it back to the house, I couldn't let go of the mystery of Patrick's ultimate demise. What had happened to him? Surely if my parents had murdered him they wouldn't have gone to the trouble of burying him, would they? Or, if they wanted to make it seem as if it was a natural death should anyone inquire, adding him to the family plot would seem to be the smart thing to do. I didn't know. I swung from one possibility to the next, never landing on an explanation that seemed right or that I could fully embrace.

The following day I scoured the property for lumber I'd need to rebuild the burial site fence. I also planned to include grave markers with their given names and, as best as possible, their birth and death years. From my extensive reading, I was aware that's what people did for graves. Years before Da had taught me to carve wood, so I determined I would carve each marker. I'd done it for Mam and Da's gravesites, though only as Mam and Da O'Shea. Now that I had their names from Patrick's diaries, I decided to re-do their markers, too. There's something about honoring the dead properly that lessens the sting of the loss. I knew carving Mum and Da's names on their grave markers wouldn't erase the pain of losing them, but the very idea of doing it lessened the hurt enough to make the next days bearable.

It took me two weeks to properly rebuild the fence for Patrick's family plots, carve their names in their placards, as well as Mam and Da's. I felt significantly better. Until I left home for good, I visited Patrick and his family once or twice a week. I sat with my mam and da every morning and every night before bed. Yes, it was lonely out in the countryside with just my pup and me. The dead, Pippa, her dolly, the livestock and my mirror twin were my only company. Soon after, my own diary would join my companion list as, taking my cue from Patrick, I began filling one of his blank diaries with my own experiences, loves, thoughts, dreams, joys, disappointments and observations. It's a habit I continue to this day, with every word I pen being a sort of homage to a man I never met, but grew to love.

As far as how Patrick died, I wouldn't find out until many years later when I finally located mam's sister, Quinn. But that's a story for another time.

10

The Bounty

∞ ∞ ∞ ∞ ∞

After tending to the gravesites, I refocused my energy once again on the attic. I'd gotten sidetracked reading Patrick's diaries and still had one more crate to open. The largest of them all, it was pushed right up against a wall. I tried to give it a shove, but it was far too heavy for me to move it even a fraction of a centimetre by myself.

With crowbar in hand, I set about loosening the lid from the crate. After perhaps an hour of prying and wrestling with unwieldy nails, I finally lifted the crate lid off. Well, to be honest, it was also too heavy for me, despite my most valiant effort. I ended up pushing, then sliding the top off the crate and to the floor. It landed on its corner with a mighty thud, cutting a gash deep into the hardwood floor.

To my surprise and delight, the crate appeared packed with first-edition, leather-bound books of varying sizes and genres. I understood why they'd been stored in the attic, as there was no room in the massive library for even one more book, let alone a hundred or more. Still, I decided a crate in the attic was no place for such beautiful masterpieces. Stack by stack, I carried the entire contents of the crate down to the library, determined to display them somewhere. It took the better part of the day to bring every book down to the first floor.

Once I'd emptied the crate, I dismantled it. I needed the wood as I had used all the excess lumber we had to rebuild the cemetery fence. The wood would come in handy for other projects. That task began at sunrise the next day. I finished in the afternoon and transferred the wood outside to Da's workshop.

As I took the crate apart, board by board, I wondered how on earth Patrick had initially gotten the crate into the attic. It was far too wide to fit through the door or the dormer window. One other thing that was quite peculiar is, it didn't have any shipping markings on it at all. All the other crates in the attic had markings, but not this one. Even the crates with Mam's belongings and Patrick's had markings, though they'd obviously been repurposed, being originally used to ship other cargo.

The next day, I went back up into the attic with the goal of rearranging it as best as I could, and bringing some furniture down, such as the mirrored bureau. The crate I'd dismantled and removed left an enormous area I could fill to help declutter the rest of the attic. I grabbed the broom I'd brought up from downstairs and began sweeping years and years of dust and cobwebs away from the wall. At a certain point, I noticed something odd. A strange sliver of light leaked through the bottom of the wall. How could that be, I wondered? At closer inspection, I could also see light coming through various seams of what appeared to be a panel. Me, being the curious cat I am, got on my hands and knees to inspect these light gaps more thoroughly. It soon became clear to me there was something on the other side of the wall!

Within minutes I had taken the crowbar to the wall, swiftly removing a panel about one metre square. The mysterious light was coming from another dormer window, blocked off by what turned out to be a false wall! Of course! Why hadn't I realised that before? You could easily see two dormer windows on the outside of the house, but somehow I never gave it a second thought that there was only one visible in The Attic. Silently berating myself for not being more observant, I crawled into the space. Once I'd gotten into the hidden room, I raised my head to see what was the mystery, the reason for a false wall. In a startling moment of revelation, I understood the crate blocking the hidden panel never came in through the attic door and why. Patrick had built it *inside* The Attic, meant as a decoy! At that second of discovery and realization, I loved Patrick Finley Mottorshaw more than ever.

Because I'd never seen money or any form of legal tender before, at first, what I'd found didn't completely register. If not for the library and my curiosity about life beyond our land, I might never have understood the significance of my find. Though, to be clear, I still had only a vague notion of what I'd stumbled upon. What was it I'd discovered? Hidden treasure. By shear luck I'd revealed a bounty far beyond my imagination. Yes, because neatly stacked against the true back wall of the attic, in a space approximate three metres square, were stacks and stacks of gold and silver bullion, along with buckets and buckets of silver and gold coins, and stacked bundles of paper money. It was an amazing sight to behild.

I hadn't the foggiest what the current value of it might be, so in the next days, having taken a thorough inventory and researching the library for clues, I ventured a guess. My calculation was what I thought might be on the low side. The best I could figure, there must have been the equivalent of at least two million Australian dollars! Not completely comprehending money or its value, instinctively, I still knew it was a significant cache. Upon entering the real world as I liked to call it and realised its true value—which I'll just say was far more than my initial guess—the impressiveness of my discovery utterly astonished me.

I knew it was far more money than I'd ever need to survive—even if I lived twice; but I knew I had to protect it and keep the knowledge of it to myself should I ever come in contact with other people. I'd read enough to know, throughout history, people had killed for less.

If not for my profound loneliness and utter boredom, I might never have found what ended up being the keys to my freedom from the farm. Until my parents died, I'd never felt trapped, or caged, or a prisoner of any sort on our farm. No, it was my home, and all I knew. Because I was happy to travel the world via our massive library, I felt content there. And, with my help, my parents made sure we had food, clothing, enough oil, wood and water to survive. I never, ever wanted for anything. Everything they knew about running our farm, I knew. I was confident I could survive alone because they taught me well; but without them, without their physical presence, our home had lost its purpose for me—along with its joie de vivre. Even though I had my Pippa with me, without Mam and Da and their enormous personalities, my world had become unreasonably quiet, and excruciatingly lonely. I cannot emphasize that enough. I felt as if I were the last human being in the world, and for all I knew, I might well have been. There was something crushing about the very possibility of it.

In the past, though they'd left me for weeks on end, I knew Mam and Da would come back at some point. So consumed was I with managing the farm and reading endlessly in their absence, time flew by. As such, loneliness was a foreign concept to me. Naturally, once Pippa came into my life, their absences became even easier to endure. Forever alone and on my own, home became a sort of desert island in the middle of a vast ocean. In my case, the vast ocean was kilometres, and seemingly endless kilometres of uninhabited countryside. I knew nothing of the world beyond our land except what I had read in books. I also knew my staple provisions would last only so long before I'd have to venture out on my own to replace them. Aside from the fact I didn't know where I was or where to go for such things, without physical money, inherently I understood I'd have had a tough time of it. The very notion of my uncertain future had weighed heavily on my mind.

Finding Patrick's money negated a significant portion of my worries. However, once I found it, a new and more pressing problem presented itself. How would I transport that much treasure without becoming an easy target for thieves, or worse? Value-wise, it was not an insignificant amount; but, physically, it was sizeable and frightfully heavy. Contemplating how I would transport it, I feared for both myself and Pippa. I knew she would do everything in her power to protect me against rogue elements, but I didn't want to be reckless, risking either of our lives in the process, just for money. Yes, I had Da's guns, and was prepared to use them to defend us against baddies, but it's the very last resort, isn't it? One doesn't want to invite any kind of trouble, let alone deadly trouble.

I felt certain once I left the farm, I most likely would never return. I don't know why I thought so, though I suppose despite my wonderful memories as a child, my attic discoveries had tainted whatever happiness the farm held for me. I knew I would never forget what my parents had done, hiding me away from the outside world and myself, and who knows what they may have done to Patrick. Chances of holding on to whatever remnants of happy memories I had with them were greater if I left and didn't have constant reminders of what might have happened staring me in the face. Knowing I wouldn't be back, I had to figure out a way to take every bit of the bounty with me.

Upon deciding I would leave the farm forever, I still had to figure out how to leave. I calculated how much food and other necessary supplies I had on hand and how long I'd have to prepare for our escape. If nothing went wrong, I had probably eight months to a year before I'd need to replenish my staples or leave altogether. Since I was alone, with only Pippa to keep me company, just keeping the farm running at a minimal level proved to be a lot of backbreaking, seemingly unending work. I had no choice. It was still my home, and it needed me to do whatever I could to keep it running until the time came to leave and say goodbye.

Letters

∞   ∞   ∞   ∞   ∞

With Patrick's bounty discovered, I refocused my attention on the rest of the attic. I moved a few things around and brought the dresser and mirror down to my bedroom. It wasn't easy to do, but bound and determined, I somehow got it out and down the stairs to the second level. Once I'd finished reorganizing and rearranging, the attic was far easier to navigate.

After I finished, I could focus on the items in the crate I believe belonged to Mam. I'd left that task to the end because each time I'd think of it, a rush of sadness would crash over me like a tsunami. I hated the feeling, and so I left it until last. When I finally sat down and began going through her belongings, I will tell you it was a tough day for me. As soon as I pushed through my grief and began the process, though, a certain calm came over me, befuddling me in a way. Had I known that would happen, I mightn't have dragged my feet for so long.

Almost immediately, I came across a stack of snapshots, wrapped with a faded green silk ribbon that itself had seen better days. There were twelve somewhat aged black and white photos. Some had Mam in them, others had people who I thought had a strong resemblance to her. On the backside of each were names printed in a child's scrawl.

One reoccurring name, as best as I could determine, was Quinn Mahoney Ó Dubhghaill, sometimes Quinn Mahoney, or simply, Q. One appeared to be a wedding or engagement photo with a man's name printed on the reverse—one Seamus Ó Dubhghaill. A few images also had the name of towns that, until I could do further research, I could only assume were in Ireland. With the pictures spread out before me, I sat on the attic floor for hours, trying to make sense of them.

The woman named Quinn and Mam looked a lot alike; I guessed they must have been sisters, or cousins, even. I remember Mam mentioning one sister in particular—her favourite—but I don't recall her ever mentioning her by name. Why not, I wondered? Why would you keep such an important part of your life to yourself? And, from your own child, no less? Truth was, I knew almost nothing about Mam and Da—Eoin and Kellen O'Shea. *Why not?* That question repeated itself in my head over and over again in the months following their deaths.

When I'd exhausted every bit of speculation I could muster about the photographs, I continued examining the contents inside the crate. Aside from some old clothes and such there wasn't much in there of interest. One item, a heavy brown wool overcoat, lay neatly folded on the bottom of the container. I lifted it out only to find it had been a tasty meal for moths as there were numerous small holes in it. I imagine Mam might have worn it in her homeland, but once in Australia hadn't needed a coat quite so heavy. We have our chilly season, but nothing, I imagined, as bitter and wet as Great Britain might be. Again, it was all conjecture as everything I knew I'd only read in books. The coat didn't fit me; but even if it had, it was beyond repair. As I refolded it, though, I felt something bulky in the coat's hem.

I examined the rectangular and bendable thing through the fabric with my fingers. Excited to discover a new potential hidden treasure, I tore at the fragile hem which came apart easily. I caught my breath as a bundle of yellowed envelopes, bound with dark blue silk ribbon, fell into my lap. They were letters, addressed to Kellen Maebh Mahoney O'Shea, 85-87 Wills St, Dunkeld VIC 3294, Australia. The return address was from QRMO, 3 Eglinton St., Galway, Ireland. The writing on the envelopes appeared to match the chicken scratch on the photos.

My heart raced as I untied the ribbon and opened the first letter. I pulled a folded piece of paper from the envelope and quickly unfolded it. The words written on it were strange and nonsensical, as if an unschooled child wrote it. I didn't understand any of it. My spirits sank. I opened the next, and the next, until I'd opened all nine of them, all with the same disappointing result. For a brief glimmer of a moment, I thought I would finally learn something about Mam and her past, but no.

Utterly confused, let down, and gravely dispirited, I refolded the papers, tucking them back into their envelopes. I examined the envelopes, noting there seemed to be no pattern to their timing. Some were months and months apart; others, years. I wondered if there might have been others, and if so, where might they be? I quickly dug through the contents of the crate again, hoping I'd missed the others, but no. I hadn't missed anything.

Carefully, I retied the ribbon around the nine letters I had. As I pulled the bow tight, the impact of what I'd just learned hit me. Fat tears slowly slipped down my cheeks. Soon, sobs wracked my body, the depth of my disappointment evidently so deep, when it erupted with such force, it took me by surprise.

For a long time I wept, but once cried out, I put everything back into the crate, keeping only the photos and the letters out. Then, I anemically climbed down the stairs and went straight to my bed. Except for minimally caring for the livestock and Pippa, I stayed there for three days. Curled in a ball, with Pippa and her dolly on the floor beside me, I felt alone and lost.

Towards the end of my self-exile from everyday life, as I lie in my bed, bemoaning my very existence, it came to me there might be more correspondence, unclaimed, in Dunkeld. At the realization, I shot up into a sitting position. After all, I mused, it had been months and months, over half a year, since Mam and Da had passed. The possibility of unclaimed postage was high and intrigued me. The more I thought about it, the more I wanted to see for myself. The mystery and its endless possibility is what finally got me up and into action.

Dunkeld

∞ ∞ ∞ ∞ ∞

About a month later, in mid-January and shy of a year since losing my parents, Pippa, Dolly, the Loadstar and I were finally on our way to Dunkeld. We'd have ventured out weeks earlier, but it took me that long to locate the road off the property. I'd never been farther from the house than not quite a kilometre, so it took some serious exploration to locate it. I'd found the town of Dunkeld on one of Patrick's maps; but even though the map showed a road to Dunkeld, finding it from our property was quite another matter altogether. All the roadways from our property, which were more like paths, led to open land, and all ended not too far from the house. Desperate to find an exit off our land, each day I'd saddle up Queenie, one of our two riding horses, and with my pup running alongside, sought a viable way out.

Queenie was one of two Andalusian horses Da brought home when I was perhaps seven or eight. They named the other one Rusty. Da said the breed was quite rare and valuable as there weren't many in Australia. Money-wise, their value was of no consequence to me. Queenie, our mare and my absolute favourite, was a magnificent animal. Her colouring was what Da called dapple grey; and so, her body was a medium grey, dappled with silver spots. Her legs, mane and face were black, and her long and beautiful tail, silver. She had a sweet personality and was also quite affectionate with me. Always calm and never skittish, she seemed to favour me, too.

Rusty, the gelding, was our other riding horse and Da's favourite. Also a fine animal, his temperament was not so sweet. He was a strawberry roan with dusky grey legs and a rusty-coloured face—hence his name—black tail and mane. Rusty never liked me and wasn't shy about letting me know it. He'd attempted to kick me several times, and even bit my upper arm once. His bite wasn't enough to break skin, but still left me with a nasty bruise. Terribly anxious around him, I'd stay on my guard whenever he was in the near-vicinity. After Da passed, I tried to ride the ornery bugger, but he wouldn't have it.

After a while, however, I think he realised he would have to tolerate me, or he'd get stuck in the corral forever. Each time I took him out, I feared he'd end up bucking me off in the countryside where I'd end up dead in a ditch. To even imagine my darling furry mate left alone without me was unbearable, so I resorted to loosely tethering Rusty to Queenie to get him exercised. If he ever bolted, for whatever reason, no one would get harmed but him.

In my search for an egress from the farm, I discovered how incredibly isolated we were. I began to more fully understand why not one person in my entire life had ever stumbled upon us. Patrick wasn't kidding in his diaries when he espoused the joys of being "as far away from civilization as possible," building our house in the center of the property. Near the end of my searching, I feared I'd lose my way out there and would likely die alone, trapped within the confines of our property. The day I finally discovered a road off the farm, I was overjoyed. To be fair, I should confess my girl Pippa is who found it. I'd actually missed seeing it as it was on the other side of a grouping of trees. Had I been searching with the truck, or alone, we'd have never found it.

From the map it didn't appear as though the tiny town was too far away. I guessed I could get there and back in a day—*if* all went to plan. I wasn't sure my calculations were correct, as I had to guess about everything. I'd been nowhere, and I had no one to ask for guidance. I also had zero references; as such, every decision made was a poke in the dark.

We were in the middle of summer and it was already evident the day would be a scorcher—far hotter than usual. I packed the truck with ample water, extra food and two fifteen litre cans of petrol; the .30-30 and the revolver, including several boxes of extra rounds. I wasn't exactly sure how money and the world worked, as I'd never had to purchase anything. Just in case, I took a short stack of Australian dollars from Patrick's attic stash.

And, because I'd not been anywhere, nor had I ever seen people beyond my family, the entire way I brooded, questioning my decision to venture out into the world. Pippa sat on the passenger seat with her dolly beside her, intently listening as I voiced my doubts aloud. Did I have the proper clothing? What would I say to strangers? What was the rest of the world even like? Was there an outside world? Was it safe? Was it dangerous? Confusing? Welcoming? If I actually found it, might I find my way back? I had so many questions and no answers.

From time to time Pippa would pick Dolly up and push her against my shoulder to show me her unwavering support, which I appreciated very much. I headed into Dunkeld blind with the hope of tracking down where Mam's letters from Quinn got sent. If I could manage that, I'd be amazed, and far beyond pleased.

The dirt road from the edge of our property to the highway was filled with endless ruts and random holes, making it a slow, rough ride. After nearly two hours of relentless and painstaking jostling, we finally reached the highway I hoped would lead us to our ultimate destination. Sadly, its condition was not much better; but by then, not much better felt fantastic. At least the roadway had bitumen paving, though a good deal of it sorely needed repair.

From when I turned west onto the two-lane highway, it only took another hour before the weathered sign for Dunkeld appeared. In that hour, I'd seen only one other vehicle. It was unfamiliar to me as it wasn't a Loadstar. I learned later it was a passenger automobile. Whatever it was, it sped by us as if we were standing still.

Not knowing what to expect, upon seeing the Dunkeld sign I got instant butterflies in my stomach. The closer I got to the actual town, the more I doubted my reasons for making the trip. How would I ever find the address I sought? It was like the proverbial needle in a haystack, wasn't it? Moreover, I was quite a sight—a teenaged girl, all alone save her dog, driving an enormous truck. I'd worn my best denim trousers, a blue blouse—both made by Mam, and my too-small scruffy desert boots. I'd grown considerably since my parents passed, as all of my clothing were shorter and tighter. I won't claim I was comfortable in my clothing, or even my own skin, because I wasn't in either, but it's who I was and what I had.

The farther I ventured on, the more anxious I became. I noticed there were signs naming side roads or streets, but I hadn't yet seen one called Wills Street. I continued driving slowly until I had completely passed through the town. Had I blinked, I might have missed it entirely. I continued on for a few minutes more before I could make a turnaround as the Loadstar had a significant turning radius. Once I made the u-turn, I headed back into Dunkeld.

I decided I would turn onto each little street until I found Wills Street. To my surprise, it didn't take long, and it actually amazed me how quickly I found it. I hadn't seen it on my first pass through town because the street ran parallel to the road on which I'd been travelling. The second I saw the street sign, I yelped with excitement. I turned right onto it, hoping that direction would take me back into town. I rode the clutch, driving as slowly as I could without stalling the truck so I could read the numbers on the modest houses as I drove. And then, I saw it!

The house-like white clapboard building with a hitching post out front had a sign on it—Post Office. Of course! Quite pleased with myself, as I pulled into a parking place facing the front of the Post Office, I couldn't believe my luck as it seemed far too easy. I was new in the world, a novice; and, yet, there I was, parked outside of a building I'd only just known as a strange address in a strange town in a world I wasn't even sure existed.

I sat studying the building, adorned with numerous Australian flags. It looked quite festive and patriotic. Later that day I learned they were in preparation for Dunkeld's Australian Day ceremonies later that month. I'd read about the founding of Australia, and had a vague understanding there was a public holiday, but I didn't realise it was an occasion for celebration.

For the longest time, I was actually afraid to get out of the Loadstar. I don't know why exactly, but I suppose I felt protected inside the truck cab. By getting out, I'd thrust myself into a world unfamiliar to me, where I'd never been. Yes, I was scared. Petrified, truth be told. I cannot tell exactly how much time passed before I finally ventured out, but I'll wager it was significant. I watched with intense curiosity as all sorts of people, arriving one after the other by horse, carriage, automobile or on foot, entered the building before coming out only minutes later, their hands often filled with papers or packages. Most were so absorbed in their mail they failed to notice me or anything else.

My experience of seeing other people for the first time really was something else. It was almost as if I were a ghost, quietly observing living people going through their daily routines. I dare say, the experience, beginning to end, fascinated me. I nearly forgot why I was there.

On the drive home I kept looking at the three unopened letters lying on the seat next to me, suppressing an intense urge to pull to the side of the road and rip them open. Before I left for Dunkeld I vowed if there were recent letters, I would wait until I returned home before opening them. I meant to keep my promise to myself, no matter how difficult it became to do so.

As I drove, I also replayed my encounter with Mr. MacKinnon behind the Post Office bench, over and over in my head. He wore a plastic placard pinned to his shirt that read Mr. MacKinnon. Behind him on the wall, a square wood frame with no glass showcased a white piece of paper with printing that said January 15, 1968. I immediately thought of the grandfather clock at home, and getting it properly reset once I returned to the house. My next thought was, it's 1968. I'd never known what year we were in, so I was immediately intrigued, thinking how I could use that information to fill other gaps in my own timeline.

Mr. MacKinnon looked ancient to me, because he was the oldest person I'd ever seen. He was also likely close to the conclusion of his working years if not his life. Nearly deaf, he also seemed to have difficulty with his vision. As if my shyness and nervousness weren't enough, because of his diminished hearing, I almost had to shout in order for him to hear me. I explained, stuttering heavily, that my mam and da had passed unexpectedly and I came to pick up their mail—forced to repeat myself three times. Each time by necessity was louder than the last. Once he finally understood what I was asking, Mr. MacKinnon was incredibly kind to me. He asked me to describe Mum and Da, and once I did, he nodded knowingly.

"Oh, yeah, yeah, yeah," he said in a different dialect than I'd ever heard before. "I remembered them two. I especially remember your mum. Sweet lady. Hey now," he queried, peering over the bench, referring to Pippa and her dolly. "Who're your little mates there?"

"Ah… um… Pi-pi-pippa, a-a-a-an'… her d-d-d-olly—D-D-Dolly's her name," I said, shocked by my stutter.

"Good doggie," he said to Pippa. Pippa enthusiastically wagged her raccoon tail in response, making muffled woof noises with Dolly held in her mouth.

Mr. MacKinnon said my parents had been coming in for mail for maybe fifteen years—even longer, perhaps. He remembered them because he was from Scotland and they said they had lived there for a time. Scotland? My parents lived in Scotland? Yet another mystery needing solved.

He inquired how they died. I told him I didn't know except that they came home weak, feverish and delirious for about a week before passing. He told me around the same time as their deaths, a minor flu epidemic had killed three in Dunkeld—a baby and two older folks. Several deaths had also been reported in a few smaller towns in Victoria. Maybe that's what it was, he offered. I shrugged. I couldn't say. He asked if I had anyone left after them. I lied and said I did. My gut instinct told me I'd best be careful with strangers. While Mr. MacKinnon seemed a lovely man, I didn't know him. He kindly offered his condolences and gave me Mam's mail. I bid him farewell, and then the three of us left.

I'm used to the sound of my own voice as I have a tendency to talk to myself on the regular. My Pip can hear but a whisper, so sometimes, even when I'm talking so softly, I can barely tell if I'm speaking aloud or not, Pippa will let me know, that yes, I'm speaking out loud. Even before losing my parents, I would, so it wasn't that I was alone, but more of a way I sorted my thoughts out. Somehow, thinking outside my head was better than letting thoughts, ideas or dilemmas knock around on the inside. Mam and Da used to tease me mercilessly about it. Yet, when I had to raise my voice to such a level where the postman could actually hear me, it startled me, making me feel uncomfortable.

We shan't mention the added humiliation that came from me fumbling and stammering my words the whole time. I'd never spoken to another human being before, other than my parents, that is. It was disconcerting, on top of everything else, to have to speak so loudly my first time out. Thankfully, while there, no one else came into the building to witness my mortification.

The sun had barely set when we parked alongside the barn. Completely knackered, I turned the Loadstar off, overwhelmingly thankful I'd found my way back home. I'll admit, when I set off on my adventure, I worried I wouldn't find my way home, especially the closer to nightfall it got. Despite my fears, I made it both ways without mishap. I was right proud of myself. I gathered up Mam's letters and took them with me to bed, tucking them under my pillow. I'd look at them in the morning.

The next day, after tending the livestock and playing with Pippa, with great trepidation, I opened the three letters in order of arrival. Why I expected anything different from the previous letters, I'm not sure, but I did. When I realised the letters contained more of the same, I only ended up sorely disappointed yet again. I couldn't figure out the words or the meanings, and the writing itself was atrocious. I know Mam's formal education was limited, if she had any at all, and she looked to me to educate her after a certain point in my self-education, but even she wrote better than what I found in the letters. I had to accept the likelihood her sister may have had even less education. Gravely disheartened again, I reluctantly moved on. Perhaps I'd figure out what to do about the letters some other day.

Before I left the farm for good, I'd managed another four trips to Dunkeld. One reason was to send the letter I'd written to Quinn informing her of her sister's passing. I couldn't know if she'd be able to read what I sent her, or if they'd even reach her, but I felt an obligation to let her know. I also needed clothes. I knew how to sew, but my seamstress skills were marginal at best, and it wasn't something I enjoyed doing. I had the means to buy what I needed, so I would. My criteria were basic: functional clothing that fit. Anything beyond those two requirements mattered not to me. My clothes were fraying, too tight, short, and way beyond uncomfortable. Additionally, I hoped to find someone who would buy my horses and the dairy cow when it came time to move on. The pigs, chooks, and goat, along with a wild boar and rabbits I'd hunted had fed me and Pippa for the last year.

What I didn't have to worry about were our two work horses who had died of old age, and the small herd of cattle my da grazed out on our land. In the first few months after my parents' passing, the mob had completely disappeared. I'm embarrassed to admit that while in the throes of sickness and then recuperation, with my focus on everything else, they'd completely slipped my mind. By the time I thought to venture out to look for and tend to them, they'd disappeared. Vanished without a trace; I suspected they were long gone.

I'd only been out with Da a few times to tend to the herd, so I didn't know where they might have gone or the first thing about hunting them down. We had such a considerable amount of land that, in all honesty, the very idea of venturing out too far frightened me, me being afraid I'd get lost forever. Every so often I'd go out to see if they'd returned, but they never did. Though I felt terrible about losing them, I was also relieved. What would I have done with fifty or more head of cattle? That was the one area of running our farm Da hadn't taught me before he died.

Nonetheless, I knew when the food completely ran out, or nearly so, I would leave, and that time would come up soon. I could resupply with ease in Dunkeld and continue to do so all my life; but, by that time in my life's journey, I just wanted to leave. I needed to put the farm behind me and go out and experience the world—or at least what I could of it.

13

Preparing

∞ ∞ ∞ ∞ ∞

Upon discovering Patrick's riches, I immediately began plotting my escape. No matter what I was doing, my mind stayed in overdrive calculating the logistics of leaving. Naturally, a part of me didn't want to leave because I loved my home. It was all I'd ever known, and the only two people I loved were buried there. But as the months slipped by, loneliness and a sense of hopelessness began consuming me. There were too many times I wanted to scream at the top of my lungs in the hopes my voice would somehow come back and keep me company. Once I fully accepted it really was time to move on, I'd already begun preparations for leaving. By my assessment, I figured I'd be ready in six months.

I'd already calculated I had perhaps another year of food and supplies, but it didn't matter. I couldn't possibly have lasted so long on my own without going 'round the bend. If I ate lavishly, it might take half a year to eat most of the livestock. I'd worried so about the horses and the cow, knowing I couldn't eat them, and couldn't just let them go. Domesticated, they'd likely die a slow and agonizing death in the country, or get eaten by dingoes, the very possibility of which I found repugnant. The rest, the chooks and goats, I'd eat. Somehow, I knew an idea would come to me eventually, and it did. After my first trip to Dunkeld, and seeing the bulletin board in the lobby of the Post Office, it occurred to me I could probably sell them, or even give them away.

My biggest and most significant challenge would be the gold, silver, and paper bills. How would I ever transport all of that treasure without getting robbed and/or likely killed? This dilemma weighed heavily on my mind, consuming me. At night, done in beyond reason from working the farm, I'd lie in my bed, staring at the shadows on the ceiling, thinking and fretting until I fell asleep. When I awoke the next morning, my worry picked up from the night before. Throughout the days hence, I endlessly turned the problem in my head, more and more certain I'd never find a solution. I knew if I couldn't solve my problem, though, I'd never be able to leave the farm where I'd likely perish, alone.

Long before finding Dunkeld, the solution to transporting my riches first began formulated when I finally moved the Loadstar out of my eyesight. I'd left it where my parents parked it upon their fateful return. From the beginning, seeing it every day, several times a day, it forced me to remember that dreadful time. I couldn't bear to look at it there, in that spot, as a constant reminder of that horrific day—not for one more minute. As I fired up the rig and moved it to just outside of the barn, almost like a lightning bolt striking, or a flash of brilliance, the solution presented itself to me.

You see, at that point of clarity, I realised I could modify the truck's bed to accommodate and hide the riches. Patrick's false attic wall was my inspiration. Might I possibly fashion a false bottom, hiding everything with no one the wiser? Why had this solution taken so long to manifest itself, I wondered? No matter, I'd found a way to proceed and achieved a certain level of elation with it I'd not experienced in a long while. I still had to smooth out the details, but the seed had been planted. I only needed time to perfect my proposed solution, and that might take a while. Another problem to solve, and perhaps the biggest of all—where would I stash the loot once I had it mobile?

I determined I'd have plenty of time to figure out that important detail while I plotted how to transform the truck to properly accomodate my riches. My initial challenge was to find enough wood for the project. I spent the following days doing just that. The boards from the decoy crate would not be near enough, so I resorted to emptying and taking apart several of the other wood crates in the attic. Though the attic ended up filled with hundreds of bottles of liquor, I had extracted more than enough boards for my truck bed transformation.

Before I got too excited about the Loadstar as the answer to my problem, I had to make sure I had enough fuel to get me wherever I hoped to go. We had a large distillate tank on the property, and about once a year Da would tow it away empty. A few days later he'd bring it back full. It sat way off at the edge of the cleared area of our homestead, far enough from the principal buildings where we didn't have to worry should it explode. Da said if it were any closer and ever exploded from a lightning strike, or something else, the explosion would be enough to take out all our buildings—and us! Naturally, the "something else," stuck in my head.

I'd watched Da check the tank level before, so I set about doing so, climbing up to the top of the reservoir. After unscrewing the metal lid from an opening at the top, I dipped a long wood pole down into it. I then pulled it back out, pleased to find the tank nearly full. Then, I ventured into Da's workshop to see if he had all the parts necessary to maintain the vehicle.

I'd need to change the oil and the filter, spark plugs and the like before setting off to Melbourne. I'd been doing that work with Da long before I even learned to drive it. Sure enough, Da being Da, he had two or three of everything I'd need, including a spare set of tyres. The truck had four twenty litre petrol cans strapped to the back of the bed at all times, but I discovered another four stashed in the workshop. I also located several metal water containers in which I could store about a hundred litres of water. Food, water and distillate were key to my survival once I set off.

Mam and Da were excellent teachers, showing me how to do almost everything they could do. A skilled builder above all, Da taught me well. The hidden truck bed was my first solo project, but I wasn't at all concerned because I had a plan. My intention was to build a foot tall false bottom with a floor you'd never suspect held something beneath it. Then, to further add to the illusion, I'd build walls around the floor with a gate in the back. You'd have to actually make an effort to look for something amiss to see all was not quite right. That was the idea, anyway. Over the next days, I painstakingly measured and sketched out my plans on paper.

Before I started building, I needed to ensure everything from the hidden room would fit in the space I planned to build. On the outside of the false wall, I cleared out and marked a space the exact dimensions as the truck's bed. Then, for two days, I carefully moved all the treasure into that space. Yes, it took that long. I imagined the transfer to the truck would take twice as long as I would have to carry paltry amounts at a time down the stairs and out to the truck. I'm so thankful for my careful and patient planning. Had I not done a trial run, I'd have been two inches too shallow. I adjusted my drawings accordingly and began building.

Ten days after, I stood back from it, bloody tired, and surveyed my handiwork. I shook my head, disappointed. Until I painted the wood, I'd continue to see what I didn't want seen. Thanks to my da, who was a bit of a hoarder, I turned up more than enough paint with a close enough match to the truck's original colour. By the conclusion of the following day, I finished. Once again, I examined the job from a distance.

"Grand!" I exclaimed with enthusiasm upon realising my subterfuge was successful.

It was perfect. In that moment I realised how proud of me Da might have been. A wave of sadness washed over me, the likes I hadn't experienced in over a year. I missed my parents terribly. Keeping myself busy every waking hour had kept my grief at bay, but that episode literally brought me to my knees. I wept uncontrollably for the longest time as the reality of how alone I was hit me again. I let myself cry unabated until there were no more tears, then I got up, dusted myself off, and got back to work.

Once I had the transport vehicle prepared, the slight problem of where I would keep everything remained. My greatest fear was I would do all the work only to get robbed, or make it halfway to Melbourne only to break down. Then what? Back then, I hadn't any knowledge about towing or repair shops. I assumed if I broke down, that was it—the end of my road, so-to-speak. Even so, if I had known, if the Loadstar needed towing for repairs, anyone who'd ever driven a truck would realise straight away it was heavier than it appeared. They might ask questions I wouldn't dare answer. I'd also have risked the treasure being discovered during the repair. In hindsight, I'm thankful I was oblivious as it would have been one more set of what-ifs to fret about. No, I needed assurance I would get where I was headed intact.

In Patrick's belongings I discovered a collection of road maps —yet another thing kept from me by Mam and Da. I can't remember how many times I'd asked them for maps of the area, only to be told there weren't any. We were so far away from everyone they said, nobody bothered making a map. Why would they? Nobody cared about where we were, they'd say. Yet, there they were in *The Attic* the entire time.

Once I had eyes on Patrick's maps, it took me a bit to orient myself. When I figured out where our property was, generally speaking, I had a better idea of where I might go. It's how I'd gotten to Dunkeld and back. I also found what I thought might be an ideal hiding place for my treasure. Off the main highway, almost to the outskirts of Melbourne, I'd located a smaller side road that seemed to go on forever. Whether it was still there, I couldn't tell for certain as the maps were well more than a decade old. However, I thought—*hoped*—if it were, I'd take it for a ways, then, if I could find a particular landmark I felt confident wouldn't likely disappear, I'd turn off there. I'd drive a ways more, look for yet another landmark, dig an enormous hole and bury my treasure. I planned on using the loads of plastic tarp sheeting I'd found in the workshop to weatherproof the loot. My plan was complete, or at least I hoped as much.

The most difficult thing about making plans to leave for parts unknown was that I felt as if I were planning to turn my back on the countryside and our farm. Up to that point in my life, they were my identity—my *everything*. All I'd ever learned about life came from books in our library or the people I'd buried in the ground. I hated the thought of leaving my family behind, and for the house itself to die from neglect and abandonment, or perhaps even become occupied by wildlife squatters, but what other options did I have? To say I lost quite a lot of sleep over leaving during the several months of preparation would be a grand understatement.

On The Road

∞ ∞ ∞ ∞ ∞

The day of my final departure had finally arrived. Not two weeks earlier I'd made my last trip to Dunkeld to deliver Rusty, Queenie, the milk cow, and my remaining sheep to their new family. Oh, to leave Queenie behind, that beautiful sweet creature, with strangers nearly broke my heart. No bones about it, it thrilled me to pieces to say goodbye to Rusty; but, Queenie was quite another story. It was obvious she, too, felt unsettled by the transfer. I managed to stuff my own emotions down to spare her any further trauma, but it was difficult. Thankfully, the new owners of my horses were a wonderfully kind couple who instantly sensed Queenie's nervousness, and mine.

I'd met Miriam and Chet Collins at the Post Office while posting a flyer advertising the horses. It hadn't been on the bulletin board for more than thirty seconds before they expressed interest, as they'd been standing behind me when I posted the sign. As it happened, they owned a mid-sized sheep ranch and had been hoping for replacements for their elderly horses. Thankfully, they agreed to take the other livestock when I mentioned they, too, were available. Mr. MacKinnon vouched for the Collinses, which was all I needed to decide. I didn't need the money, but I had to ask something for them lest I invite unwanted scrutiny. By the time we parted ways, Miriam had already formed a bond with Queenie, easing my own concerns. The Collins' got a tremendous bargain and at least one magnificent horse, and I could tick off another item off my departure list.

Prior to my last day on the farm, I'd packed the truck with food, water, and distillate, the extra tyres, along with a few belongings. Once the packing was completed, I took one last walk around the property, seeking to memorize every detail. At one point, I sat on the ground between Mam and Da to say goodbye. I looked towards the house, weeping buckets and buckets of tears. I didn't want to leave, but I couldn't stay, could I? Nothing was the same, nor would it ever be. If I stayed, I knew I would eventually go mad. Human beings aren't meant to be solitary creatures.

I know some people prefer solitude, those self-professed hermits like Patrick, but even he ended up seeking the company of my parents. I knew for sure I wasn't the hermit type. That evening, unable to sleep, I endlessly mulled over my plans, worried I'd left out some important contingency—some crucial detail that forgotten might dash everything. I hadn't, but still, I fretted all night. I rose well before the sun, and though whacked to my bones, I found myself filled with a strange combination of exhilaration and trepidation.

That morning, two hours before dawn, Pippa, Dolly, the Loadstar and I set off for our new adventure, heading for the closest big city on the map—Melbourne. Driving in the darkness of night made everything seem dreamlike. Was I really leaving the farm, or was I only dreaming; or worse, hallucinating? Was this really my life now—a travelling vagabond with her companion dog and a dolly? There were many times during that first leg of the trip I doubted it all, convinced none of it was real.

Within not quite an hour, as the sun breached the horizon, and after driving over a wretched dirt road, I'd found the landmark I sought. It's the place where we'd leave the road. Not only was I thrilled the turn off was still where the map indicated it would be, and where I hoped it might be, but the timing was perfect. Any sooner and we'd have driven right by, missing it in the dark. Once I turned off it, though, I only drove a short way until the road behind us was barely visible.

I stopped the Loadstar, grabbed the rifle and leapt to the ground from the truck cab. Leaving the engine running, I asked Pippa to guard the truck, then ran back to the road from where we came. I gathered some sticks and branches for my makeshift broom. Taking my time, I systematically swept the truck tracks and my footprints, continuing down the dirt road back to the Loadstar. I left no detail unattended, so determined was I to keep our location and movements undetected.

Nearly a full hour later, we arrived at the proposed stash location. I parked under an enormous tree and shut down the Loadstar before climbing down from the cab, Pippa right behind me. I slung my rifle over my shoulder and stuck the revolver inside the front of my waistband. I did a quick survey of the area for an ideal place to hide my treasure, and where we might camp for the duration of the burial process.

The chosen area was unimpressive, but it had some hills and hilly mounds surrounding it, creating a marginally protective valley. I walked a perimeter near the distance of about a kilometre and saw no evidence humans had been there—at least not for a long, long while. Splendid news. After our afternoon tea, I began marking where I'd bury my cache. The next morning, with the rising sun I began the arduous process of excavating a hole big enough for my precious cargo.

Initially, I figured it would take me three to four days to dig the hole, then fill it and camouflage it. Armed with a shovel and pickax, it actually took seven days and part of the eighth to complete the project. We spent another two days at the encampment so I could physically recover and recoup my energy. Despite leather gloves purchased in Dunkeld, at the end, my hands were raw with a few deep and ugly blisters. I'd had the foresight to acquire antiseptic salve and wrapping gauze from the Apothecary in Dunkeld; but still, my entire body, head to toe, was completely done in.

Each night, to protect ourselves from the cold and wild animals, Pippa and I slept in the back of the truck, relatively safe within its gates. Prescient plan, as each night dingoes and wild boars boldly ventured into our camp. Pippa did a brilliant job of staying quiet, though it was she who alerted me to our nightly visitors with a gentle shove from Dolly. I entertained the possibility of shooting one of the boar for food, but I had no energy left to butcher it, nor did I wish to attract scavengers who would no doubt show up at our camp demanding scraps.

The days were sweltering and the nights quite chilly; but being natives, we were properly prepared to survive the elements be what may. Each night, as we settled into our bed on the back of the truck, and just before I fell asleep, I'd marvel at the endless blanket of stars above us. In all my travels around the world since, I've yet to discover a more soothing lullaby than Australia's stunningly dramatic night sky. There's nothing quite like it.

Ten days after leaving the farm, and satisfied my burial job was completely undetectable, we hit the road for Melbourne. After taking the usual precautions, of course—leaving before dawn, covering our tracks both at the burial site and our exit onto the turnpike, and so forth. The afternoon before, wandering around the area of our camp, we'd found a sizable watering hole. For the first time since leaving home, I bathed and laundered my clothes. What a relief to be clean and not have to arrive in Melbourne looking like a right grimey hobo.

We arrived at the Melbourne city limits just at sunset. Rather than trying to navigate a strange city in the night, I headed back in the direction from which we came, travelling for about ten kilometres and searched for a place to pull over until morning. I discovered the perfect spot where we would be off the highway enough not to have to worry about being bothered by passersby.

That night did not provide the most restful sleep as I stressed over what the next days might bring for me. Not only did I worry about entering the enormous city we'd witnessed earlier, but whether I might actually find answers I so desperately sought. I suppose what kept me awake, and frightened me more than anything, was the niggling idea that in the end I might not cut it in the outside world, finding myself back at the farm, isolated and alone for the rest of my days. Needless to say, the coming days could hold the answer to my entire future. No, nothing to lose sleep over—nothing at all.

Part Three

15

The Brown House Inn

∞ ∞ ∞ ∞ ∞

Upon our arrival in Melbourne the following morning, I set my sights upon locating The Brown House Inn. I'd read about it in Patrick's diaries. From what I could gather, his best chum since childhood, Hugo Brown, was the proprietor of the inn. Patrick had mentioned Hugo many times throughout the decades in his diaries. When the boys were ten, Hugo and his family immigrated to Melbourne. The two friends had remained ardent pen pals throughout their lives until Patrick also emigrated from England.

Unfortunately, I'd found no letters from Hugo to Patrick in Patrick's crate. I thought if I could locate the inn and Mr. Brown, he could perhaps answer some nagging questions I had about my parents and Patrick, the true owner of our farm. I also hoped

Patrick might have shared something about Mam and Da with Hugo beyond what I'd found documented in his diaries.

Driving the Loadstar in an enormous city proved difficult and had me on the verge of panic from the second I entered city limits. Best as I could tell from Patrick's diary entries, I would find the inn in an area he called Surrey Hills—a section of Melbourne. Unfortunately, Surrey Hills is east of Melbourne, which meant I had to travel right through the city to the far side of it. By my standards and experience to that point, Melbourne was enormous.

Once I exited M1, or the Monash Freeway as it was called, I quickly realised I'd need to find a place to park the truck, and as soon as possible or face certain calamity. The M1 itself was a harrowing experience, bringing me to a near emotional breakdown the whole time I was on it. With all the other vehicles travelling so fast, and seemingly erratic, my whole being experienced stimulation overload. Until I could exit the highway, I was convinced certain death was imminent.

Though not sure of the inn's exact location, once I felt I might be near the vicinity of it, I parked, hoping I could find my way back. Upon exiting the freeway, I began seeing signs about parking, alerting me to be careful about where I parked. Not sure at all what consequences I'd experience should I park incorrectly, I looked for any street signs forbidding or limiting parking before I stopped. When I did finally park, I hoped with every part of me the Loadstar would be there upon my return.

Now, Dunkeld had been somewhat of a culture shock for me, but Melbourne was off the charts different from anything I'd ever experienced. I cannot stress enough how intense the experience was for me. From the moment we drove by the Melbourne city limits sign, I teetered on the ledge of what I imagine could be a massive meltdown. I'd already hidden the rifle behind the truck bench seat, though I carried my revolver tucked into my waistband, concealed from view.

I debated with myself whether I should leave Pippa in the truck to wait for my return; but, in the end, I couldn't leave her. She knew what I was thinking as she became agitated, pushing Dolly onto me as she softly whimpered, as if begging me not to leave her alone. I relented immediately, regretting I'd let the notion even dare cross my mind.

"Okay, darlin'… my Pippa BlueBlack'nWhite O'Shea… I shan't leave you 'n Dolly here." Reassuringly, I kissed Pippa's wet nose. "C'mon, girls, off we go," I proclaimed, opening the drivers' door for them.

As I stepped onto the sidewalk, with Pippa on my heels, I hoped beyond hope I wasn't making a mistake. At the time, it never occurred to me to put her on a lead, but I did worry how Pippa might behave in such a foreign environment and around strange people. As it happened, she was perfect, staying right beside me at all times—sometimes so close to me I got the sense if she could have managed it, she would have climbed right onto my back. We were both on edge.

I didn't know where we were going or how long we'd be gone, so I brought my suitcase with me. It was Mam's, brought from Ireland, and had seen better days. Still, it brought me comfort and a sense of home to have it with me. Worn tan tweed, with brass latches, it wasn't terribly large, but it contained some clothing, Mam's letters, her pictures and a few of my favourite books. It was all I had that hadn't been left behind.

Upon leaving the safe confines of the truck, the shear bigness of Melbourne loomed over me like something I cannot really explain. I'd not seen such a concentration of concrete, glass, automobiles and people before. We weren't even in the city's heart, but near its edge, and the noise of civilization was so incredibly loud to the point it physically hurt. The noise didn't assault my ears so much as my brain; perhaps, even when I think back on it, it adversely affected my entire being.

With my feet on the ground, the first unexpected hurdle I encountered was a fear of strangers. Before Dunkeld, I'd never seen another human being other than Mam and Da. Still, Dunkeld itself was tiny compared to Melbourne. Dunkeld was country, and Melbourne was... cosmopolitan—a large, *large*, seemingly endless city. Later in life, as I travelled the world to some of its largest cities, I'd laugh to myself having thought Melbourne huge, when in fact, by comparison, it was quite small.

While completely and utterly fascinated by the people I saw around me in Melbourne, they also terrified me. The way they walked and dressed seemed so foreign to me. The best way to describe them, I suppose, is they were clean, sharp and... fancy? I'll admit, I felt unduly self-conscious. I was so far from fancy in my Dunkeld store-bought clothes I could have been a vagabond. I worried how strangers would take me, so the first few I approached I'm sure were made wary of me by my own skittish awkwardness and self-consciousness, which likely oozed from my pores.

At first, it took every single ounce of courage I could muster to approach them. I presume I came off peculiar, as well I would. Aside from growing up in complete isolation, I'd been on the road nearly two weeks, living in the elements on little food and not much rest. Despite having bathed and changed clothes, I'm certain I was a frightful vision. I felt frightful, especially coming in contact with fancy people. Nonetheless, in spite of my discomfort, I pressed on. It was imperative I find the mysterious Hugo Brown and his inn. I also needed to quickly find a place for us to stay or the cab of the truck would remain our home for the unforeseen future.

I must have approached a dozen strangers, with each reaction a cool variation of the previous. Once I addressed them, they'd jump slightly, as if startled, briefly glance at me, then Pippa, before looking away. They'd scurry past as quickly as possible. It took that many, if not more—I'd lost count—awkward attempts for me to fine-tune my approach and presentation into a successful conveyance of my inquiry. Still, I remained unsuccessful and frustrated. I'd gotten to a point where I believed I'd failed, resigned to the farm as my destiny. As a result, I'd about given up when a beautifully-dressed middle-aged woman, holding the hand of an adolescent boy, actually stopped and answered my question.

"Why, yes!" she exclaimed. "I do know of the inn! You're quite close, actually. It's over on Union Road," she pointed 'over there.'

She seemed pleased to know the answer to my question and told me where it was and how to get there. Meanwhile, the young boy and Pippa made their acquaintance. I listened intently to the woman's directions while watching Pippa from the corner of my eye, fascinated to see how she interacted with the boy. I was pleased to see how sweet, gentle, and seemingly happy she was with him.

"What's her name?" the boy asked with a dialect similar to the woman's. Pippa took the opportunity to slather him with kisses, prompting giggles from the boy.

"Pippa," I replied with a smile. "Her dolly's name is... erm, Dolly."

The woman paused only long enough for me to answer the child, then continued on. I tried to comprehend her directions as her thick Australian dialect still threw me. It was English, but it sounded so foreign to me compared to my parents' Irish, even after my time in Dunkeld. When Australians spoke it always sounded to me as if they were smiling—hard. So hard, in fact, their Rs disappeared and so many of their words sounded stretched tight, or over-worked. After she left, I wondered if I'd deciphered her instructions properly.

"Good luck, dear," she said with a bright smile before continuing on her way with the boy in tow. As they walked away, the boy strained to look over his shoulder and awkwardly waved to Pippa with his free hand. Pippa's tail wagged with great appreciation of her new friend.

Although I'd lost my way, at least three times before I found Union Road and the inn, when I had to ask other strangers to assist me, each new encounter only got easier than the last. The moment I saw the inn, I became ecstatic, soaring high with confidence that upon speaking to Mr. Brown, many of my life mysteries might finally get solved. Too quickly, and to my great disappointment, my hopes were dashed.

In short order, from behind the bench, The Bartender and his substantial handlebar moustache, that would have put my da's to shame, informed me Mr. Brown had passed on.

"He's dead, miss." The older gentleman continued to wash, then dry glasses before placing them on the counter. "Aye. Kicked it nigh on not quite a year ago. Sudden. Here, then gone. Good man, Hugo was. Ain't been same 'round here without 'im."

Oh, to have only begun my journey earlier! My arrival might have preceded his death! Crestfallen is what I was. I just stood there, watching The Bartender continue his work, stunned by the news. By any stretch of my active imagination, I never expected to find Hugo Brown dead. After several minutes of choked silence, I finally spoke. My words caught in my throat as I fought tears that threatened to burst forth without notice.

"Did... um... did Mr. B-b-brown have a... wife? O-o-o-or... children?" I asked, my voice timid and quivering.

"Hugo?" The Bartender chuckled as he shook his head, "Ah, no, missy. Not likely. Not likely a'tall." He placed his hands on the edge of his side of the counter, still holding the white towel in one hand as he leaned towards me, peering over the far edge of the top of the bench. "Now, who's that there?" he asked, referring to Pippa who sat to my left, watching attentively, Dolly having been carefully laid at her feet.

"P-p-pippa, a-a-an' dat's her D-d-dolly."

"G'day, there, mate," he said to Pippa with a kind smile. Pippa stared at him, her blue eyes sparkling. He reached below the bench and came up with a small, hard biscuit. "Can she have a biscuit? Y'mind?" His Australian dialect was the strongest I'd heard since my arrival.

"O-o-oh… erm…" I stammered. A biscuit? For a dog? I'd never heard of such a thing. I shrugged. "Y-y-y-yeah… ch-ch-cheers."

"Here y'go, girl," he said, holding the biscuit over the bench. "Catch it!" he said, tossing it to Pippa. A bit startled and unprepared, the round biscuit bounced right off her nose; but the moment before it hit the floor she recovered brilliantly, catching it in her mouth, not even chewing it before gulping it down.

"That's a girl!" he exclaimed with a hearty laugh. "She's a right beauty, she is. Righto, then… I'll have ya talk to The Cousins, hmmm…? They'll sort yas out."

"Th-th-the C-c-cousins?"

"Yeah, yeah… Hugo's kin from America. He left the place—whole kit 'n caboodle—to 'em. Hang tight…"

He turned and left his station, exiting from behind the bar through an opening at its end. He slowly ascended a flight of dark wood stairs I initially thought was but a doorway to another room, his brown leather boots treading heavily all the way to what I presumed was the top. I waited for what seemed like aeons, taking in my surroundings in his absence.

From the outside, the inn didn't strike me as a warm or welcoming place. The exterior paint was weathered and brown, as one would expect, with an off-white wood trim creating diagonals along the front of it. Even the sign itself was unremarkable. But inside? It was warm, welcoming and homey, engulfed with the tantalizing aroma of fresh-made stew. It smelled like lamb. In an instant, I never wanted to leave.

The decor was what I would describe as a comfortable mix of masculine and feminine. Dark, heavy wood beams and paneling beautifully complimented the heavy pieces of upholstered furniture scattered throughout the establishment, along with dark wood tables and chairs. The draperies were brightly coloured, however, and they'd adorned every table with a vase of stunning, fresh-cut flowers. Richly coloured paintings of myriad artistic styles adorned nearly every space of the interior walls, in some spots, from floor to ceiling, and even *on* the ceiling. At the far end of the large common space was an impressive fireplace made of craggy stone, covering a good portion of the wall. A small area on another wall had some type of platform. I later learned it was the stage for the house band and visiting musicians who performed every night of the week the inn was open.

The clomping sound of The Bartender coming down the stairs faster than he went up pulled me out of my surveillance mode. He stopped as he reached the floor and casually beckoned me to join him.

"C'mon up. They'll see yas upstairs—in their flat." He beckoned again.

"Oh… oh, all right," I muttered, unsure. I picked up my suitcase and walked towards him. Pippa picked up Dolly and followed me.

"Y'can leave it, miss. I'll keep eyes on it. C'mon, then…" he urged, waving once again.

I hesitated for a moment before setting my suitcase down, then continued walking to him. He stepped aside, making room for us to enter the staircase.

"Just at the top, miss, take a right and go to the end. You'll see their place at the end. They're waitin' for ya."

I hesitated, peering up into the darkened staircase, afraid of what I might find up there in the unknown. Meeting strange men in a strange place didn't seem like a particularly grand idea, but at least I had Pippa and my revolver with me. Still…

The Bartender sensed my trepidation.

"Ah, now… nothing to worry about, girl," he soothed. "Joan and Trix… why… they're good, *good* people. You'll like 'em— everyone does. Fair dinkum. Go on up with yas now…"

I sighed with great relief—The Cousins were *female!* I nodded, slowly beginning my climb up the staircase, with Pippa and Dolly bringing up the rear.

The Cousins

∞ ∞ ∞ ∞ ∞

The steep wood stairs creaked with each step I took. At the top I encountered an impossibly long hallway to my right with light emitting from a doorway at the end of it. To the left were closed doors on either side of the darkened hallway. As instructed, I walked towards the light, cautiously, all the while tamping down my ever-growing fear as best as I could. Pippa's nails clipped softly behind me on the hardwood flooring.

What only took perhaps a minute felt like forever to me as we edged along the hallway, both of us filled with trepidation. The women, older than myself by perhaps two decades and younger than The Bartender by nearly the same, stood waiting for us as we reached the entrance to their flat. They were each attractive in their own way.

The slight one and shorter of the two held out her hand to me, expecting me to offer mine as The Collinses had when we met.

"Hallo. I'm Joan. Joan Haversham. Please, come in, doll," she said, her strange accent completely unfamiliar to me. "Who's yer little bloke there?"

"H-h-her n-n-ame is P-P-Pippa, a-a-a-an' dat's... dat's D-d-d-olly," I replied, already embarrassed. I hated that I couldn't get my words out easily, but it always seemed to happen when I was especially anxious.

Joan's long, fine blonde hair fell easily around her tanned, freckled shoulders, framing a golden brown, yet delicate face. A full head shorter than I, she had a petite build, but wasn't in the least bit frail. She wore a light blue sleeveless cotton shift-style dress adorned with a busy flower pattern, the length reaching right above her knees. It buttoned up the front to a v-line neck. The three buttons at the hem were unbottoned, as were several at the top, partially revealing an ample bosom and a deep, tanned cleavage. I tried not to stare; still, I couldn't help myself. I forced myself to move my focus to her eyes, which were a colour I'd never seen before, instantly captivating me. Green, but brown; grey, but blue...? I couldn't decide.

Still riveted on her face and eyes, timidly, I entended my hand to Joan's, jumping a little when she took mine in hers, as she was the only person other than my parents and the Collinses I'd ever touched. Her hand was soft, but firm. She gave mine a gentle squeeze, gesturing to the other woman as she released me from her grip. "This is... *Beatrix* Brown," she said with a broad smile. "We're Hugo's nieces."

Beatrix couldn't have been more dissimilar from Joan. She was nearly as tall as me, but her build and colouring were almost the exact opposite of Joan's. With dark brown hair that was significantly shorter and wavy, and I dare say, almost mannish, her shoulders were broad, but not overly so. Beatrix wore rumpled khaki shorts with a simple white cotton t-shirt. Neither woman wore shoes nor socks, and I noticed Joan's toenails were shiny and bright pink, which I thought was the most peculiar thing I'd encountered in civilization to that point.

As Beatrix extended her hand to me, I acknowledged her with a slight nod, offering my own hand. I was immediately shocked by the strength of her grip.

"How do? And, call me *Trix*," she added with emphasis, shooting a playful scowl at Joan as she enthusiastically shook my hand. "*Nobody* calls me Beatrix," she scoffed with an accent similar to Joan's, though hers sounded similar to what I'd heard out on the street, and a milder version of The Bartender's.

"H-h-hi," I replied softly and nervous as could be. "I-I-I'm... m-m-my name... I'm..."

Trix laughed. "Don't be scared, girl. We don't bite. Come on in and sit." She eyed Pippa with a smirk. "She doesn't eat cats, now, does she?"

I shook my head vigorously, despite not being entirely sure what she'd do if she ever met a cat. Pippa had never seen a cat before—nor had I—not in the flesh, anyway.

"No matter. Cats must know a doggie's here—they both disappeared. Probably under the bed," she said, chuckling. "So, now... Reg says you were looking for our Uncle Hugo... said ya got questions for him?"

I couldn't find the words, so I just nodded as they led me to an area with an overstuffed sofa and numerous chairs. On the way, I absorbed every detail of their flat. It was decorated in the same style as the establishment downstairs, which made me wonder whether they had left it as they found it, or if the feminine touches were theirs.

They directed me to a small upholstered settee; themselves sitting on a similarly styled but larger piece across from me. I sat on the edge of the settee, self-conscious of how dirty I must have been from travelling. Despite having bathed and wearing clean clothes, I still felt road-worn. The furniture was so nice I feared soiling it. Looking at my clean and tidy hostesses, I became even more self-aware. My girl sat at my feet, gently placing her dolly on the rug. Sensing I wanted to bolt, Trix was the first to speak.

"Now, doll, can I get ya a cuppa? A pinta, perhaps?" she asked. Her smile was warm. "You look like you could use a bevvie."

I sputtered, not knowing how to answer.

Joan gave Trix a quick jab with her elbow. "Shush! Don't mind Trixie, dear. You're fine. You want anything? Food? Bevvie? Water?"

I shook my head ever so slightly.

"All right," Joan said with a nod. "Before we get to the brass tacks, what's your name, doll?"

"Sio… Sio… bhán. Siobhán… um… O… O…"

"Well, c'mon, now. Spit it out, hon," Trix interrupted me, then grinned mischievously.

Joan immediately rolled her eyes and chuckled. "See what I have to put up with? You were saying, Siobhán?"

"O-O-O'Shea. My name… is Siobhán… O'Shea."

Joan smiled. "That's a lovely name. Irish, yeah?"

I nodded.

"Where're ya from in Ireland?" Trix inquired, relaxing back into the settee, leaning slightly into Joan.

I stared at her, not knowing how to answer. Where was I from? Not Ireland, but, I actually didn't know… not precisely, anyway. "De… erm… out… a ways outside um… from here. Near Dunkeld…?"

"That's near Grampions National Park," Trix interjected. "Remember, Joan? Yeah, we've been there. Nothin' there… park's grand, but…"

"Y'don't mean…" Joan interrupted. "Dunkeld in Victoria?" she asked, somewhat incredulous. "Where were ya born?"

"S-S-Same," I answered, somewhat puzzled.

Joan looked to Trix. "I woulda thought Ireland, wouldn't you?"
Trix nodded. "Nah, yeah. Sounds Irish to me."

I cleared my throat. "I-I-I..." I said under my breath. "M-M-My mam 'n da... were I-I-Irish."

"Huh. Guess that explains it. So... what brings ya to us? How do ya know Hugo?" Trix demanded.

"Oh, I... I... I didna... know... him," I stuttered. "I..." Where should I begin, I wondered? How much should I reveal to these strangers? Both women stared at me, waiting for an answer to Trix's question. "I... my... my m-m-m-am and m-m-my da, dey... d-d-ied. 'Bout... erm... mebbe, erm... t-t-two years ago? I-I-I'm not... not really sure... not e-e-exactly."

They both spoke at once, uttering condolences that overlapped, and became unintelligible.

"After dey... erm... passed... I learned sum tings... I found..." I stopped, feeling a wave of panic about to fold over me.

Joan could see I was near losing my composure. "Now, now..." she purred. "Take your time, doll. Take a deep breath..."

I looked right at her and, without a second thought, did as instructed.

"We've got all day, don't we, Trixie?" Joan quipped, shooting a beaming smile at Trix.

"All day, love." Trix beamed back.

"What happened to your parents?" Joan inquired with a gentleness in her voice I'd not heard from her before. I wanted to cry, it touched me so.

"I'm not sure... erm... dey... dey came home from d'city sick, 'n... a... a week... a week later, well, dey was, um..." I looked at my knees. "... dead."

Trix and Joan looked at each other, and said in unison, "Flu."

I cocked my head to the side. I remembered that's what Mr. MacKinnon thought it might be.

"Tore through parts of here like a prairie fire," Trix said. "Killed a few. How d'you not get it?"

"Oh, b-b-b-but I did!" I exclaimed. "I-I-I… I was surprised dat I… dat… I didna die… too," I admitted, more to myself than anyone else.

"Were your mam and dad older folks?" Trix asked. "It seemed to only do in the little ones and the old folks."

"Mmmm… I don't tink so." I shrugged. My parents' ages never came up before. I also had no reference with which to figure it out.

"You have other family?" Joan asked.

I pursed my lips together and shrugged.

"No one?" Trix inquired, somewhat incredulously.

I shook my head no.

"Why, hon, that was… two years ago," Joan stated. She looked to Trix, then back to me. "You been on your own all along?"

"Well… me, and… P-P-Pippa."

"Out in the country?" Trix prodded.

I responded with a slight nod.

Both their faces went awash with astonishment.

"How the devil…?" Joan whispered.

Once their initial shock wore off, we ended up talking for hours. Well, what I mean to say is, Joan and Trix did most of the talking, drinking white Australian wine as they did. I only listened. Without going into any detail about my story, I gave them an abbreviated accounting of my story as I knew it. They were shocked I'd survived for such a long period in the countryside by myself. To be fair, once off the farm and in Melbourne, I was, too. Naturally, I left out the part about the treasure I'd discovered and had buried out somewhere outside Melbourne. Straight away I took a huge liking to the two women, but I was still cautious enough to know I needed to keep the knowledge of my found wealth to myself.

The Cousins were lovely in every sense of the word. They laughingly referred to themselves as middle-aged spinster cousins.

They told me all about themselves, beginning with how they'd inherited the establishment from their bachelor uncle Hugo not too long before I arrived looking for answers. He was the much older brother to Trix's father and Joan's mother. While The Cousins had other siblings—Joan had four older brothers, and Trix had a younger sister and brother—Joan and Trix were Hugo's favourites, as evidenced at the reading of his will. Together, they inherited quite a substantial amount of his wealth in addition to the inn.

Upon learning of Hugo's death and their subsequent windfall, The Cousins left their jobs in the U.S. and returned to Australia, having emigrated from Melbourne with their families when they were adolescents. The families originally lived within a mile of each other until, as they explained it, the lure of America grabbed onto Hugo's siblings after WWII. In 1946, when Joan was ten and Trix thirteen, Joan's family landed in a place called Denver, Colorado, where her father taught Art History at the University of Denver. Trix's family ended up in Los Angeles, California. Her father was a banker, specializing in film finance at a movie studio called MGM. Trix's mother also worked in the movie industry as a seamstress. Although they were apart for several years after moving to the U.S., the best friends remained close, writing letters every week until after Joan graduated from high school.

As The Cousins told their stories, I sensed something about them I couldn't quite understand. They had a closeness between them I'd only ever seen between Mam and Da. Still, I never saw such genuine affection between my parents; leastwise, if there was a similar thing between them, they never expressed it in front of me. As my parents were the only other people I'd ever known, I had no experiences with which to compare them. Still, I think my natural instincts were on high alert. The way in which The Cousins finished each other's sentences, the intimate looks between them, subtle touches... there was something there—a lovely tenderness is what I figured out later—but right then, I had no words or understanding to describe what I observed.

As it happens, while first cousins, they were also lovers. Slightly drunk, or indeed, more than slightly, they laughed nervously when they confessed their secret to me. I suppose they instantly doubted whether they should have revealed themselves to me then, if ever. I imagine the third bottle of wine had something to do with their candor. As I'd never heard of such a thing—women being lovers—the puzzled look on my face must have given them pause.

The three of us were quiet for a long while. Me pondering the oddity of what they revealed to me, and them, I suppose, quietly drowning in regret and an overabundance of wine.

At last, I asked, almost whispering, "Isn't dat... erm... would dat be... is it... I dunno... kinda..." What was the word? I wracked my brain for the right word. Ah! "... *Incest?*"

I wasn't certain, only knowing what I'd read in Patrick's library. All of this newfound and immediate civilization confused me, and swiftly became almost too much to process in a single afternoon.

Trix chuckled heartily. "Ah, well, if ya wanna get right technical about it, doll, I suppose... eh, um... would it be, love?" she asked Joan. "We are first cousins, true, but..."

Joan took Trix's hand, patting it, and then addressed me. "Siobhán, I doubt we'd qualify for incest as we cannot procreate, cannot marry; but... we are considered... erm... how can I say this...?" she turned to Trix.

"Just say it. We've gone and dipped our toes in the Rubicon already, lovey... Might as well cross the bleedin' thing."

Joan nodded. "By law, Siobhán, cousins or no, we're considered... *deviants.*"

My eyes opened wide in response. *Deviants?*

Trix nodded. The Cousins consulted each other in silence.

"Yeah, so," Trix began, "we've taken a tremendous risk in telling ya, Siobhán, but..." she glanced at Joan who finished Trix's sentence.

"... we trust you, don't we, Trixie, love? Right?"

Trix grinned. "Righto. Ya got one of the most honest faces I've ever seen." She giggled self-consciously, then downed the remains in her wineglass, which was slightly more than half full.

"Thing is, darling…" Joan continued, "you… well, you're on your own, and…" she shrugged, struggling for words, and turned to Trix for clarification. "You get what I'm saying, Trix, yeah?"

"Yeah, yeah. Shiv, love," Trix said to me, "would you… you wanna be… erm… our cousin? I mean…" Her disarming and sweet smile wasn't enough to tamp the panic that immediately engulfed my whole self.

"Your… wha… what?" I sputtered. Oh, my… Was *cousin* a code word for… whatever they were? I sat up as if to leave, but realised, where would I go if I did leave? I quickly sat back, feeling a mite trapped. "I… I…" Beside myself, I wondered what I'd gotten myself into. "… should go…?"

The Cousins roared with laughter.

"Siobhán… darling… calm down," Trix began, giggling. "Shiv, love… we don't mean…" she snickered uncontrollably as Joan continued unabated.

"We're not asking you to be…"

"Nah, yeah…" Trix giggled.

"… like us."

"Or *with* us," Trix added, emphasizing *with*.

With? The room bobbled.

"No, no, no…" Joan stated with sincerity. "You get that, right? Right, hon?"

I nodded, though I wasn't convinced, feeling woozy with sudden anxiety.

"No, we're saying, if you'd like, we'd… y'know… want you to stay with us. Here at the inn. You'll have your own room, natch. C'mon, join our strange little family."

"We are a bit strange, yeah?" Trix asked Joan with an awkward wink, then giggled.

"Oh, yeah. Right strange," Joan answered with a snort and a suppressed chortle.

"Right," Trix continued. "Shiv… you're all by your lonesome, love—you and your pup—you've nowhere to go… is what you said, anyway."

I nodded, though unsure.

"Y'know… you'd be ever so welcomed here—as you are. The two… I mean, the *three* of ya." Trix winked at me. "You could work here… your choice. Not a requirement to stay here, though."

"No, no, you could work anywhere," Joan added. "We're only saying we'd find something for you to do here… at the inn—for work. If you want. You'd have your own room… board… pay…"

"Why?" I asked. "I mean… I-I-I appreciate… it's so very… nice of ya, but… y-y-y'dunna even... I-I'm a stranger to yas."

The Cousins didn't answer my question right away. They looked to each other as they had before, without words exchanged between them, as if having a telepathic conversation.

Trix spoke first. "We like ya, love. We think you're a good egg, and we—"

"We can tell these things," Joan interrupted. "We're never wrong. Ever."

"Never," Trix agreed.

"You're a decent person come on hard times," Joan continued, "and… we wanna help you out. It's that simple. We just…" her voice lowered conspiratorially, "…but y'know, ya can't mention our erm... about… erm... y'know… *us*. You understand, right? Not to anyone, yeah? *Ever.*"

Shaking my head emphatically, I replied, "No, no… I wouldn't. I'd never…" I promised to keep their secret, though, at that moment, I didn't entirely understand what I was promising. I hadn't been a part of the real world for even an entire day, and already I was making promises to complete strangers, and keeping secrets I couldn't comprehend. Who would I tell? Who'd even want to know? Why…? I had so many questions, and some I'm sure I didn't even realise yet. I decided I'd figure out the ramifications of my promise later, but for that moment, I swore my loyalty to The Cousins, and I meant it.

"Well, then… Whaddya say, love? Ya wanna stay here?" Trix asked. "I mean, if ya don't like it… us…"

"We'd understand," Joan interjected.

"Of course we would," Trix added.

Joan continued, "But we have a right agreeable time here, eh, Trix? The customers are grand, we're in an excellent area of town, and… pay's not bad," she said, then smiled a brilliant smile.

What was there to say? I looked into their faces… their *sincere* faces… They were irresistible. I couldn't say no, so I refrained from doing so, because they were right. I had no one, nowhere to go, and despite my millions buried in the country, but for Pippa, I had nothing but the clothes on my back, the Loadstar, and a few meager belongings in an ancient tweed suitcase.

The next day, The Cousins drove me in their little sports car, a pastel blue MGB roadster convertible to where I'd parked. Pippa and I rode in the tiny backseat with the wind rushing wildly through our hair. Though a short ride, it was still grand. It relieved me greatly to find the truck right where I left it. The Cousins assured me if I'd gotten a ticket they'd take care of it. Once back at the inn, they let me keep my truck behind the inn where they kept their own car.

From the first, Joan and Trix introduced me to everyone as their cousin from the sticks, and true to their word, treated me as part of their family. Only Reg knew the truth. They called me their cousin, but they were more like aunties to me than anything else. The only other woman I'd known before meeting The Cousins was my mam, but they were so different from her in almost every possible way. Physically they were practically polar opposites; but beyond the physical differences, their personalities and how they dealt with people—me, especially—was so foreign to me as far as what I'd known prior.

The Cousins talked to me. I mean, really talked ot me. We had deep, deep, meaningful conversations. They cared what I thought, what I wanted from life. They taught me things. There wasn't anything I felt uncomfortable talking to them about; and, believe me, we had conversations about subjects that would have sent Mam apoplectic. Not to say some of our conversations didn't just about send me there myself, because they did. Still, I loved The Cousins so much... like I'd never loved Mam and Da, and probably more than I'd ever loved anyone since. In short order, they became my genuine family.

Early on, The Cousins taught me how to properly use th in words. I noticed right away they said certain words different than I knew them, using an unfamiliar sound; and me, being the curious sort, I straight up asked them about it. In no time, with their help, I had adopted a more Australian way of speaking. It was an easy transition for me.

I began working at the inn first as a chambermaid, which I didn't mind. I'd cleaned up after barnyard animals my entire life— in my mind, the worst of our guests were not much different. Then, I worked as a waitress, and in a short time worked my way to the barkeep position.

Years later, I managed the entire inn. It pains me to admit it, but when Trix offered me the barkeep job I lied about my age. I was likely only sixteen when I first arrived at the inn, though I can't say for sure what age I was; but I was tall, quiet and educated— informally, but educated all the same—and often mistaken for someone of age. About six months after I arrived, Reg met a woman from Sydney. With little notice, he up and moved there, leaving his position open. I'd only been waiting tables for about three months when Trix asked me if I was old enough to tend bar. I asked how old that would be?

"Nineteen," she said.

"Ah, what a coincidence! That's just how old I am," I replied without hesitation, promptly concerned how easy it was for me to lie—not just to her, but in general.

17

Tea Sundays

∞ ∞ ∞ ∞ ∞

The inn closed every Sunday and Monday. Every so often The Cousins would entertain the possibility of staying open the entire week, but the consideration never lasted more than a few minutes. We all appreciated our time off. The only overnight guests we allowed on those days were what we called FOTCs—Friends of The Cousins'.

Every other Sunday, after our Saturday guests had checked out, Trix and Joan would host a tea for their artist friends—a handful of locals and most who travelled from Sydney. Some came from abroad even, from as far away as the States to attend. Though it began as tea, or the evening meal, the eclectic gatherings never dispersed until well after two or later in the morning. Artists, writers, sculptors, poets, musicians, stage and movie people... they all came.

Quite a few were homosexual men, or gay as some called themselves, but those who were not didn't seem to mind. I didn't. The gay men were always the most amusing and animated attendees of the parties. A small contingency of women like Trix and Joan would sometimes appear. The lesbians. They liked to refer to themselves as The Lezzos.

"The Lezzos have arrived!" they'd announce with great fanfare as they entered the inn.

I don't know why, but the sound of the word lezzo always made me giggle—no matter how hard I tried not to. Thankfully, I wasn't the only one. Most of the lesbians were writers and poets, though occasionally a musician or artist might join their cadre. They didn't attend every week, but when they did show up, the energy in The Cousins' flat dramatically transformed. It wasn't negative; it wasn't positive; it was just... charged and almost exhilarating.

Either way, I lived for Tea Sundays as we called them, especially when The Lezzos came. They were the best storytellers; and, if I'm being honest, they couldn't resist flirting with me, which both thrilled and entertained me immensely. The Cousins warned me to be mindful of them. Even though I wasn't their kind, they cautioned, The Lezzos could be cunning and wholly persuasive. Add in a few pints, and they could be dangerously persuasive. I honestly didn't know what my kind was exactly, but The Cousins were convinced I wasn't a lesbian. Despite their warnings, I quite enjoyed The Lezzos' attention.

While the bi-weekly gatherings happened in the privacy of upstairs, the downstairs remained closed, thankfully so. Somewhere around nine the live music would kick into top gear. Tea Sundays were wonderful and populated with some of the most talented people I've ever known. Such an array of gifted people came representing various genres, never ceasing to amaze me with their brilliance. Oh, we had the finest times singing, dancing, telling stories, arguing *all* the taboo subjects—sex, politics and religion. I absolutely adored it.

Joan and Trix's connections in the entertainment field in America were how they initially developed their infamous tea crowd. While living in Los Angeles, they'd had a similar event once a month where their artistic circle of friends and acquaintances would gather. Most of their incredible art collection that hung in the inn were gifts from their talented mates prior to becoming famous or successful. Although The Cousins' decision to move back to Australia when Hugo left everything to them was a tough one because of their prohibited relationship, both women missed their native home enough to risk everything. Word spread upon their relocation to Oz, and soon after their Tea Sundays resumed in Melbourne, albeit with a mostly new crowd, continuing for many years after.

Overall, I think they made the right decision coming home. They were Australian to the bone, despite their Yank influenced accents and ways; though, as the years passed and their native dialects reemerged with a vengeance, unless informed otherwise, you wouldn't guess they'd spent a good portion of their younger years in America.

On Mondays and alternating Sundays, when not sporting a terrific hangover, I would set off to explore the city and its surrounding areas. Not a heavy drinker per se, from time to time I would overindulge. We all did. Every week I'd go to the movies as the cinema was probably my most favourite pastime of all. Next after that, were the library and the local bookstores. I mostly stayed within the Surrey Hills district, though there were occasions when I'd venture into the city itself. I found the inner city far too loud and fast-paced for my liking; and the suburbs, though pleasant enough, seemed almost prison-like to me. There, at the Brown House in Surrey Hills, I could relax and maintain a modest life— except on Tea Sundays—and avoid the bombardment of never-ending noise and commotion. I was truly content. Besides The

Cousins, I had a few friends I'd first met as customers, some I'd met at the local bookstore and library; and, of course, aside from my loyal companion, Pippa, there was my darling Fionn, who'd been my closest mate and ally almost since my arrival in Melbourne.

Deniel Andrei Constantin

∞ ∞ ∞ ∞ ∞

Yes, right after Pippa, my best mate in the entire world was Fionn Ambrose. I loved him like I imagine I would a brother, though he was old enough to be my uncle or father, even. We had a grand relationship, having bonded almost from our first meeting, shortly after I began working and living at the inn. Each evening at the same time, he'd stroll into the inn, taking his reserved spot at the bar. We didn't have to officially reserve it for him because everyone knew it was Fionn's. Whenever he was out of town, which was often, my nights just weren't the same. But when he'd return, never really saying where he'd been, it was like a special occasion. He'd sit down and order his whiskey or beer, or both, depending upon his mood. He'd raise his glass to me and say, "Hiya, Shiv. How's it go?" Then, he'd wink at me and add, "I missed your face, mate."

I'd pretend I was bothered, and retort, "Just my face?"

"Yup. Just your face, mate."

"Better'n nuthin', I expect."

I loved him as no other.

Ours was an odd pairing, not just our ages, but he was such a worldly bloke, and I… well, anything I knew was from books, and not from living or experience. I learned so much from him and I'd venture to say he enjoyed teaching me. I'm convinced I learned something new from him every time I saw him. Still, he never disclosed anything personal about himself—nor did I about myself. It was as if we had a mutual understanding. There were times I wanted so much to tell him about my hidden treasure, because I felt I could trust him implicitly; but something in me told me not to, so I didn't.

I wanted to know more about him, such as where he came from. I knew he wasn't native Aussie because his accent was different from anyone else I knew. At first, he sounded authentic, but quite soon I began noticing his accent was a blend of something from somewhere else. From where, I couldn't say as my world experience was limited, but I did have a good ear and picked up the difference fairly quickly. I also wondered why such a handsome and lovely man was not married or coupled with anyone. I assumed he didn't have a wife or children or grandchildren as he never mentioned any family members. Oddly, I knew the marital and familial status of every single regular who came into the pub, but not one thing about my best mate's.

Even though I was fine with the way things were, I will admit I often wondered about things like, what he did for a living—another subject never broached. He always dressed casually—khaki pants or shorts and usually a short-sleeved, white collared shirt, but I got the sense they were not purchased from an average store. The quality of his clothing was well above that of our usual customers.

Yes, I had questions about my bestie, but I was satisfied with how things stood believing he'd clue me in when he wanted to, or not. After a while, I had come to accept the fact he probably never would. Then, one particular evening, when I least expected it, I learned the mystery of Fionn Ambrose's life.

The evening began as any other, filled with routine and habit. Fionn, as ever, sat at his favourite seat at the bar, and I tended to my patrons. Almost from the moment he sat down I noticed he was different. I couldn't quite put my finger on why I thought so, just that he was acting peculiar. If my calculations are correct, at that point in my life I believe we'd been friends for nearly three years. As I mentioned, we saw each other every night the pub was open, spending each evening deep in conversation in-between me serving patrons. That particular evening, I suspected Fionn had something going on with him; what exactly I cannot say—an inner struggle of some sort—causing him to be more reticent than usual.

Near closing, I finally asked him straight out. "Fionn... you're a bit off, mate. You alright?"

Expecting a casual denial or a smooth brush off, as was his way, instead, Fionn looked at me, almost as if he were looking through me, and replied softly, "I have a thing to confess, Siobhán."

"Yeah?" I answered, cocking my head. All at once, the seriousness on Fionn's face and in his voice proved my instincts were right on.

"Yeah... yeah. I've wanted to tell you for a long while, and... erm, looking for the right occasion, y'know, and erm... well, it came to me... today... it's time. It's time to... to spill the beans, as they say."

I drew a strong breath in, exhaling through my teeth. "Crikey, Fionny... now you've got me all... I dunno... sounds serious. What's up with ya? Not gonna die on me now, are ya?" I glanced quickly around the place—it was empty but for us. "Need to bury a body, or...?"

Fionn smiled wryly and studied his wristwatch. "Closing time, yeah?" As he stood up, I feared he intended to go home and leave me hanging. Instead, he motioned to an empty table near the fireplace. "May we sit?"

"Yeah, yeah… want another pint?"

Fionn barely shook his head, but held up two fingers. "Whiskey, please."

"Right, mate."

Along with a pint glass of water for myself, I set two shot glasses filled with Bushmills, Fionn's favourite Irish whiskey, on the table in front of him. I pulled my water towards me as I sat down across from him. I said nothing, waiting for him to tell me what was on his mind. While I waited, I studied his face, a face that had fascinated me from our first introduction.

Before the two of us got to be besties, the only other bloke I'd ever really known was my da. Da was a slight man with olive skin, straight black hair and dark grey eyes. Strong, yes, but you would only appreciate that watching him work. Fionn was as dissimilar to my da as… hmpf, well, as I was.

Fionn appeared strong. He stood a little over six feet tall with a confident, fit and rugged build. Not overly so, yet you wouldn't want to challenge Fionn to a bar fight—not unless you were pissed to the tits or had a couple kangaroos loose in the top paddock. He had a full, almost unruly beard and moustache, with tousled salt and pepper hair. Both his beard and hair had remnants of auburn from his younger days, only visible when the late afternoon light from the window hit his hair just so, even though there was barely enough auburn remaining to catch the light.

Too often, when speaking to me, I'd get lost in Fionn's deep brown, soulful eyes—eyes that betrayed he had lived a life. What kind of life I didn't know, and never dared to inquire, but his eyes held promise of quite a story. When I think of Fionn, I suppose the one thing I especially loved about him, aside from his generally serious facade, was that he loved a good laugh. His head would tip back as his baritone laugh resonated through the inn, while showing off beautiful white, perfect teeth behind full, though pinkish lips. I'd never seen teeth so bright, made even more so against his dark skin. True, my friend was dark-skinned, but because of the Australian sun, I suspected, not heritage.

Except for Joan and Trix's special male friends, in contrast to other local men who frequented the pub, Fionn stood out; but in such a subtle way, it's likely no one else realise how much. He had a refinement that didn't reconcile to his appearance. In spite of being impeccably dressed, he was also rough hewn. I suppose rugged is probably a better adjective to describe Fionn. Despite his ruggedness, Fionn was gentle, kind and soft-spoken with a honeyed timbre baritone voice that could lull me to sleep if I'd let it.

More than anything, Fionn was sure of himself—wholly and brilliantly comfortable in his own skin. I think what set him apart the most, for me, anyway, was his intelligence and keen observance of his surroundings, however understated. I was aware of it, and certain Joan and Trix were as well, but others? It was as if he consciously masked his mental capacity from everyone else but the three of us.

From my first shift working for The Cousins, I took note that Fionn would come in at the same hour each evening, sitting in the same place at the bench. There were times I wouldn't see him for several days to more than a week. When I'd ask where'd he'd been, he'd only smirk, letting me see he'd heard me, yet never answered my question directly.

He mostly kept to himself. Nevertheless there were rare instances when another patron might engage him, striking up a conversation. Rather than ignore the overture or act hostile for the interruption of his solitude or our conversation, Fionn always responded in a personable, polite and quite entertaining manner. Other than those infrequent intrusions, aside from Joan, Trix, or Reg, I was the only person Fionn spoke to regularly. For the longest while, I remained certain Pippa was the attraction. Pippa took to Fionn immediately, him being the only other person besides myself who she'd purposefully greet, pushing Dolly into his leg, vying for his attention.

Our initial engagements were hit and miss, innocuous, as I waited on and bussed tables through the night. Once I got promoted to behind the bar, however, we only got closer, our conversations often continuing uninterrupted, but for me dealing with patrons, until closing. Fionn taught me about the three taboo subjects: sex, politics and religion. Naturally, we worked hard to break those rules on the regular. As such, we discussed everything you can possibly think of under the sun and moon, including the weather, local and international politics, religion, sex, evolution… *all*, that is, but our personal lives.

Neither of us ever brought up our past histories, as if we'd made a silent pact to avoid divulging anything too personal. Despite that curious omission, over the years, much of what I've learned about the actual world I learned primarily from Fionn, and has proven invaluable.

At The Cousin's Tea Sundays, with Pippa lying on the floor next to me, you would undoubtedly find Fionn and me with our heads together, oblivious to our surroundings. Joan and Trix would often refer to us as "partners in crime." The term escaped me at first, but as it was always said with a laugh, I surmised it probably wasn't a terrible thing.

Fionn began his story, jostling me to attention as I'd been lost in my own thoughts waiting for him to proceed. He spoke softly with an unusual hesitance. I leaned into him, listening with significant interest.

"You should understand, right off… All I'm going to tell you must remain between us until… I'm gone. Can you do that?"

I nodded, my interest piqued. But… gone? Was Fionn going somewhere?

"Straight away, I will tell you... I... ahem... erm... Fionn Ambrose is not... it's not me... What I mean to say... It's not my given name."

My eyebrows raised.

"True. In fact, I'm Romanian-born, Shiv. From Bucharest," he said. His rich voice—with the barest hint of a strange, foreign accent intermingled with a distinct Australian dialect—remained quiet, but even. He pulled smoke from his signature hand-rolled cigarette, blowing it out slowly through pursed lips. "Deniel Andrei Constantin... that... that was the name given to me at birth; and remained so until... my eleventh year." He paused for several moments—whether to gather his thoughts or pay mental homage to his given name, I wasn't sure.

He went on. "My family... they were wealthy financiers in Bucharest. Even during the communist rule. Through clever politics and ample bribes they were allowed to pursue their trade unmolested by the government. Their clientele were government bureaucrats and their families. Compared to most, we lived extremely well, despite living under communism.

"During my tenth summer, I'd overheard my father and uncles arguing with my Uncle Nicolae. He was my papa's eldest brother. It seems Uncle had made the fatal error of cheating an important state official's elderly aunt. By doing so, he put my family's businesses and status in terrible jeopardy. The official, Bogdan Ionescu, was also a rich and powerful man. But more than that, he was wicked—I'm convinced he was Satan's twin brother, if not Satan himself. My uncle was considered a brilliant financier, but... he was not an honourable man. He was nothing like my papa, nor was he terribly bright in any other way than finances. He was the family's, how do you say... erm... black sheep?" He shook his head. "Ah, believe me when I tell you, Uncle was a bad man... and, I promise, I could say worse."

I nodded.

"He either failed to discover the dangerous connection; or, he never considered the consequences should his thievery get discovered. Who can really say? Upon discovery of his misdeed, Ionescu accused Uncle of being a filthy capitalist, and anti-communist. He was, in fact, those things, but it wasn't information one wanted known. In Romania then, those accusations were far more heinous than being a fraudster and embezzler.

"A public trial of sorts was held, but Nicolae, well-schooled in the ways of communism, successfully bribed the apparatchiks presiding over his inquisition. I, myself, heard him bragging about it to my papa after the trial. The officials declared him innocent of Ionescu's charges. After the acquittal, publicly embarrassed and outraged he'd been out-manoeuvred by my uncle, Ionescu vowed revenge. True to his word, one year later—to the day, in fact—Ionescu exacted his revenge. He decimated… he had my *entire* bloodline… slaughtered."

I gasped. "He… *what?*"

"And, then?" Fionn proceeded, his voice barely above a whisper. "He disappeared them. Hence, I was the *only* surviving member of my people. There's no one left but me."

"And… it was him? The official?" I asked, stunned by Fionn's revelation. "How can you be sure?"

"Oh, indeed, Siobhán. I have no doubt he was the one. Sadly, I speak the truth, because… *I was there*—witnessed his evil, or at least part of it."

"How…? I mean…" I breathed.

Fionn peered across the room, but I knew mentally, he was elsewhere. I watched him, still processing the horror of what he had just revealed to me. I waited until after several long, silent minutes when he continued.

"We were all together outside of Brasov—that's to the north of Bucharest. Raina and Boleslav were my aunt and uncle, and it was their country retreat where we gathered. Raina was Papa's youngest sister. He had eight siblings in all. Boleslav and my papa had been chums since childhood and were also business partners. The gathering was the occasion of my great aunt Violeta's ninetieth birthday, the only remaining sister to Papa's mama. She wasn't expected to make it to her next birthday as she'd been ailing since the previous year, hanging on to life only by sheer will. I still remember it like it was… yesterday.

"Ah, it was a grand, but private affair, Siobhán. Only blood relatives and those related by marriage were in attendance as no expense was spared. "

He saw my eyebrows furrow as I didn't understand.

"Let me explain. In the communist bloc, you understand, if you weren't a state official, it was unwise, deadly, in fact, to appear well-off. To avoid scrutiny, we gathered in secret—or so we thought." Fionn closed his eyes and breathed in. He then drew another deliberate pull from his considerably smaller ciggy, held between his index finger and thumb, letting the smoke escape from his nose and mouth while speaking. I remained focused on him, utterly mesmerized by his history.

"It happened—the massacre—during the party. I only survived because I was out in the timbers hiding from Dumitru, Nicolae's bully of a son. Dumitru, a few years older than I, never wasted an opportunity to torment me during family gatherings—Aunt Violeta's party was no exception. As much as I hated him, ironically, I owe my life to him. Yes, because of that scoundrel, I was half a kilometre away from the festivities, hiding among the timbers. I'd been crouched behind a significant boulder for quite a long while, scared to death what Dumitru might do to me if he found me.

"I listened intently, fearing his footsteps and my ultimate discovery. Sounds of the woods surrounded me, as well as the faint sound of music wafting from the house and through the thick timber. Then, in a moment I'll never forget, all sounds, even the surrounding nature, fell silent, as if someone had flipped a switch.

All sound completely ceased. Everything became still, unimaginably so… just… eerily quiet.

"I don't know why, but in that instant I had a deep understanding something was terribly wrong. I waited, hoping it was my imagination, but when the silence continued, I stealthily returned to the party. My instincts had kicked in, I suppose, making me cautious of the unknown. Once I got back to the house, my fears were realised, far and beyond my imagination."

Fionn paused, likely mentally reliving whatever it was he had found upon his return. I clenched my fists from my growing angst, fearing to the deepest part of me his next words.

He drew a deep drag from his fag, swiftly exhaled and threw back the shot of whiskey he'd been toying with throughout his narrative. Though his eyes watered from the burn of alcohol travelling down his throat, it appeared to give him the strength he needed to continue.

"To my horror, I found all seventy-seven members of my family—my pregnant mama… my papa, my three sisters, my two brothers; aunts, uncles, cousins, grandparents, *Aunt Violeta*…" He closed his eyes for a moment, then sighed as he opened them again. "Every living blood relation I had… dead, stabbed and sliced to ribbons, with all of their throats slit as the ultimate insult —children and babies, women and men—all lying in an ocean of fresh blood."

My stomach churned with threatening bile as the scene Fionn painted for me took horrendous shape in my mind's eye, rendering me speechless.

Crushing the remains of the ciggy butt into the tavern ashtray, Fionn proceeded rolling another. With practised precision, in mere seconds, he filled the paper-thin smoke paper with tobacco from a pouch he kept in his pants pocket, rolled, lit and pulled his first draw from the fresh-made cigarette.

Bloodline

∞ ∞ ∞ ∞ ∞

"Initially, seeing what I saw, I could not move… I was frozen. The scene before me was so… heinous, immediate, and… surreal. It was far beyond my ability as a child to comprehend. In my young life I'd never seen one dead body; but in a moment, death itself overwhelmed me—surrounded me. I literally smelled the blood.

"Was I in a nightmare? Had I somehow died in the timbers and gone straight to hell? What kind of evil would mete out this sort of terrific destruction? It was as if my feet were made of lead, holding me in place, as my mind barely held onto sanity as I stood at the entrance of the ballroom. In horror, I watched what appeared to be a swag of blood on the floor slowly creeping towards me.

"Siobhán, I cannot tell you how long I stood there, but right before I believed I might lose consciousness, I heard men's voices approaching from outside. In a split second I came alive, realising if I didn't move immediately, I would soon join the massacre on the floor. Where to go? What to do? And then, I remembered a place we children would often hide to spy on the adults when visiting.

"It was a long wooden hinged bench seat under the picture window located in the family room. It had storage underneath the seat. If you didn't know of it, you would never think of it as a potential hiding place. Quickly, I darted across the room, careful to avoid the numerous pools of blood on the floor. I lifted the bench seat and quietly slipped inside, only moments before several men entered the house, closing it on top of me. My body quaked uncontrollably from fear.

"Tucked into the cupboard where I hid, through a narrow space between the wood slats, I was only just able to make out the men coming into the room. One of them I recognized from the newspaper. It was Ionescu! Though I struggled to see through the narrow space, I could still hear each and every wretched word of their conversation.

"Ionescu had come to see that his orders had been properly carried out. More than anything, he wanted assurances every last member of Nicolae's family—*my* family—were properly exterminated, and... *erased from existence for all time*. His men assured him more than once the entire Constantin bloodline was gone. Extinct. Did they suffer, he asked? When told, yes, horribly so, he laughed. Yes, Shiv... he *laughed*.

"I wanted to leap from my hiding place and rip out his throat with my own hands; but thankfully, common sense prevailed. Ionescu then commanded his henchmen to take every single body, burn them in a mass grave in the woods, and clean the premises as if the Constantins never existed. He commanded no evidence of our family be found, or that anything bad ever happened. Ionescu was well aware if news of a massacre got out, it would likely lead straight back to him." Fionn fell silent, nodding. "There is no doubt in my mind, if they had found me, I'd not be sitting here today, telling you my ghastly story."

I slowly nodded in agreement, trying not to imagine Fionn's fate had the daemons discovered his presence.

Fionn picked up the second shot glass, stared into it for what seemed like an eternity as I'd stopped breathing, and in a flash, threw his head back, downing the whiskey. He brought the glass down to the wood table with purpose, the sharp crack of glass against wood, making me jump a little.

He swiftly rolled another cigarette. Before lighting it, my friend looked right at me and stared into my face, though I feel certain it was not me he saw. Strangely enough, I wasn't made uncomfortable by his look; rather, I stared back into his face, gazing directly into his brown eyes as I waited for him to proceed. Fionn blinked, then shook his head, which was more of a twitch than anything. He lit his fag and continued.

"For hours I listened to men with blackened hearts discuss the most foul things as they disposed of my immediate family and relatives—as if they were rubbish. Sometimes, I had to cover my ears, the things they said were so foul. They were not men as I knew men. They were not animals, even, as animals have dignity and innocence—a pure purpose dictated by nature. No, they were fiends, most certainly sent up to the surface of earth straight from the depths of Hell by Satan himself.

"That first night, I prayed to God I might escape the coffin-like hiding place once evening fell, but Ionescu had instructed his men to stand guard in case of any late arriving family members. My prayers went unheeded by the same god that allowed my people to get butchered. Trapped, I endured the torture of listening to them clean up, forced to soil myself repeatedly; to suffer the night's cold, the insufferable closed and cramped space inside the window seat during the day where I dared not move a muscle for fear of exposure, and the lack of food and water.

"Besides everything else was the realization *if* I survived, I would spend the remainder of my life without my beloved family, and the memory of their slaughtered corpses burned into my brain and my innermost self. Worse still, on the final day of the disappearing, came the unimaginable smell of burning flesh—of my very own people—permeating into the interior of the bench."

While I watched Fionn's face change as he recounted his nightmarish history, silent tears rolled slowly down my cheeks. My own story was unusual and tragic, but listening to Fionn, watching him relive the horror of his life? I felt beyond grateful to have lived mine instead of his. I quietly waited for the story to continue.

"Tide's gone out..." he said, lightly tapping his index finger next to the pair of empty whiskey glasses.

"Of course," I replied, jumping to my feet as I reached for his empties. Just as I was about to snatch them up from the table, I changed my mind. Instead, I went behind the bench, grabbed a near-full bottle of Bushmills, as well as a glass for myself and then returned to our table. I was a moderate drinker, preferring beer, and never hard liquor; but this occasion warranted a diversion from my norm. I filled the shot glasses to the top, then sat down to await the rest of Fionn's horrific tale.

"Ta," Fionn said, reaching for one of his whiskeys. Picking it up, he held it out to me, encouraging me to pick up my own, which I did, willingly. We solemnly brought our glasses together with a gentle clink.

"Cheers," he said, downing his drink before I even got mine to my lips. I'd never drunk a whiskey shot before, so I hesitated, but only for a moment.

"Cheers, mate," I muttered, tilting my head back, letting the warm liquor rapidly pour down my throat. Its bite surprised me, causing a spontaneous cough, but the effect was immediate and a pleasant surprise as the warmth of the liquor affected my entire body. While I continued processing the whiskey experience, Fionn resumed his tale, rolling and lighting yet another smoke as he spoke. As long as I'd known Fionn, I'd never considered him a heavy smoker. He might draw a few puffs from a ciggy, and roll one but one every hour or so; but that night, he chain-smoked, letting very little of each go to waste. I couldn't blame him.

He inhaled the fresh smoke deep into his lungs and exhaled, talking as he did.

"It took three long days and nights for Ionescu's men to dispose of the dead bodies and purge the premises." Fionn softly pursed his lips and gently spit a bit of loose tobacco from them, wiping his lips with his thumb and forefinger. "I don't know what they did with all the vehicles, along with all of my aunt and uncle's personal belongings. When I finally exited the bench, that I could not spot a shred of evidence that anyone had ever been to the house, or even lived there, confused me.

"I thought I must be delirious from lack of sustenance and sleep. How was it that such a thing could happen? Then, in an instant of terrifying clarity, I understood I had become far more than an orphan. I was the last of my kind—the last remaining Constantin. As Ionescu ordered, my family had been erased— disappeared forever.

Fionn sighed, pausing for a painfully long while.

"Yes," he began again, "once I felt certain it was safe to exit the cupboard, even though the will to do so was there, physically I was unable. My limbs had frozen from not moving for all those days and nights. It took more than an hour even before I could finally extract myself. When my limbs finally moved, as they woke up, the agony was excruciating. At times, I wanted to scream out loud from the pain. Sadly, I realised at least I was still able to feel pain as a living person as opposed to my dead and burned-to-ashes family.

"I feared to my bones Ionescu's killers remained somewhere on the property, so I stealthily made my way through the house, sneaking from room to room, looking for any proof of my family's existence, but there was none. Not even a speck. *None!* Had I indeed gone mad? No, but Ionescu's men had so completely sanitized the property of evidence and everyone's belongings, I didn't recognize it as the home I'd visited numerous times a year since before I could remember.

"I'd not eaten since breakfast since the morning of the gathering and was starving. I searched high and low, but not a morsel remained; there was not so much as a single bread crumb in the house.

"By the time I'd made my way through the household, dusk had begun in earnest. I needed to decide. If I stayed indoors, I most certainly risked discovery, so I headed back out to the timbers. Though mid-June, the evenings remained chilly, and I wore only trousers and a dress shirt. I stopped at a small stream about a ninety metres from the residence as my pants were horribly soiled with my own filth. Erm, I'm sorry for the…"

I shook my head as if to say, go on, I'm not bothered by it.

Chagrined, he nodded.

"Once I reached the stream," Fionn continued, "I immediately took my pants off intending to wash them, but stopped myself right away, realising, if I were to clean them before nightfall, I would surely freeze to death overnight. I also realised if I left my mess inside the window bench, Ionescu's men might eventually discover it, realising a witness had survived. From what I'd heard from Ionescu's own mouth, if he suspected there might be a survivor, he would never rest until there wasn't.

"With great regret, I put my filthy, disgusting pants back on, vowing at the first break of day I'd clean myself, and then I'd go back in and clean out the window seat. In the meantime, I needed to find shelter for the night, which I did. There was a place where I used to hide from Dumitru, a rotted out space in an old tree, not too far from where I'd been during the massacre. As far as I was aware, no one knew of it but me, so… that's where I hid, and… where I spent the next forty-three nights."

My eyes opened wide with disbelief. "Forty-three nights?"

"Yes, Shiv. Forty-three, cold, lonely, miserable nights. I kept reminding myself each morning as I'd scratch another mark into my tree, 'But at least I'm alive.'" Fionn nodded as he cleared his throat. "After the first night in the timbers, I… erm… I went back to the house and cleaned the hiding place, burying everything in the timbers. The entire time, worried Ionescu or his henchmen might discover me and kill me, fear nearly overwhelmed me.

"When I finished, relieved beyond measure, I slipped back into the woods, never to return to the house. It was not an easy thing for me to do, but there was no other choice. Remember, I was but eleven years old, and had lived a privileged city life to that point. I knew *nothing* of wilderness survival, or any other survival, for that matter. Despite that, I somehow managed to stay alive, if only barely, because… what else could I do? I survived on sheer will, for the sake of my family—but only just until the forty-fourth day. That's when Gasper Jancek found me at death's door."

"Gasper… Jancek?"

"Yes, my adopted father."

I tilted my head, questioning Fionn without words.

20

Andrei Jancek

∞ ∞ ∞ ∞ ∞

"After my forty-three days and nights in the timbers, with little to eat, exposed to the elements and winter close on my heels, I became convinced I would die within the next few days, if not sooner. I could hardly walk without falling, and had begun hallucinating, seeing dead family members at every turn.

"Late that afternoon, while hunting, Papa... erm... Gasper happened upon me lying on the ground near a tree root I'd stumbled over in the morning. I hadn't the strength to get up, lying there, I prepared to die. Dazed, and in and out of consciousness when he happened upon me, before I passed out, I believed he was yet another of my hallucinations. Three days later I awoke in an unfamiliar bed, a strange house; and, as I learned much later, in an entirely different country."

As if Fionn's story could not get any more fantastical, my fascination rendered me speechless.

"Gasper was a Slovak living in Bratislava, Czechoslovakia. He spoke several languages other than Slovak, including Romanian. Despite travel under the communists being severely restricted, especially between countries, Gasper... hmmm... how shall I say? He had special connections? Later on, he explained how he suspected I'd been orphaned because of my condition, which is why he took me home with him to Bratislava. He felt certain if he hadn't, I'd have died.

"Officially, he was not supposed to be in Romania, so if Gasper had handed me over to the authorities, he'd have found himself under unpleasant, and perhaps deadly scrutiny himself. Confident he could attain the best medical treatment available for me, something he knew might not be as certain were he to turn me in to the Romanian authorities, and, sensing I needed his protection beyond my current health needs, he... adopted me. Gasper had highly attuned instincts.

"When I awoke, not sure of the situation, though in a frail state, I quickly concocted a story I hoped would secure me in his care. It was a clumsy story, full of holes, but it was the best I could do. I told him my name was André Luka and my parents had perished in a terrible accident—somewhat true—and the state had placed me with my cruel uncle Vlad, who beat me daily and starved me near to death. I'd run away and had been hiding in the timbers from Vlad when Gasper happened upon me.

"Though I had no physical signs of previous beatings, Gasper appeared to believe me. Years later he confessed he had quickly concluded I had fabricated my story, and he could find no records of such an orphan or an evil uncle Vlad. Based on my physical condition and my phony story, Gaspar suspected something awful had happened to me, which was all he needed to know.

"Until I regained my strength and my health, Gasper kept me from the public, afraid they would accuse him of unseemly behaviour. However, after three months recuperating, once I was presentable and agreeable to the ruse, he claimed me as his long-lost son, Andrei Jancek, recovered when my Romanian mother took her own life while residing in Moldavia. He had to somehow account for why I spoke Romanian and not Slovak, but didn't want my origin to be Romania where I might be more easily traced. From then on," Fionn shrugged, "he was my Papa. Since my entire family got disappeared, I didn't mind in the least; and, I grew to love him as if he were my own flesh and blood.

"Papa was rich. Though he lived under communism, he and his wealth were protected. Much like my actual family, he, too, was a financier, but more of an... erm... *unconventional* sort. There was nothing legitimate about Papa's work. Nothing. No," Fionn chuckled softly, "Papa laundered money and worked with gangsters at the very top of the criminal food-chain, many who were high officials in the government, to hide, protect and grow their ill-gotten gains.

"Even though he was a master criminal himself at the height of his profession, my papa was also kind, funny and highly intelligent; but, at the end of the day? Savage gangsters hadn't anything on my papa. Almost everything I know about finances, self-preservation and the underworld, I learned from him.

"I learned about finances, how to create fake companies, how to clean... erm... illegally acquired cash, how to make friends with the 'right' people, and how to keep clients in line, and... erm... *dispose* of the wrong people. Papa was who I am today; though, to be honest," he added matter-of-factly, "I have surpassed Papa's abilities tenfold."

"A-a-are y-y-you a... a... a g-g-gangster?" I whispered, searching his face as I did.

Fionn drew a long breath and sighed. I noted a hint of sadness in his half grin.

"Yes, Shiv... I suppose I am. But... I'm only, erm... dangerous to... dangerous people. Ask Ionescu how dangerous I am—if you can find him." With a subtle smirk, he took a drag on his ciggy as he studied my response which I imagine was one of confusion and perhaps even concern. I cannot say as I was stuck on Fionn being a gangster who probably did bad things to people.

"You needn't worry, mate. Yeah? I live two separate lives. That other one, the dark one resides in Sydney... it never comes here, right? This one... ah," Fionn chuckled softly, "well, let's just say, this bloke right here with you... this is who I'd have been if I'd never lost my family." He looked me right in the eyes, and I swear, in that moment, I thought I could see right into his soul.

I pressed my lips firmly together and nodded. What can I say? I trusted Fionn. I loved him with all of my heart. He was my best mate and his eyes never lied—not to me, anyway.

Fionn picked up the half-empty Bushmills bottle and filled all three shot glasses. He swiftly downed one of his, before pushing mine towards me, nodding with encouragement. "Go on. Don't make me drink alone, Siobhán," he urged.

I complied, instantly appreciating the warm, relaxing effects of the whiskey.

"You alright?" he asked.

"Yeah, yeah," I answered, and I was. "Yeah, I'm good. Please, go on, Fionn."

"Right, now... where was I?" He regrouped his thoughts for nearly a minute, then, "Ah, right, right. When I was twenty-five," he continued, "Papa had a massive stroke. Suddenly. While discussing a potential client in my office, he just... gave me an unusual, questioning look. Mid-sentence. He dropped to the floor like a sack of potatoes, dead.

"Before I could even properly process his abrupt departure, his accounts came to me, expecting me, demanding, actually, that I continue his work. I did—without hesitation. Soon, they found I, his apprentice, was better, more... *creative*, and far more fierce than

Papa had ever been. My reputation grew fast and exponentially. Within a few years, I sat on top of the world, making more money than I could ever spend in several lifetimes."

Fionn looked at me, nodding slightly.

"You're wondering, if I'm such a success, why am I on the edge of Melbourne living this quiet, unassuming life."

I sputtered, attempting to answer him, because of course, he was correct.

"There is a reason." He pulled a drag from his cigarette, then swiftly threw back another shot. "About a decade ago, a serious and determined rival emerged, almost from nowhere. I scoffed at his relevance. A tragic miscalculation on my part. I failed to take his threat on my business seriously until he brutally tortured and killed off a third of my clientele—those poor fools who refused to leave me for him. Another third, out of self-preservation, almost immediately jumped ship. Before I could properly act on the threat, an assassin came for me."

My eyes opened wide.

Fionn nodded. "Oh, yes. He'd been lying in wait in my garage. The instant I stepped out of my car, unsuspecting, he hit me square in the mouth with a club."

I gasped.

"Lucky for me, if you want to call it that, he didn't swing quite hard enough. Knocked off balance but for a tick, I recovered, which he was not expecting. To be sure, I was a bit wobbly, but we fought. It was an epic battle, Shiv, but short-lived as I soon put an end to him, the details of which... well, let's just say it was his last day as an assassin."

I sat and stared at him, aghast by the physical violence Fionn had suffered, while trying not to think of his would-be assassin's own demise.

He tapped his front teeth. "These are an everyday reminder of the potential danger lurking out there for me."

I didn't understand what he meant, which must have been evident on my face.

Fionn chuckled to himself, then tugged on his upper teeth, pulling them partly from his mouth! I reared backwards, shocked, which made him roar as he quickly returned them to their rightful place. I'd never seen dentures before, but I had heard of them.

"Yeah. Loads of stitches with only scars under this beard, but all my front teeth got knocked out, upper and and lower. I was a right ugly mutt for a long while." Fionn shook his head, then sighed. "My motivation to act upon the threat to my company had been thrust into top gear. So, before the rest of my clients either joined him or were also killed, I... erm... I... well, I dispatched the rival." Fionn looked at the table, then to me. "He's been, erm... neutralized. And, now has barely enough faculties remaining to comprehend he is this close," Fionn held up his thumb and forefinger but a hair apart, "to a vegetable state."

I shivered at the image Fionn managed to create in my mind.

"Since then, I've grown increasingly cautious, fearing other potential challengers in my future. As a result, I went underground where I remain to this day. All of my business is in Europe; yet, I operate solely out of Sydney as Andrei Jancek. Here in Surrey Hills, I purposefully live a quiet, humble life as Fionn Ambrose, staying well under the radar. I have enough money to live like a king three lives over, but... I daren't. Not yet. Nor can I quit doing what I do because my current accounts, who are nearly as ruthless and cunning as I, won't allow it. *No* is not a word they understand.

"However, I no longer take on new accounts—no matter the offer. In time, my existing clients will exist no more. Literally. In time, they, too, will be... properly... erm... *dispatched*. Though... as I said, it takes time to affect such dramatic changes so as not to attract too much attention to my pursuit of freedom. I must take great care to... erm... extricate myself from certain individuals who are at best considered monsters of the worst kind."

One side of Fionn's mouth raised in an attempted smile as I immediately understood his meaning.

Suddenly, another piece of the puzzle came together for me. "Ahhh, Sydney," I said, nodding. "It's where you go when you're not here."

Fionn winked at me, returning my nod. "Smart girl."

Three hours past closing, and after telling me his amazing story, Fionn left for home. Off his face, having killed a nearly full bottle of Bushmill's on his own, he seemed lighter, having finally told his story after decades of keeping it to himself. Pissed as a fart myself, I locked up the inn and practically crawled up the stairs to my room. All the while I felt overwhelmed with gratitude that of everyone in the world, Fionn chose to share his deep, dark secret with me.

The following evening, like clockwork, Fionn returned for his daily spirits. We were both a bit hungover, but acted as if nothing had happened the night before. Carrying on as usual that day and every day thereafter for the next fortnight, neither of us mentioned a word of his shocking revelation.

Throughout that strange period, I deliberated whether to tell Fionn my story. It had been two years since my last visit to my buried riches. I'd reached an impasse on that visit as to what to do with it all. Given my dilemma, Fionn telling me his story inspired me to possibly share my own. But, he'd also revealed himself to be a ruthless man. What if I told him of my riches buried in the country, just outside of Melbourne? Might he kill me for it? Or take everything?

In my heart of hearts, I felt certain I could trust him with my life. With every part of me I believed I knew Fionn, but still, something held me back. Unable to figure out what it was, despite my yearning to divulge my own story to him, I refrained. At some point in the future, I'd know when to tell him everything. Until then, I'd wait.

Darwins

∞ ∞ ∞ ∞ ∞

When I first arrived in Melbourne, straight off I discovered music —for the first time in my life. I haven't let a day pass since without it because music fills me in a way I cannot easily explain. If I could say it completes me without sounding terribly cliché, I would, because it does. When I'm happy, it makes me happier; when I'm sad, it makes me less sad. When I'm down, there's nothing better than a heaping dose of music to boost my spirits. And, truth of it is, I do get down.

By nature I'm a happy, positive person; but every so often, darkness can envelope me like a shroud, and I'll find myself in the deepest, blackest of doldrums. I'll let myself wallow for about a day; and then, I force myself to move on. I have to give myself that time, because it's necessary, especially for me, to acknowledge my blues rather than stuffing them down. I've tried that method, and it's not good for me or anyone around me.

Though I am a cheerful person, generally speaking, since losing my family, I've struggled terribly with a lingering sadness. It'll come upon me, sometimes so hard, I have to stop and just let it be for a tick. The realization that not only was my life not normal, but rather tragic as well, is quite a burdensome thing to live with day to day, because it *never* leaves. So yes, from time to time, when I can no longer ignore the reality of my life, I get down. Thankfully, music always brings me back from what I like to call my lower depths and back to my happy place.

Despite my odd childhood and the loss I unknowingly suffered, I've actually had a good and interesting life. Knowing that, I try not to dwell too long upon unfortunate things, if at all. I can look around me and see my life, kept in proper perspective, is damned bloody good. Which is why, when the darkness comes upon me, usually without warning, I'll only allow myself a brief time to indulge my melancholy. To get it out of my system, I suppose, so I can enjoy life as I normally do.

Until music entered my life, my melancholy was unbearable— sometimes overwhelming so. On the farm, we had no music whatsoever—no records, instruments, radio, singing, humming, or even whistling. To be sure, I'd read about music, musicians playing instruments and such, but it's difficult to imagine such a thing if you've never listened to it before. I'd frequently ask Mam or Da what is music, but they only shrugged and said I wasn't missing anything. Having experienced music and how magical it can be, I can't imagine how they could be so blasé about it.

As Pippa and I came into Melbourne, searching for The Brown House Inn, a street musician stood on a corner playing an instrument I recognized as a violin. I couldn't believe it! My ears had never encountered such beauty. Mesmerized and soothed, as I was experiencing intense loneliness and anxiety having arrived in a place where the visual stimulation engulfed me, so much so I thought I might go mad from it. The music instantly erased any negative feelings and emotions I had, replacing them with pure joy. I sat on a wood and metal bench across the street, completely elated until the musician packed up her violin and left. It wasn't a long time, but enough to touch me for life. Since then, music has been my elixir of happiness.

My first night at the inn, I knew I had to have died and gone to heaven when I learned the pub had a house band. They played every night of the week the inn was open. I didn't know what to expect, but after hearing the violinist on the street, the possibility of hearing music every night absolutely thrilled me.

I'd settled into my cosy room down the hall from The Cousins. Before I ventured downstairs for my tea, I decided to take a bath, my first ever with indoor plumbing and running water. It was wonderful. While I dressed and prepared to go downstairs for my tea, the house band had already arrived, set up and were in the midst of having their tea. As part of the band's compensation, The Cousins provided food every night before their initial set, and alcohol after. As The Cousins' boarder and newly hired employee, I was offered the same accomodation.

When I finally came down from my room, Pippa close behind me, there were far more patrons in the pub area than when I arrived earlier in the day. One of the largest tables had filled with a group of people I guessed might be band members and their mob. I counted twelve. The way they laughed and joked together fascinated me. They seemed so alive, happy and carefree. Not surprisingly, me being as new as a person could be in society; I found myself inexplicably drawn to them. I chose to sit at the table closest to theirs, where I could more easily observe their merriment. Oh, I loved them right away, and though I couldn't hear a word they said, I felt somewhat guilty for even wanting to eavesdrop on them.

Right before six, one by one, the band members took to the small stage and began making obnoxious sounds with their instruments. I didn't comprehend what they were doing and feared they were playing some horrible type of music. There was nothing beautiful about the sounds they made. I immediately feared that music might not be all I expected it to be, or what I yearned for it to be.

There was a large violin type instrument as tall as the man handling it. He stood it bottom up on the floor and began plucking its deep resonating strings. I now know it's called a standup or double bass, but then I hadn't a clue what it was. All the others plucked their strings as well, but none together. One had a little thing called a mandolin, two others had larger things called guitars, and the fifth man sat at a worn upright piano that needed a tuning. Don't ask me how I knew it was out of tune, but my ears knew straight away something wasn't right with it.

Music was already so new and foreign to me, but when the tuning up cacophony ended and I finally heard the band called Darwins actually play, the word *swoon* comes to mind. My only experience regarding music, prior to hearing Darwins, had been that street violinist earlier in the day. Then, because it was my only ever experience, I thought the violin was the most amazing thing— until Darwins. From the early notes struck by the band, they bowled me over. That evening I became a fan for life.

To be clear, the band name was Darwins. Period. Not *The* Darwins, or The Darwins *Band*; and certainly not Darwin. No, just Darwins. I'd made the mistake early on referring to the band as The Darwins Band to which they swiftly and roundly corrected me. It seems the band's proper name had always been a rather delicate issue with its members. Rest assured, after the tongue lashing I received, I never made that mistake again. Darwin is Australia's Northern Territory capital city. Despite its grand title, with a population of not even 50,000, in the late 1960s, it was a small city—at best. Though extremely proud of and loyal to their hometown, the band had exhausted its opportunities in Darwin, ending up in Melbourne.

Within weeks, the band and I were on a first-name basis. I can't say we were more than acquaintances because I only ever saw them in the pub. Initially, I was too shy and awkward to have any meaningful conversations with any of them, and mostly listened to them and theirs, making keen observations and taking mental notes as I did.

Jimmy O'Rourke from Darwin was twenty years old, a bass player and the band's leader. He was tall, gangly, with a mop of unruly red hair and a sad attempt at a beard. Then, I didn't have a proper description for him, but now, after many years and thousands of faces along the way, I can write with confidence the bloke had a head like a dropped pie—he was a homely man. My opinion, of course. His girlfriend and eventual wife, Maggie, had her own opinion. She thought he was the handsomest thing she'd ever seen. Different strokes, I suppose.

Maggie herself was adorable, and a little twink of a thing with her head only just reaching Jimmy's chest. Born in Ireland, with just a hint of an Irish dialect remaining, she had long, straight, jet black hair; big and round blue eyes, with a smile that lit up the room. Maggie never missed a performance, maintaining her role as the band's most energetic promoter and fan. We'd often sit together during the groups' performances, with her doing most of the talking. Anything I ever needed to know about the band, the town, her family, her friends, people she knew, people she didn't... Yes, Maggie was a bit of a stickybeak. Still, I learned loads, and then some, from her.

Also from Darwin, nineteen-year-old Dodo Monroe played the mandolin and sometimes the banjo. He founded the band with Jimmy, his best mate. Dodo's given name was Donald, but when he was born, his older brother stuttered and Dodo was what came out. Dodo didn't seem to mind at all.

Not too much taller than Maggie, Dodo was a charmer, and quite the looker. His combination of curly, wavy and straight blond hair looked strange, and a bit like an untended bird's nest, but his features were striking—broad shoulders, straight nose, strong chin, tan skin, rosy lips and the hint of blush in his chiseled cheeks. Dodo's cow eyes and thick sandy eyelashes had a way of pulling me in where I felt almost hypnotized as I watched him perform. He was a smooth talker, too, but his most wonderful singing voice elevated him to extra special status. Everyone in the band sang, but Dodo could put the room, men and women alike, into a collective faint with his velvety baritone voice.

Shep Davies played the piano. At eighteen, he was also the youngest member of the band. A bit on the chubby side, and average looking, Shep's musical genius made Darwins the band they were. He'd never had a lesson, and couldn't read or write music, but he could play any song, and any genre of music at will. I was never privy to his actual name, but though he came from Darwin, he'd actually been born in New Zealand.

The name Shep, it seems, was a shorter and kinder version of 'sheep shagger,' something Aussies playfully call people from New Zealand. That and Kiwis. Personally, I'd have preferred Kiwi, but Shep had a terrific sense of humour and fully embraced his nickname. Chocolate brown eyes, with freckles sprinkled across his upturned nose were his best features. He had an unkempt, mop of Sixties' hair with no rhyme or reason to it other than he'd likely not had a trim in months or more, nor had a comb or brush been within a mile of him.

His least attractive feature were his teeth. They were as much of a mess as his hair. Overlapping and protruding, and in various stages of decay, and terrible breath, I often had to suppress overwhelming urges to implore him to go and brush his teeth. My parents were fanatics about keeping clean teeth; and, it seems, I am, too. I held my tongue, but it saddened me greatly to think he'd someday end up toothless (and, as it happened, he did).

The oldest Darwins musician, Mick "Grandad" McDougall, played an old, weathered Gibson acoustic guitar. He said he was twenty-five, but Maggie confided in me he was actually twenty-nine. I thought he looked closer to twenty, but I wasn't much of an expert when it came to ages. He was my height, 5'10", and lanky. His short-cropped hair was thin and dirty blond, but his moustache and goatee were a coarse coppery red. I'd seen nothing quite like it. As the band's most quiet member, Mick kept mostly to himself; but onstage, *he* was the showman. He sang high, he sang low, pure or rough depending on the tune. His guitar playing was also top-notch. Compared to the rest of the band, Mick had top-rate musical skills, second only to Shep.

Originally from Adelaide, he'd originally met the band's founders while on a visit with his family in Darwin. At the beginning, Jimmy and Dodo didn't want Mick in the band because he was so much older than they were. Jimmy feared "Grandad" would want to push him out as the bandleader, but Mick convinced them he'd never want to be in charge of anything. He proclaimed himself the quintessential follower.

Petey Ryan played a beat up white Fender Telecaster electric guitar. Out of all the players, he leaned more to rock-and-roll, whereas the others clung to their folk and traditional music roots. Petey was Jimmy's older cousin by two years. They were friends, though occasionally they'd have a row about what kind of sound the band should have, and fall out for a week or two and not speak. Those were interesting times, especially while they were onstage.

Now, me, I think their two styles came together quite nicely, but to try to convince either Petey or Jimmy otherwise was a fool's errand; so, during their periods of not speaking to each other, we'd all suffer. Despite being first cousins, Petey and Jimmy looked nothing alike.

Petey was just a tad shorter than me, perhaps by two inches at the most, thin as a reed, and his near black hair was so curly you could pull a piece of it six or more inches from his head only to have it snap back when you let go. He had dark green eyes with eyebrows like delicate black caterpillars sitting atop deep eye-sockets. Petey had a smile and infectious humour that naturally drew people to him. And, he loved a good laugh. Petey's laugh affected *everyone*. His singing was no better than average, but when he got his chance for a guitar solo, his passionate and creative playing could practically take your breath away.

Darwins mostly played original songs written by Dodo and Jimmy, or if requested by the audience, they'd acquiesce and play traditional music. Jimmy refused to play what they called cover tunes by famous bands, which upset some patrons, but only for a short while. Once people heard Darwins' own tunes, that was it, they were fans.

The obscure house band should have been international superstars, they were that good. They were terrific and every bit as good, if not better, than many famous bands from that same era. I suppose timing is everything—being in the right place, at the right time and all that. Nonetheless, I have wonderful memories of them and feel extraordinarily grateful for that time in my life when we were friends.

I suppose you're wondering, if they were as great as I proclaimed, then what happened to Darwins? All I can tell you is what I've learned, having kept in touch with Maggie off and on through the years. Like so many favourite bands, they eventually broke up. Petey wanted to tour the world, but the others had started families and wanted to stay close to home. Shep always had bigger plans than being in a pub band, as did Mick.

Petey moved to America, trying his luck there, but found the music industry more cutthroat than he'd ever imagined. He stayed and became a sales manager for Ford Motor Company. He's now a retired widower with three children and quite a few grandchildren. Petey still has a cover band that plays oldies at birthday parties and special occasions.

Jimmy and Dodo opened a music store together in Darwin that, for all I know, is still in business. Jimmy and Maggie have four sons, none of whom are musicians. Dodo got married and divorced twice, with a daughter from each marriage. Both daughters are music teachers. Mick moved to London, got hooked on cocaine, then heroin and died of an overdose in late '70s.

I'm saddened thinking of such an ending for him, but when I think our initial introduction I remember sensing a profound darkness about him, so it didn't surprise me to learn of his demise. Shep works in Los Angeles as a popular studio musician and has for decades. He left the band about a year before it disbanded to play with a band in Sydney, then got an offer to work in the States. He's been there ever since and still does session work. Married several times, there are rumours Shep has fathered eight children by eight different women.

Radio

∞ ∞ ∞ ∞ ∞

Not long after I took up residence in Brown House, I got my first transistor radio. I was scheduled to bus tables for the afternoon and evening shifts and needed to eat first. I wore my outfit de rigeur—khaki shorts, a white t-shirt and white sneakers. Joan would tease me mercilessly, calling me 'Lil' Trix' because Trix and I had similar tastes in clothing. I wasn't trying to copy her, I just liked my clothing to be easy and comfortable. The second I pulled the door to my room shut, Joan called out to me from their flat.

"Oi, Shiv! *Shiv!* C'mon here, mate. I got something for ya."

I turned on my heel, sidestepped Pippa, and hurried to the end of the long hallway.

"Yeah?" I answered, following her back into theirs. "Wassup?"

"Glad I caught yas before yas went down," she replied, and held out a little red radio and a beige wire to me. "Trix 'n me, we're getting rid of stuff. Annual thing, y'know... Givin' it to the women's shelter across town, but... we thought ya'd like this. Yeah? Whaddya think?"

I took the two unfamiliar items from her. "What are they?" I asked, staring at the foreign objects, my brow furrowed.

She smiled broadly at my innocence. "It's a transistor radio, love. That little wire there? It's so you can listen by yourself. Trix got it in the States... has to be... oh, I dunno... six, seven years ago, now, but she hasn't used it in a monkey's. Still works."

I turned the rectangle contraption over in my hands. It was a right smart looking little yoke, small enough to fit in the palm of my hand. The back and sides of it were red plastic, with gold trim and lettering on the front of it. TRANSISTOR was across the top with numbers below on a cream-coloured background. The lower half of the radio looked like silver mesh. A small circle on the bottom left corner of the silver part said Trancel. On the back it said Made in Japan.

"Y'never seen one before?" she asked, somewhat incredulous.

I shook my head.

"Ah, y'little..." she laughed with obvious affection. "Here, lemme show ya how it works."

I handed the radio and wire back to Joan. She quickly slid a small switch on the side of the thing and with a click strange static sounds sprung from it. I jumped a little, making Joan laugh again. She then turned another wheel on the other side of the radio. As she rolled it, more strange sounds crackled from it until she stopped. A song I'd heard before on the jukebox downstairs came out of it. It had a thin, metallic sound quality to it, but it was beautiful all the same.

"This is my favourite station, Shiv—3UZ? Every hour of every day and night they play all the Top 40. And, here..." she pushed a silver thing at the end of the wire into a small hole on the edge of the radio and the music immediately stopped. I frowned as she handed me the other end of the plastic wire with an oblong-shaped yoke on the end of it. "Here, put this end in your ear."

I reared back slightly. "My… ear?"

Joan laughed again. She took the end of the wire from me, reached over and pushed the rounded end into my ear canal. I gasped as the music I'd heard when she first turned on the radio was now coming directing through my ear and into my head. It sounded better. Instantly filled with wonder and awe, my eyes opened wide as I gasped softly. I tilted my head and listened for a few seconds. Joan's face beamed.

"This is brilliant!" I exclaimed. "I love it!"

"Ah, we knew ya would. It's yours. Enjoy it, mate. It'll probably need a new battery soon. Dunno how old that one is. When Trix gets back, I'll have her dig up a new one and show you how to change it. Yeah?"

I nodded, mesmerized by my new radio.

Joan chuckled softly. "Right. Gotta get back to the purge 'n make room for new crap. Y'know how Trix is…" She snickered as she turned and headed back to her bedroom.

"Cheers, Joan!" I turned and left the flat, mesmerized by the beautiful thing in my hand and the music flowing into my ear, brain and soul. "C'mon, Pip!" I said, practically skipping down the hall, my girl close behind.

For years after, you would rarely see me without my AM radio, or the ever-present mono earphone stuck in my ear. As the years ticked on and electronics became more sophisticated, I'd upgrade accordingly. But, that first little hand-me-down Japanese transistor was as constant a companion as my Pippa. Before long, listening to the station every waking hour (and, honestly, every sleeping hour, too) I knew every DJ, all of their shifts, and every song in the Top 40. Natch, I had my favourites, both songs and DJs, and ran through 9 volt batteries like mad.

Holidays

∞ ∞ ∞ ∞ ∞

Much like birthdays, something we never did on the farm was celebrate any holidays—religious, cultural or public. I knew of them, or at least the concept of them from my reading; but as usual, when I inquired about them, Mam and Da gave an excuse or skillfully demurred. We also followed no religion. I remember asking once about Catholicism and The Pope one time after reading something on the subject. I learned right away it was a taboo subject and never dared bring it up again. Da said, in no uncertain terms, the subject was not up for discussion. At all. Ever. Mam held her tongue, but I could tell she had an opinion on it, only she wasn't telling.

When I first arrived at The Brown House Inn, I knew nothing of traditions or culture or holiday celebrations. It was there where I was first introduced to them. My very first holidays were Good Friday, Easter Sunday and Easter Monday which happen during our autumn time. To that point in my life, no one I knew was religious, so my experience was centered more on the holiday and party spirit than anything else. Because I was connected with the inn, those three days and festivities were focused on our guests and neighbors as we hosted parties and barbeques for them. Darwins was our entertainment, of course, and the kitchen staff went above and beyond providing their version of the traditional roast beef dinner and the famous hot cross bun.

Joan and Trish would hire a local man to wear a bilby suit to play the Easter Bilby on Easter Sunday, handing out chocolates to children of all ages. They tried to get me to do it one year when their fella couldn't make it, but I didn't want to get inside the sweaty suit. There were numerous games, fun prizes and a popular dance contest.

The Cousins loved a party and went all out for their holidays. I loved it as I'd never experienced anything quite like it. Easter Monday was both more relaxed and more festive than Easter Sunday; but, on Monday, we wrapped everything up around two in the afternoon so we and the inn staff could enjoy the other activities around the area, or be with family.

Christmas was such an interesting holiday to me. Again, the religious aspect escaped me because I knew no one who really embraced that aspect of Christmas; but the festive and giving nature of it spoke directly to my heart. I remember how puzzled I was when Trix and Joan first dragged out boxes and boxes of decorations in the beginning of December. The two of them were giddy with excitement as I'd never seen them. When I inquired about what they were doing, they soon learned I had never celebrated Christmas before. I never let on about Easter, but I couldn't manage to keep my ignorance in regard to Christmas to myself. My revelation floored them. From that point on, The Cousins were determined to make my first Christmas the best of all time—until my very last Christmas, they said.

The next few weeks were a crash course on all things Christmas. They had made it their life's work to make up for all the Christmases I'd never had, and it was brilliant. The inn itself was decorated so that there wasn't a milimetre not covered with something Christmas. The Cousins' flat was almost as over-the-top. They were so happy to use the Loadstar to pick out trees at a Christmas tree farm just outside Melbourne. I had never heard of such a thing! They let me pick out the trees for the inn and their flat, and insisted I choose a small one for my room, too.

Almost every day one or the other of Trix or Joan would take me shopping with the hopes of teaching me the art of buying presents. They insisted upon giving me money to do so, even though I didn't need it; but it made them happy—especially since they knew it would most likely get spent on presents for them. From that experience I learned what each woman liked, and how to buy the perfect present for almost anyone.

On Christmas Eve that year, the inn threw a mad bash we talked about for years. The band was absolutely grand, playing mostly Christmas holiday music I'd never heard before. As it was summertime outside, the inn had a barbeque for anyone who wanted to come and enjoy the festivities.

After the party and just before midnight, The Cousins invited me to their flat. All of my presents to them and theirs to me were wrapped and beautifully displayed under their magnificent tree. Almost reaching the ceiling, the tree was strung with little candle-like lights filled with liquid in the candle part that bubbled when the lights warmed up. They mezmerised me.

Colorful glass ornaments of varying shapes and sizes hung from the branches, and the shiny silver garlands wrapped around the tree sparkled as a color wheel sitting on the floor projected onto it, changing colors from red, green, blue and yellow as the wheel slowly turned. More Christmas music softly played on The Cousins' console record player.

I stood in their doorway, wondering why they'd asked me to come to their flat so late in the evening.

"Come in, Shiv," Joan said with a warm smile. "Don't be shy, doll. 'Allo, Pippa. Come girls… come si'down."

"'Kay…" I went in and sat down on a club chair. Pippa laid at my feet.

"On Christmas Eve," Trix began, "well, at the stroke of midnight on Christmas…"

"Yeah, yeah," Joan nodded. "It's actually Christmas…"

"Yeah," Trix continued, "we have a tradition…"

"Goes back to when we were little…" Joan interrupted. She shot a look of apology at Trix. "Sorry, love."

Trix grinned with a wave of her hand. "We each open one gift from under the tree. Usually the smallest."

"At midnight," Joan added. She looked at her watch. "Ten minutes to go," she giggled, obviously excited.

"Sound good?" Trix asked me.

I nodded. "Yup." I was agreeable to most anything at that point. I'd had a couple pints with Fionn. I knew The Cousins both had their wobbly boot on, too, but they seemed no worse for wear as they were old pros at imbibing.

"So… how it goes," Trix said, "y'pick out a prezzie… something small. The idea is, it'll give ya something lovely to sleep on 'til the mornin'. Yeah?"

"Dream about…" Joan said to Trix with a grimace. "'Sleep on'… sounds like y'mean a pillow…"

Trix looked at Joan like she was crazy, then to me. "Did y'think that, mate? I meant a pillow?"

I shook my head.

"See?" Trix chided Joan.

"Bollocks!" Joan snorted as she glanced at her wristwatch. "Five minutes!"

The Cousins stood up.

"C'mon, Shiv," Joan beckoned to me as she and Trix moved towards the tree. "Let's pick our prezzies!"

"Five, four, three, two, one… Bob's your uncle!" Trix and Joan exclaimed in unison.

Joan and I tore at our presents as Trix looked on.

At first glance I caught my breath. My present was a gold watch with a black leather band from Joan. It was beautiful. I looked at the brand name on it—Certina. Round with a gold bezel and gold face, it had narrow rectangles in place of numbers. It was so elegant and grand, it rendered me almost speechless as I muttered, "Thank you so much, Joan."

"Glad ya like it, Shiv. Put it on. Let's see it on ya." She'd already removed the wrapping from her present from Trix, but hadn't opened the box that held it. "What've we got here, love?" she asked as she pulled the cover from the white cardboard box. Once she saw what was inside, she looked up at Trix as a magnificent smile crossed her face.

"Y'like 'em, babe?" Trix asked, blushing a little.

Joan pulled the pearl earrings from the box. "Ah, I love 'em, doll." Joan leaned over and kissed Trix tenderly on her lips. It was the first time I'd ever seen affection of such a physical nature between them. They were so sweet and dear, my heart seemed to swell inside my chest.

They parted, then Joan prodded Trix. "Well, whaddya waitin' for? What did ya get from our Siobhán?"

"Lemme see…" Trix said as she pulled my wrapping off the hard black case. She pried the case open, smiling broadly once she saw what I'd gotten her. "Ah, Shiv… I love it! Look, Joannie," she exclaimed, holding the sterling silver chained bracelet up for her to see. "Ahhh… nice! It's that ID bracelet I've been wanting for so long. Thanks, mate!"

I grinned as I watched Joan clasp it onto Trix's wrist, knowing Joan helped me pick it out. It was a grand finale to a fantastic evening. I couldn't have been happier.

Later in the morning, The Cousins pounded on my door, rousing me from my slumber at six a.m.. We had no guests registered, so no one but me was disturbed.

"Ho, Ho, Ho! Merry Christmas, Shiv! Wake up, mate! Time to open more prezzies!" they hollered from the hallway.

"Bloody hell," I muttered, but rolled myself out of bed. Pippa and I followed The Cousins down the hall, all of us still in our pyjamas. When I entered their flat, I immediately saw that a multitude of wrapped presents that were not there just five hours earlier filled the underneath of the tree, spilling out far beyond it.

"What...?" I began, completely befuddled, and truth be know, still half-asleep.

"Santa Claus!" Trix exlaimed. "He comes at night when we're sleeping and drops off more prezzies!" she explained, clapping her hands together as her face filled with mirth.

Those two were like children, so excited by Christmas and all that it entailed in their own traditions. We spent the next two hours opening presents, one at a time, admiring each as they were revealed. At the end of it, the living room was filled knee-high with discarded wrapping paper, boxes and so many presents I'd lost count. They gave me so much, I was overwhelmed by it all.

I loved the entire experience and all their gifts, but the absolute best presents I got from Joan and Trix were a suitcase record player and a stack of LPs. To this day, it is the best Christmas I've ever known. I couldn't have asked for a better or more grand first time. Every Christmas since, I've paid homage to the women who taught me how to properly do Christmas and holidays in general. On that particular day, I try to remember the joy and innocence that survived so brilliantly in them well past their childhoods.

Birthdays

∞ ∞ ∞ ∞ ∞

Until I got to Brown House and met The Cousins, I'd never celebrated my birthday, nor had a birthday party, or cake or presents. One, I didn't know when I was born. Two, well... I suppose there is no "two." I just didn't know when my birthday was. Mam and Da insisted it wasn't important. I accepted it. I was alive, so I was obviously born sometime—I just didn't know when. And, how do you guess? How do you just pick a birthday out of the air? There are three hundred and sixty five days from which to choose, and every four years there's an extra day. I could never do it—I just couldn't decide—so I never did.

Joan's birthday was May 10th and Trix's was January 3rd. Their birthdays were always celebrated on a Tea Sunday, and those teas were heavily attended and by far the most festive. I thoroughly enjoyed those teas, but admittedly, the first birthdays I was secretly envious, maybe even a little sad. I never said as much and put effort into hiding my feelings. It was my problem, not anyone else's.

After the first round of birthdays, though, The Cousins apparently decided I'd been woefully left out of the birthday ritual, because on the first Tea Sunday closest to Summer Solstice they threw me an enormous surprise birthday bash. Oh, it was so grand, I just couldn't believe it was all for me.

The entire time we were getting set up for the party, Joan and Trix, with straight faces, told me it was for a special customer's birthday party. I never questioned them. I realised later The Cousins were magnificent liars, and I was ridiculously naïve.

I nearly fainted from fright when more than fifty people jumped from their hiding places and shouted "Happy Birthday" at me when I entered the strangely darkened pub. How they all managed to sneak in without alerting me is still a mystery. Yes, it was a grand affair. I won't mention how I cried like a baby once I realised it was all for me, y'know, because… it never happened.

Naturally Darwins were our entertainment, and the guests, Tea Sunday regulars and not-so-regulars, all brought me presents—so many the pile of them was nearly as tall as I am! That first time the Cousins proclaimed my birthday as "officially" June 21st. I don't know how official it was, but they made quite a spectacle of declaration. Both cousins were pretty blotto by that point in the celebration—I think I was as well (I might have had a Schooner… or four)—but it didn't matter to me whether it was official or not. After so many years without, I finally had a day that was mine, and it was all because of The Cousins.

Every year since that first birthday they celebrated the occasion of my birth with gusto. Sometimes I think they made a point of going overboard to somehow makeup for all the birthdays I'd missed before I met them. They were generous like that, and just one of the million reasons I loved them so. I never felt so much a part of the Brown House family than on my "birthdays." To this day, I have an extra special day of celebration on Summer Solstice.

The Girlfriend

∞ ∞ ∞ ∞ ∞

About three months after I arrived at Brown House, just before teatime, a woman unfamiliar to me sauntered into the inn with a large, well-worn backpack slung over her shoulder. One hand held onto the shoulder strap, the other carried a beat up tweed guitar case. From my table in the dining area, I watched her pause at the entrance and give the place a quick look over. Then, she made a beeline straight to Reg at the bar. I continued giving her a thorough suss up as she appeared to ask Reg something, then turned and strode confidently right up to Jimmy on the stage. Jimmy continued tuning his bass as she spoke to him, then nodded.

"Yeah, sure," he said. At least, that's what my lip reading eyes told me.

The woman looked to be in her early twenties, perhaps younger, maybe older; but in my opinion, she was a beaut. Golden tan, five feet six inches, give or take an inch, shoulder-length summer blonde hair with dark, natural roots. Tight faded blue jeans with both knees torn and frayed, tucked into brown cowboy boots, and a sleeveless darker blue blouse showed off a body in excellent physical condition.

That girl had more confidence than I'd ever seen in three bodies combined. When I got an opportunity to get closer to her, her big blue-green eyes, pert nose, dark and slightly arched eyebrows, and full lips got me. Freckles sprayed across her nose. Yes, I had an instant pash for her. Why, I wasn't sure, because the strange feelings she evoked in me were confusing.

Her name was Frances Elgin, but she called herself Frankie. Frankie came from America and had been travelling around Oz for the past year, sitting in with other musicians wherever she found them. She travelled to our inn specifically to perform with Darwins. Someone she'd met while visiting Darwin, who knew Jimmy, told her all about the band. Jimmy said he'd let her try out. She came to sing and play, and she did both in spades. I'm sure my mouth hung open while she auditioned with the band. Her singing voice, her speaking voice, her face, her body, the way she moved… Oh, my goodness, I experienced sensations in my entire being as never before.

For three months, almost every night while working in the pub, I had watched single people couple up, fall in love, fall into bed (so I was told) and fall apart; but I'd grown to believe I must somehow be immune to the human love experience because I felt nothing. Absolutely nothing. No man or woman prior had prompted any feelings of discomfort, joy, desire, emotional euphoria, or pain— remotely or otherwise… until Frankie.

At the end of that first evening, as the band packed up, I hung around like a lovesick pup, afraid I'd never see her again. Even the possibility of never seeing her again nearly sent me into a quiet fluster. I waited around all night until Jimmy finally introduced me to her. Unfortunately, as I recall, only garbled sounds barely resembling words fell from my mouth. And, then… her incredible eyes almost dancing with delight, Frankie winked at me.

Oh, dear readers, whatever feelings I'd felt before were mere child's play compared to what roared through specific, and unmentionable, parts of me that brilliant moment. When I learned she'd be staying with us for the rest of the month and continue sitting in with the band, elated, I nearly yelped with glee.

Reg asked me if I wouldn't mind showing Frankie to her lodgings later.

I stammered, "Y-y-y-yeah s-s-sure, Reg… e-e-easy as."

Embarrassed, the heat rushed into my face, likely turning me scarlet. The other band members continued packing up and milling about. As Frankie only had her guitar and case to pack up, she invited me to sit and have a beer with her. Rather than embarrass myself again, I simply nodded. I grabbed two tall boys, Pippa at my heels. I found Frankie sitting at the farthest table from the stage and the bar waiting for me.

I handed her a bottle, trying to hide the nervous shake cleary evident in my hand.

"Cheers," she said in an accent I'd not heard before, with a hint of Aussie, but the rest something else. She hoisted her bottle in my direction, urging me to toast.

"Ch-cheers," I muttered, clinking my bottle to hers.

"Who's your little shadow?" she asked with a sweet smile, referring to Pippa.

"P-p-pippa. And," I quickly added, "that's her dolly… erm… Dolly… is the, erm… that's Dolly." I blushed.

"She's a good dog. Well trained. You had her since she was a pup?"

I nodded.

"Nice. I'm gonna have a dog someday. Hard to do now, though…"

Intrigued by her accent, I had to ask, "Wh-where… where ya from?" I asked, my voice barely above a whisper. My shyness painfully obvious, it surprised me I managed to make even those words form.

"America. Northern California. Redding, actually," she replied. "Small town. There's *nothing* there. I lived in The City for a while… San Francisco? Yeah, then I was in The Haight for a couple years before I came down here."

She smiled at the obvious confusion on my face.

"Haight-Ashbury—it's a district in The City? Yeah, it was too crazy there for this country girl. All the hippies, drugs, and… hmmm… what's a proper word for it?" She thought for a moment. "*Debauchery*. It was everywhere." She shook her head. "Not really my scene, y'know?"

I nodded. "Why here?"

Frankie smiled, showing dim white, slightly crooked teeth. "I've always wanted to come to Oz." She smirked. "Got a bit of a thing for kangaroos."

"Really?" I decided right there and then I'd refrain from mentioning how we'd routinely hunt and eat kangaroo meat on the farm. My instincts assured me it might be a bad idea.

Frankie's laugh was hearty. "Nah. I'm pullin' your leg."

I breathed out with relief.

"No, I just…" After a few moments, she said, "Y'know, I loved the idea of Australia since I was little. My uncle Paul wanted to move here, so he sent away to some agency for information. They sent him a big yellow envelope back with all these brochures and stickers… all about Australia. Once he decided it wasn't for him, he gave it all to me. I read every brochure and every word probably a thousand times." She cast a smile at me. "I fell in love with the country and… everything in it."

"Ah." I loved watching her talk and couldn't think of anything to say in response. My cheeks went hot again. I must have been ten shades of beet by then.

"I never want to leave."

"H-h-how long have you been here?"

"A year."

"Ah."

"I can trust you, can't I?"

"Me? *Erm*… nah, yeah." I nodded.

"My visa expired nine months ago, so, um…" Frankie chuckled nervously.

I cocked my head. I was confused. What's a visa? I wondered.

"I'm a fugitive. They find me, they deport me. Send me home." She snapped her fingers decisively. "Just like that."

"*No…*"

"Oh, yeah. It's why I gotta keep moving around. I mean…" She shrugged one shoulder. "I don't mind. I'm a bit of a gypsy in that way, but… I… I don't wanna go back."

I didn't want her to go back, either. *Ever.*

The two of us sat at that table for the better part of three hours, talking, drinking, laughing until we were both rotten. I'd never been drunk before in my life. I'll admit, it didn't take much to get me there. I wasn't entirely sure I liked it, but I didn't hate it, either. The more I drank, the easier it became talking to her. The more Frankie drank, the more physical and funny she became, carrying on like a right pork chop.

I honestly don't remember laughing so much or so hard before. She told the best stories about the people she'd met along her travels, impersonating them in such a way she almost became each person. I'm pretty certain in that time span I tumbled head over in love with her. It could have been the first minute, or the last. It didn't matter. By the time I showed her to her room, I was completely mashed.

The next morning, I awoke to Frankie's sparkling eyes staring at me; her face mere inches from my own. Just staring. Once she saw I'd awakened, she smiled a sort of come-hither smile.

"Good morning, hot cheeks."

I gasped softly when I realised where I was—in Frankie's room, in her bed, entangled in arms and legs, and both of us completely starkers. Pippa sat by the door, patiently waiting. A slow panic crept into me as I desperately fought back a growing urge to bolt from her bed and to my own room down the hall—or maybe even to another country. I stiffened, head to toes, as every part of me wanted to run.

"Hey, hey, hey, babe…" she soothed. "We're okay. Hmmm…?"

The honeyed tone of her voice soothed my agitation. I immediately relaxed back into her embrace. "I'm sorry…"

"For what? Last night? Mmmm… babe, last night was amazing. I mean… mmmm…"

"I-i-i-t was?" For a tick, I couldn't remember anything before that moment, and then… heaven help me, in a split second, it *all* came flooding back. "*Ohhhh…*"

Making love with a woman, with anyone… with Frankie for the first time, and several times after that was… almost too much to take in. Wonderful… amazing… but all at once I was vulnerable, embarrassed, and a mite confused. More than anything, and most confusing of all, I got excited—*again.*

"Mmm hmm… hey, come here," Frankie purred, pulling me to her. I melted into her arms as her hands began exploring my body. She kissed me deeply on the mouth as my insides pounded with desire. Nearly lost in the moment, I remembered it was a workday for me. Not only that, but Pippa needed to go out. "W-w-w-ait…" I stammered, pulling my lips from hers. "What time is it?"

"Hmm…?"

I pushed Frankie from me as I entered a new stage of panic, but this time for a different reason. "*What's the time…?*" I leaned over the side of the bed, pawing through my clothes on the floor until I found my discarded wristwatch. The second I saw how late it was, I gasped and leapt from the bed. "*Crikey!* It's half-past nine! *Oh no, oh no, oh no…* I'm late for work! *Two and a half hours!*"

As Frankie watched on, somewhat amused, I quickly dressed and fled the room, hoping against all odds The Cousins hadn't noticed my absence, but no such luck. The instant I exited Frankie's room, before I could even pull the door shut, I ran straight into Joan, nearly knocking her down as Pippa ploughed into me from behind.

"Hey, hold on, kid!" she laughed. "What's your hurry?"

As if a criminal caught in the act, I quickly shut Frankie's door, and stammering, "I-I-I-I..."

Joan grinned knowingly. She took me by my shoulders and looked me straight in the eyes. "Hey... Shiv, Shiv... honey... it's okay. Nothing to be ashamed of. We've all been there." She could hardly contain her smile. "You alright?"

I nodded, as the heat climbed my neck once again.

Joan chuckled. "First time, yeah?"

Sheepishly, I looked at the floor and nodded.

"Good on ya, girl! I got a good look at her last night—she goes *alright!*"

"I'm sorry I'm late, Joan, I-I-I..."

"Bollocks! No worries."

"No, I have to—"

"Don't be a wanker, Shiv," Joan said with a laugh. "Just... Hey, y'know what? Get back on in there. You girls get a bath, get changed, some brekky, and... take the day off, Siobhán. Yeah? It's a slow day. Trix and me? We'll handle it. You go..." Joan gave me a wink and a click of her tongue.

"Ya sure?" I asked, surprised.

"Have a rip snorter day, love. There's only one first time—savour it, yeah?"

That first day, Frankie and I stayed in her room, leaving only to take ourselves and Pippa out for the necessaries. I'll never forget that day. I had no idea my body had such a vast array of reactions. I shan't go into details, because I wouldn't want to kiss and tell, except to say… *there wasn't just kissing*. What I will say is this: with Frankie, I reached an unreasonably high level of personal and physical satisfaction. For too long after we were no longer together, I convinced myself she had properly ruined me for anyone else. Eventually, I got over the effect she had on me, but ahhhh… *what delicious memories!*

Lest you think Frankie and my love affair was pie in the sky, I can assure you, it wasn't. We were together for nearly a year, but always with the threat of Frankie's deportation hanging over our heads. That year was mostly wonderful, except for Frankie's terrible jealous streak. While with Frankie, I never had eyes or desire for anyone but her; but so often, she'd get it into her head it might interest me to root other people. Men or women, there was no difference to her.

My previous experience, or lack thereof, unnerved her it seemed, planting suspicion I might someday yearn for more and different experiences with other people, other sexes. The entire time I was with her, though, I just never did. She made me happy. Her bouts of jealousy were tough, tough days for me. I'd be absolutely drained; and each time it seemed as if I'd lost a part of myself, or something. Whether it was love or respect or desire, I'm not exactly sure, but her suspicion slowly eroded the innocence from our relationship.

Because of Frankie, I now have zero tolerance for jealousy of any kind. Not one little bit. It's ugly and creates unnecessary doubt and unhappiness. You either trust someone or you don't. It's just that simple.

Trix and Joan's friends, and most of their regulars, loved and adored Frankie. Sometimes, I'd just sit and watch her with our customers or our Tea Sundays guests as if she were my own private entertainment. I could never get over how comfortable she was in her own skin. Honestly, I've known no one like her before or since.

One month into our second year together, Frankie was apprehended by immigration just outside Brown House and got swiftly deported. It happened so fast there was no opportunity for goodbye or even to properly process her expulsion. One minute we were a couple, and the next, she was gone. Just... *Gone*.

I suppose it wouldn't have been so awful if she'd have written to me or called from America once she arrived safely, but she didn't. Not ever. I'd no idea whether she was alive or dead. I attempted tracking her down, but as she had frequently reminded me, a gypsy never stays in one place too long. There were times in the months after I wondered if immigration had done me a favor by deporting her.

The following year I shed a million tears, feeling abandoned and bereft; though, if I'm being honest, my tears were more for believing myself inconsequential to here than anything. If not for the support of The Cousins and Fionn, I don't know how I might have coped during that dark, grim year.

On the one-year anniversary of Frankie's abrupt exit, Maggie casually informed me, almost in passing, that while we were together, Frankie had managed to "sleep" her way through Darwins, their girlfriends, their wives, including Jimmy and Maggie. What? No! The news stunned me. I couldn't believe it. When? How? I was *always* around, I protested. Maggie assured me it hadn't been Frankie's first go at the fair, so-to-speak. She was a born sneak. I asked Maggie why she waited so long to tell me as I mightn't have wasted a year of my life in mourning. Maggie apologised, but until she told me, she didn't think I'd appreciate hearing the truth. I'd have likely killed the messenger. I hated to admit it, but she was right, I would have. I'd have been mad at Maggie for hurting me instead of Frankie. On that day, I officially quit mourning the loss of my first one true love, who, as it turned out, was apparently everyone's one true love—almost literally.

For a long, long time, despite knowing about her cheating, I missed Frankie so much, wondering what ever became of her; but, mostly I'd just think how grateful I was that *she* was my first love.

In the first spring after the turn of the century, while living in America, I visited Palm Springs, California, for the Dinah Shore festivities. Some friends from Los Angeles had invited me to stay at their desert home for the week. The Kraft Nabisco women's golf tournament, widely referred to as Dinah Shore, was an annual lesbian-centric event. Thousands of women, gay, straight and otherwise, descended upon the area every Spring for golf, partying, hookups—and everything in-between.

My friends brought me to a concert at one of the country clubs where the performance lineup was all lesbian performers—musicians and comedians. The icon of women's music, Cris Williamson, was the headliner. To my shock and surprise, I discovered the opening act was none other than Frankie Elgin. I hadn't thought of her in years. Excited to see her again, I purposely sat in the back row so as not to disturb her performance, though I doubted she'd even recognize me. It had, after all, been thirty years since we'd last seen each other.

However great she'd been during her Australian days, she had improved a hundredfold. Understandably, she'd lost any trace of her Aussie accent; but still, there she was. The truth is, though I thought it interesting to see her again after so long, in the end, her performance bowled me over. Frankie exuded an incredibly sexy, rock star vibe. If I didn't know better, and thank goodness I did, I'd have fallen for her again. After she finished her set, Frankie headed right for the bar. I waited until they had served her before I dared approached. Surprisingly, she recognized me right away.

"Shiv!" she exclaimed, genuinely surprised. "Oh, my god! *SHIV!* How the bloody hell are you? You look fantastic! What the hell are you doing here?"

I was no longer Siobhán O'Shea by then, but I didn't correct her. We hugged for a long time, chatted for about twenty minutes, and then… that was it. I never brought up my name change or her infidelity. What was the point, right? I'd moved on, she obviously had, and years before I'd made peace with her disappearing. My heart had healed (and been broken many times since), so why ruin a perfectly congenial moment?

I also no longer saw her as the Frankie I'd been in love with and a woman with whom I'd shared intimacies. No, she was just someone I once knew; which, truth be told, I found disconcerting. I listened to her talking while I tried to reconcile my emotions, or lack of, when a young dykish-looking woman came up wanting Frankie's autograph. Before I knew what had happened, they left together with nary a goodbye.

I never saw Frankie again. She looked a little worse for wear—too much alcohol, cigarettes, and fast food—but despite her shortcomings, she still maintained more than a touch of the sexy allure that had captured me so many decades before.

In 2017, I learned Frankie had succumbed to brain cancer the year before. I'll admit, when I first learned of her demise, I hoped it was another Frankie Elgin. It just couldn't be my Frankie. Once I researched further, I learned the deceased Frankie Elgin and mine were one in the same. When she passed, I was up in North Idaho writing Dot in the Weeds, completely immersed in the project. Had I still been in or nearer Palm Springs, I'd have known in time to attend her memorial service, though I'm still not sure I would have.

I did shed a few private tears, but wonder if they were for Frankie or the stark reminder that death's door is getting nearer to me by the year. Who knows? Grief can be such a complicated mess, can't it? I heard her memorial was quite an event. It would have surprised me to learn otherwise. RIP Frankie.

26

The Promise

∞ ∞ ∞ ∞ ∞

Three weeks after Fionn shared his story with me, he came into the inn later than normal, only minutes before closing time, and sat in his usual spot at the bench.

"Fionny," I greeted, puzzled. I smiled. "Missed seein' ya earlier, cobber. What brings you in so late in the evo?" I immediately set a shot glass in front of him, filling it to the rim with Bushmills.

"Evenin', Siobhán, love. Ah, well, I… I have a reason."

"Yeah? What's that, mate?"

"I wanted to come in later tonight, 'cause… erm…"

"Go on."

He tossed back his drink, emitting a satisfied grunt as he set the small glass on the bench top.

"Yeah?" I asked, noting his uncharacteristic hesitance.

"Well, darling… I've, *erm*… y'see… been thinking…" Fionn cleared his throat as he toyed with his drink. "Yeah, since that night, I think… you… y'might want to say something to me—what exactly I cannot say—but it's a thing you're not sure ya should say. To me. Or anyone, for that matter."

I swallowed hard. It took all I had not to betray the truth of what he said.

"Hmmm…? Do I have it right?" he asked, propping both elbows on the bench. Casually, Fionn clasped his long fingers together while his dark brown eyes peered into mine, deep into my being—or at least that's how it seemed in the moment.

I said nothing, frozen and unable to move or speak. Yes, of course, I wanted to tell him my story and all about my treasure; yet, despite my abiding confidence and love for him, I worried my naivete could get me robbed, killed or both. I couldn't imagine how or why he knew I had a secret to share, but he did.

"You see, Shiv, you can depend on me. Perhaps you don't know, but… you should. I wouldn't tell this to anyone else in this world, but you, and… one other. And I mean it with all of my heart. In the two, or… has it been three years already?"

I nodded. "Yep. Three."

"Righto. Since you arrived, you have become… Well, Shiv, you're my mate, natch, but more… you're like family… a… well, like a niece to me; which, you now realise, given my circumstances, is… well, it's—ripper."

I nodded. Yes, indeed, that was quite something, I thought. Ripper. Couldn't have said it better myself.

I snatched a shot glass for myself from behind the bar, filled it and Fionn's with a nip of whiskey. I picked up mine, held it out to Fionn, inviting him to join me, and tossed the liquor into my mouth and down my throat. The alluring concept of liquid courage was becoming clear to me.

"Give me a tick," I said as I came around to turn our open sign hanging in the window. "Time to mosey on home, boys," I called to the few remaining patrons. "Get along with yas, now," I added with a no-nonsense smile, while holding the door open. "Out, lads!" A collective grumbling arose, but one-by-one, the laggers slowly made their way out. It hadn't been the first time I'd sent them along right upon closing, but it didn't matter. I'm convinced, given the opportunity, some of our patrons would have moved into the pub permanently.

"Cheers, mates!" I called out when the last man exited the inn. "See yas tomorrow!" I closed and locked the door before returning to the bar. I grabbed the whiskey bottle, our glasses, and with a tilt of my head, invited Fionn to follow me to an empty table which he did. Pippa, who liked to lie at the end of the bar where she could monitor me at all times, dutifully got up and followed us. Once we settled ourselves, Pippa curled up at my feet.

That evening, I told my closest friend everything I knew about my life, including the fortune I had buried just outside the city. I held nothing back, figuring it was all or nothing. I worried the information I shared would stun or surprise him, but it didn't. Not at in the least.

Who can say how many drinks we'd consumed, but by the end of my history, we'd killed yet another bottle of Bushmills. Joan and Trix wouldn't mind, but still, I felt guilty—but only a little. Pissed again, I was but a single nip from not caring at all. Fionn, on the other hand, an old hand at drinking, wasn't nearly as pissed as I was. He sat quiet for a long while, nodding continuously as he absorbed the information.

With his words slurring slightly, Fionn finally responded.

"Thank you, Siobhán. For telling me about your life, love. The moment I met you... I knew you were extraordinary. I meant what I told ya. You can believe me—I will protect your life *and* your wealth. As such... erm... I'd like to help you manage your hidden treasure. Buried somewhere in the sticks is... well, it's not safe, darling, nor is it a… a good strategy. There may come a time that either a stranger will find it by accident, or they'll find it through you. Either way, it'll disappear—and, likely, you with it. I don't want either scenario for you. If you'll let me, Siobhán… erm… can we give it a squizz? Get an idea what we're dealing with, yeah? Then I can help you secure it. I'd also want to have a look at your farm. Would you mind taking me out there?"

"The farm?" I inquired, somewhat incredulously. When I left, I thought I'd never see it again. My first instinct was to say, yes! Absolutely! Let's go now! But a niggling part of me urged caution. Still, I promptly ignored the cautious me.

"Yes, Fionn! I *do* trust you—fair dinkum! Y'want me to take ya out tomorrow? We can go after brekky…?"

He shook his head. "No, no, darling, I'm just about legless… I mightn't wake up much before midday—if I even get it home." We laughed because we both knew he had been in far worse shape before and made it home all right. Obviously he'd gotten safely home before, only I wasn't sure how he'd actually managed it. In the shape I was, I wasn't even sure I could find my way up the stairs to my room, let alone six blocks away where Fionn lived; and he'd drunk twice as much, if not more, than I had.

We agreed to meet across town on Monday, when the inn was closed and I had the day off.

For three years my secret had weighed heavily on me. By transporting my wealth from the farm to where I buried it, I had far and away exceeded my ability to manage it on my own. What was I to do with it after that? The tremendous effort I'd expended to get it there would have been for naught if I could never enjoy it —and I hadn't. Every so often I'd venture out to the cache, just to check it was still there, but nothing more.

Fionn, my knight in shining armor, stepped in and solved my problem. He had the means and connections to safely transport the bullion to offshore banks. Being in Australia, a somewhat remote location, it might make the transport more complicated for most people, but it was Fionn's business of which he claimed he was the best. He said it would take him three or four trips to organize everything, getting it to where it needed to be, and about one to two months, tops to completion.

Six weeks from when I showed Fionn my hiding place and the farm, giving him carte blanche with my gold, silver and paper money, we met at our favourite cafe across town from the inn. I hadn't seen him since he offered to take care of my riches. Had I worried? You might think so, given my earlier hesitation, but, no, I hadn't. Not for a moment. Despite my initial qualms borne out of insecurity and fear of my own naivete, I trusted that my friend would never cheat me. To be honest, from the instant I revealed my treasure, I was awash with relief having handed over its management to him.

We each ordered lamb stew and pints. While we ate, we exchanged pleasantries, talked about the weather, some regulars at the pub, the upcoming dinner party being thrown by The Cousins, and speculating about who might attend. Once the waitress removed our emptied bowls, Fionn quickly rolled a cigarette and lit it, pulling a deep drag before expelling the sweet smelling tobacco smoke into the cafe.

"It's done, Shiv. Your wealth is secure, safe and growing." He smiled. "You think you have more than enough—you're wondering why make more? Yeah?"

"Well, actually…" I nodded, puzzled. "Yup…"

He shrugged. "It's the nature of good financial management, darling. If you're not growing, or making more, you're failing. You're letting some other reap the potential gains. I don't fail, Siobhán, and… I don't share with strangers." He pulled a long drag from his cigarette and chuckled softly. "It's not in my nature," he added, blowing a stream of smoke from his lips.

I shook my head a little, not understanding why he was being so generous to me. Though we were grand friends, mates, oddly enough, I somehow still considered us strangers. Who does such things for a stranger, I wondered? As always, Fionn seemed to read my mind.

"I believe in serendipity, Siobhán," he began. "A stranger once saved my life. He not only took me in as his son, but he taught me a valuable skill. You met me so I could protect you. That is what I believe. I trusted you enough to share a confidence I have only shared with one other." I looked at him quizzically. There was another? Who might that be, I wondered?

"You trusted me and shared your own secret with me," he continued. "Had you told this to anyone else, you'd likely be broke or dead. Someday, I believe... I hope... you, too, will meet someone you'll help."

Puzzled, I asked, "Should I learn your trade, too? Like your papa taught you?"

"No, no, Siobhán. I won't ever teach you how to do what I do. The last thing I would want for you is for you to become me. What I know, you must *never*. Your heart is pure, darling. I would...could never be a party to destroying the beauty of who you are. No, I'll inform you where I've invested your riches and where they're held; and, how to get to them if you must—though I would strongly advise against it. The less you're seen connected, the better.

"The extent of your wealth shall remain private, unknown to anyone. The way I've structured things, there are walls and walls between you and your holdings, which, by the way..." he smirked, "... is close to five million Australian."

"*What?* F-f-five?" I exclaimed. "But... I... I figured maybe two, and... I thought it was a ridiculously high estimate!"

"Precious metals, love. Your figures were no doubt calculated using old values."

I couldn't wrap my mind around it. *Five million?*

Fionn chuckled, watching me try and comprehend the reality of my financial status.

"I've created assumed identities for you should you ever need them," he went on. "Each identity has appropriate documents in the safe deposit box. They are the best forgeries money can buy— *anywhere*. You'll know exactly which accounts go with each identity. I've set up corresponding postal boxes in various places around the world. I'll continue managing your affairs for you until you say otherwise. If you need funds for... well, whatever, just contact me and I'll get it to you. No matter where we are. Anywhere. Understand?"

I nodded, still stunned.

"With your permission, natch."

I didn't hesitate. "Yes, yes! Of course, Fionn... I..."

"Good. Now... Should anything happen to me, Shiv, I've left details in your safe deposit box of how I've structured everything. Take only the identities, one at a time, from the bank. Ever. To do otherwise is an invitation for calamity. You'll also find the deed to your countryside property. All in your name." The corner of Fionn's mouth twitched.

I gasped softly.

No longer able to hold back, he smiled warmly and winked at me. "All four thousand forty-seven hectares—it's all yours, love— legally. And... I took the liberty of securing another five hundred thousand adjoining your property. You got a great deal, Shiv— couldn't pass it up." He snickered.

"H-h-how?" I whispered.

"Oh, Siobhán, darling... if I told ya..." he chuckled. "Ah, what the hell. Here it is—Y'bought the original property from Patrick Mottorshaw... with *his* money. He is now living on a remote island in the Pacific, though he'll die soon—natural causes, natch. The other land is from a neighbor's son. He inherited it, wanted the money more than the land. Stupid bloke, but..."

"He... you bought my farm from Patrick... *what?*" I asked, utterly confused. "But, he's... he's dead now."

"Shhh... No one will even question it, Shiv. He is a notorious recluse. He's old. He'll die soon, be cremated, his ashes spread into the sea." Fionn shrugged. "Now, I placed the purchase funds in a Swiss bank account, which by the way, also belongs to one of your identities." He chuckled when he saw what must have been shock on my face. "This is what I do, Shiv. May I remind ya...? I am the absolute *best* at what I do."

He grinned with obvious affection and continued, amused, I'm sure, by my gaping mouth. "You'll want for nothing, darling. I have diversified your assets, so much so, the world itself would have to end before you'd ever be penniless. And... when I'm gone—"

"No!" I interrupted, protesting even the notion of Fionn leaving the earth and me, but he raised his palm to stop me.

"When I am gone, love," he began again, gently, "I have an associate—I trust him with my life. He'll go on managing your wealth, and nothing will change."

My eyes questioned him.

He nodded. "It's okay, Shiv. He's... my son."

I gulped air. "Your...?"

Fionn's smile and face emoted a tenderness I'd never before seen in him.

"Yes, my dear, I have a son. Lucas Mikael Daniels. Daniels is the surname I assumed when I first came to Australia. I lived a double life to protect myself and my family. I raised Lucas from the age of four when his mother, Ina... erm... she, ah... she left him. Unavoidable. Cancer, I'm afraid. Ina was a beautiful girl, but so much more than her looks. Funny, intelligent, sweet, talented, kind... whatever you can imagine makes a perfect person, an angel —that's who Ina was." Fionn fell silent as he remembered Ina, then continued. "We discovered each other at a produce market in Sydney. She was also an... *ahem*... how shall I say? A bit of an... experiment for me. A test of my genuine nature, I suppose."

I studied his face, noticing a mischievous glint in his eyes, as it appeared he had just shared another confidence. Joan and Trix had often alluded to Fionn's sexual bent; but, until that moment, I had never considered he might actually be homosexual—a gay man. Many of Joan and Trix's male friends were homosexual, but they were polar opposites from Fionn. Most of them were what I would call effeminate, so unlike the masculine Fionn. I didn't care either way and actually felt privileged he was comfortable enough with me to reveal a thing so personal, controversial and dangerous.

He nodded knowingly as he knew what I'd just figured out.

"As expected, and feared," he continued, "I failed the test, miserably. But, Luke? Ah... my Lucas... *he* is my greatest success, far and beyond all my riches. And, I'm proud to say, he is a legitimate, brilliant, businessman. Believe me, dear Siobhán, he knows all about you, but most importantly, he understands how important you are to me. He won't cheat you. I swear on his blood and mine.

"When the time comes, and I have departed this realm, whether it's tomorrow or fifty years from now, he will contact you. Until then, he and I severely limit our time together, always taking extreme precautions when we meet. He must *never* get perceived as having any connection with me or my work. At least not until I've sorted everything out." Fionn chugged down the rest of his beer. He wiped his moustache with the back of his forefinger, followed by his thumb and forefinger. He smiled at me.

"When you and Luke finally meet? You'll know he's mine." Fionn chortled. "He is a tragic reminder of me and my own lost youth. *I* was *him*. Now...? *Ugh...* I'm just an old fart."

I just smiled at his self-deprecation. In fact, I wondered if he realised how lovely and beautifully handsome he was; but, I would not have said that to him then. Instead, I simply grinned, reflecting on how much I loved my bestie. I smiled mischievously, replying, "You're not old."

He cocked his head to the side, then, realising what I meant, snorted as he broke into a hearty laugh.

27

The Boyfriend

∞ ∞ ∞ ∞ ∞

Although he is but a blip in my life story, I should tell you about Robby Byrne, my first and likely last boyfriend. I feel an obligation to do so, despite his seeming insignificance, because of his overall importance in my own self-discovery.

Prior to Frankie entering my life, on my days off, I often visited a bookstore in Downtown Melbourne called Wordy Byrd Books. About thirteen or so kilometres from the inn, it was but a short drive away. It was owned and run by a late middle-aged couple, Agatha "Aggie" and Ned "Byrd" Byrne, retired professors from the University of Melbourne. Aggie had been an English professor, and Ned ran the university's history department.

I loved the store and would sometimes spend an entire afternoon there, often into the evening, reading a newly purchased book while drinking copious amounts of caffeine. They never bothered me about Pippa, though there was nothing really to bother about as she followed me, as quietly as a whisper, rendering herself nearly invisible.

It's there where my love affair with coffee began, in particular, Italian espresso. University students filled the ten or so small, round tables in the cafe part of the store, drinking espresso shots and mostly studying. The store was well ahead of its time, I believe, with an impressive brass espresso machine imported from Italy featured on its cafe service counter, churning out shot after espresso shot. The aroma in the shop was divine, never failing to illicit a bit of a heady rush each time I entered the store.

In addition to having an incredible mind for all things historic, Ned was also quite the audiophile with an extensive and eclectic collection of vinyl LPs. He'd hold court in his corner of the store, playing requests for his young and eager patrons. Then, with great authority, he'd expound on every little detail of the album and its artist or artists as the record played. I thoroughly enjoyed sitting as near to him as possible so I could properly eavesdrop on his amazing and educational conversations.

During the Frankie era, I'd stopped going to the bookstore entirely. Oh, sure, sometimes I'd miss it, but Frankie, well, she demanded all of my attention—and I didn't mind the sacrifice one bit. After she got deported, I went through a rough period in my life where I zombied through my days. I got up out of bed, went to work, went back to bed. My days off were much the same, except I didn't go to work and I rarely got out of bed. I suppose that phase of grief went on for several months. I cannot say for sure as most of that time is but a blur. Thankfully, The Cousins and Fionn let me work through my grief with little bother.

As my melancholy slowly ebbed, I began yearning for a change of scenery. Eventually, I found myself back at the Wordy Byrd. I distincly remember walking into the store for the first time in over two years, and how the tantalizing aroma of fresh coffee beans and printed books filled me with instaneous joy. I realised in that moment how much I'd missed the space and that all that time with Frankie and after, I'd only suppressed my own needs for another's. Never again, I vowed.

After that initial return visit, I made it a point to go downtown every week on a day off. I'd sit and read, listen to Ned's music and drink espresso (beginning with shots, then easing into cappucinos, and ending with lattes) until my eyes ached and my body quivered from caffeine overload. The next day at work I'd drag from coffee-induced insomnia the night before, but my soul was fed and satisfied, so I didn't mind in the least.

Around a month after my return, I noticed someone new working in the books area of the store. He was a tall, lanky lad with moppish red hair. I knew he might be older than me, but there was a boyishness about him that instantly endeared him to me. From my table by Ned, once I discovered him, I watched The Clerk as he straightened and dusted books on the shelves and assisted customers. I'd watched him with mild interest until the first time he flashed a smile. Oh, it was glorious! From the moment I first saw it, his smile had me. I adored it. He mostly kept a serious expression on his face, but from time to time he'd break out in that impressive, toothy smile, showing bright white and perfect teeth. Large, they were, but perfectly straight and aligned all the same.

Somewhere around my fourth visit since first seeing the redheaded clerk, I actually needed assistance finding a particular book. I'd remembered a book in Patrick's library, Magnhild by Bjørnstjerne Bjørnson, but I couldn't read it because it was in Norwegian. I'd tried, but there were no Norwegian to English translation books to help me translate it. One day while sitting in the bookstore, it occurred there might be a translation available. I decided to inquire whether The Clerk could find a translated copy for me.

"S'cuse me," I said in a low voice to The Clerk. His back was to me when I approached him.

He lazily turned around, holding several books stacked in his hands. He was about six two from my estimation, about four or five inches taller than me. The second he saw my face he broke into that amazing smile I loved so much. He tossed his head to the side in an attempt to move the thick red mop of hair from his eyes. His hair flipped away for a brief moment, then fell back over his eyebrows, framing his bright blue eyes.

"Heya," he said in the most beautiful baritone Australian accent I'd heard yet. "Whatcha need, mate?"

"I-I-I…" I cleared my throat, instantly self-conscious. "I'm l-l-looking f-f-for a, erm… a-a-a book. In N-Norwegian, I-I-I mean… I-i-it's in N-Norwegian, b-b-ut…"

"Y'lookin' for an English translation?" he asked with an indulgent grin.

"Y-yes!"

He set the books he'd been holding onto a cart with wheels, combed the fingers of his right hand through his hair, sweeping it away from his face, and then rested both hands on his hips. Within seconds his hair fell back to where it began. He flipped his head again. "What is it? Who's the author?"

"O-oh, erm… I-I… I don't r-r-really know how to p-p-pronounce it all, b-b-but…"

He swiftly pulled a nearly done pencil from behind his ear and a small notepad from his trouser back pocket. "No worries. Y'wanna write it down for me?" he said with a flip of his stubborn hair.

I nodded and took the pencil and pad from him. I quickly wrote down the author's name and the book title, then handed it all back to The Clerk.

"Ah, Mahgnill by Beeornstyearn Beeyornson," he replied, the foreign words flowing with ease from his lips. He smiled at me, seemingly pleased with himself.

"H-h-how…?" His pronounciation sounded nothing like what I'd imagined in my head.

He chuckled, with a head flip. "My mum's Norwegian. From Norway, yeah?"

"Fair dinkum?" I asked, incredulous at my luck.

He chuckled again. "Yeah. Mum's Norwegian, Dad's Irish, but, erm, he's born here."

Responding to my obvious confusion, he added, "They met on holiday in The Caribbean. That's when I got made," he said with a self-conscious snicker. "They got married three weeks later and she immigrated soon after. The rest, as Great Uncle would say, is history." He giggled at his own joke.

"Ah…" I replied, not knowing how else to respond.

He looked at the paper I'd given him again. "I dunno if there's a translation available, but I'll have my Great Auntie check it out for ya."

I cocked my head.

"Aggie?" he lifted his chin towards one of the owners behind the cafe bench. "That's my Great Auntie… my dad's Auntie. Ned over there? He's my Great Uncle. My dad's uncle—in fact, my dad's *dad's* brother. He's actually from Ireland. Came over, I think, as a teenager." He chuckled again at the look on my face. "What? Too much info?"

"N-n-nah… I just…"

"What's your name?" he asked, his stub of a pencil poised over the small notepad.

"S-S-Siobhán… erm, O'S-Shea."

"Y'want Auntie to give you a bell on it, or…"

"Y-Y-Yeah, nah, I'll j-j-just…"

"Just ask then, whenever you come in next, yeah?"

I nodded and looked at my shoes, suddenly shy.

We both stood in silence, not sure what to do next.

"Erm, I'm Robby," The Clerk said, breaking our awkward silence. "Robby Byrne."

I smiled. "H-hi, Robby. G-Glad to meet ya."

He flipped his hair, then nodded. "Yep."

More silence ensued.

Finally, "So, erm, would ya like to have some coffee or tea sometime? I, erm... I work here and go to Uni, but... we could... I dunno..."

"O-o-oh... erm... erm... y-yeah... sure." My face went hot.

"Cheers. I get off in an hour..." he looked at me, his face hopeful.

I glanced at the sizeable clock above the cafe section. It was just after three. I'd planned on staying for a few more hours, anyway. "Yeah, sure. Th-that would b-be nice."

"'K. See yas in a bit." He picked up the books from the cart and turned his back to me. I returned to my table where Pippa patiently waited.

An hour later Robin "Robby" Arthur Byrne and I had our first date. We talked and drank coffee until after the store officially closed, only leaving when Robby's auntie kicked us out. I learned he was twenty-one and in his third year at University as a literature major. He was highly intelligent and exceptionally bright, but his greatest, and only, ambition in life was to read every book ever written. That's it. Nothing more. He had no interest in writing or teaching, or reviewing, publishing, or... well, he had zero interest in doing anything but reading. I wish I were joking, but alas, that's who he was.

His parents, due to his mother's significant inheritance at a young age and his father's profession as an engineer, were well off and overly indulged him. Robby knew it. I could never discern for certain whether it embarrassed him, but I'd lean towards no, he wasn't embarrassed—not at all. No, I'd say he revelled in his spoiled status. I know, you're wondering why he worked at the bookstore if he were so spoiled. I wondered, too. As it turns out, he wanted to. He worked for free, just so he could be around books. Honestly, I have to admire that in him.

Robby was the eldest of four sisters, all redheads of varying shades and texture. Neither of his parents had curly or red hair, but the red hair gene apparently came from his maternal grandmother and the curly hair from his maternal grandfather. Two of his sisters had tight curls, and the middle sister had hair like his—thick, straight and moppish, the fourth, light auburn and wavy. They were a close-knit family and quite a lot of fun. Every sibling of Robby's was as different from the next as I was. Each had such distinctive personalities and interests, and if they didn't look so much alike, you'd never guess they were from the same family.

Robby and I dated, if you want to call it that, for about a year, but we drifted apart shortly after he graduated from university. He ended up moving to London, and then to New York after his parents died, where I believe he is to this day. We'd go to films and then spend the next several hours dissecting them; or read to each other at the park, stopping after nearly every paragraph to hash out the author's meaning or intent. Oh, I could listen to Robby's beautiful baritone voice and Australian accent for hours and hours, and then want more. His smile, what made me first love him, was brilliant and those blue eyes of his were quite something to behold.

Truth is, I loved Robby, and I know he loved me, too, but I'd known passionate, unbridled love with Frankie, and it just wasn't there for Robby and me. I knew it never would be. Well, I should say it wasn't there for me. I know Robby had stronger, more passionate feelings for me, but I just couldn't find it in me to even try to reciprocate.

He was an affectionate bloke, but respectfully so. We'd hold hands and snog on the regular, but we never went any farther than what you might call heavy petting. I suppose if he'd initiated anything, I might have gone along just to see what the fuss was about, but he never did. We'd go to a certain point, and then… that was it.

I'm thankful he didn't press for more, and that we didn't go farther than we did. I just didn't love him the way I thought I should to be intimate with him. Yes, I know it wasn't like that with Frankie, but that's my point, isn't it. For us, Frankie and me, it was all about the sex, sex, and more sex, and not much more than that. With Robby, I loved him, but not in a passionate way. I didn't yearn for him, to be near him, or ache for him to touch me. No, I enjoyed being around him, being close to him, but no more. I realised way back then, for me to be happy, I needed some combination of what I had with Robby and what I'd had with Frankie. Balance. Truth is, I may be hoping for a unicorn, because I'm still looking for that perfect balance.

28

Machu Picchu

∞ ∞ ∞ ∞ ∞

Joan and Trix loved the outdoors, and all that it included. They camped, they hiked, hunted, fished, climbed mountains and went on safaris. Their many adventures each year were legendary, followed by especially entertaining teas and the obligatory slide show. Those were, by far, the best teas of the year. I accompanied The Cousins on a few camping trips; but in all honesty, those girls were too hardcore for my liking.

I enjoy comfort—to the extreme. I grew up in the countryside in what some might call primitive circumstances. That's about all the "roughing it" I'll ever need. I now prefer sleeping in a soft bed, with indoor plumbing, air conditioning and heating that turns on or off with the flick of the switch... well, in short, I want every creature comfort at my fingertips. I admired the girls for their adventurous spirits; but after a few trips with them, I was content to hold down the fort whenever they travelled.

I'd been at The Brown House for not quite five years when The Cousins boldly announced they wanted to climb Mt. Everest —someday—*soon*. Their announcement might have shocked anyone else, but not me. No, I couldn't muster any response but ambivalence. Not at first, anyway. It was so much like them. In time, I grew skeptical they'd follow through on such a huge undertaking. Whenever the subject came up, I'd simply nod in agreement in order to avoid conflict.

"Of course you are," I'd scoffed good-naturedly. "Grand plan, girls."

In hindsight, I wish I'd been more enthused, more involved in their preparation; and, yes, more supportive. Instead, I determined it was a mad idea, a waste of time and money, as such an endeavour is quite costly; and, I worried about them. They were in their late forties, and though reasonably fit, neither were super athletes. Joan and Trix were middle-aged women who drank and smoked on the regular; and, aside from Joan's three mile runs once or twice a week, and their leisurely weekly hikes which were more akin to lackadaisical strolls than hikes, strenuous exercise wasn't high on their list of priorities.

I made zero effort to hide my disdain for their harebrained idea. Thankfully, they finally gave up on climbing Mt. Everest. Certain disaster averted. Next up on their agenda? Machu Picchu. The Cousins convinced themselves such a climb was far more manageable than Mt. Everest and were terribly excited about their new target.

Despite my herculean efforts to dissuade them, feeling somewhere deep inside me it was a terrible idea, I could not. Much to my dismay, they had latched onto the possibility of Machu Picchu and the terrific adventure it was guaranteed to be. Try as I might, and believe me, I was relentless; I could not get them to budge on their resolve.

Six months later, in June 1971, ignoring my pleas to reconsider, The Cousins set off for Peru, convinced they would conquer Machu Picchu, and bring home the best stories of their lives. Eight weeks later they did come home; rather, I brought them home, but with the worst story imaginable.

They'd planned on being in South America for two or more months, depending on how things progressed. Most of that time they wouldn't be accessible to me because of the remote locations where they'd stay. I didn't like the arrangement one bit, but their upcoming adventure thrilled them to pieces. So that was that. I finally had to accept their terms with a promise they'd contact me whenever they were able. Meanwhile, I was to run the business during their absence, which I did.

After the first two weeks of their absence, and not hearing a peep from them, I realised it was too quiet with The Cousins out of country, and concluded eight weeks or more was far too long for them to be away. I missed them both so very much. Another week went by without word, then another, and another. Each week that went by, worry creeped in until finally, it took up full-time residence. After more than a month of not hearing a thing from them, I was beyond worried. At six weeks of complete silence, I'd catapulted into a full-blown panic.

Convinced something had gone terribly wrong, I commenced my search at the starting point of their itinerary to see if I could catch them somewhere along the way, or at least retrace their steps. I started in Lima, and found they had checked in and out of their hotel as planned. So far, so good. Then, they travelled on to Cusco by bus, then, onto Machu Picchu. After that, we'd scheduled them to continue on to Santiago, Chile, followed by Buenos Aires, Argentina, and then back to Melbourne.

It shocked and surprised me to learn, although they had reached Cusco and checked into their hotel; it was as if they had both disappeared from the planet. In the process of tracking them down, I racked up a substantial phone bill, but as money was no object to me, I didn't care. Even if it were an issue, I wouldn't have cared. I would have spent my last dollar, or gone into debt for life because my family was missing—I had to find them!

After thirty-six hours of near constant phone calls and telegrams, I managed, through numerous official agencies and the Australian Embassy in Lima, to locate Joan and Trix. The next day, bereft and in utter shock, I left my continent for another. Thanks to Fionn and my fake Siobhán O'Shea Australian passport, I could travel outside the country without scrutiny or complication.

Until I could get to Peru to assess the situation for myself, all I could determine was there had been an accident shortly after The Cousins' arrival. Unfortunately, prior to me inquiring as to Joan and Trix's whereabouts, the authorities hadn't known who to call. From when I learned what happened to leaving The Brown House for South America, I hadn't any time to properly process the news. As such, my trip to South America was fraught beyond measure with internal panic, worry and fear beyond anything I'd ever experienced in my life.

On the third day of non-stop, tortuous travel, by some miracle I arrived in Lima, bedraggled and beat to the bone. From the decrepit bus depot—if you could call it that as it was a nondescript spot on the side of the street where the bus stopped, people got off the bus and people got on—I headed straight to the hospital.

Upon arriving at the hospital, in spite of the significant language barrier, I somehow managed to communicate to a staff member who spoke no English who I was and why I was there. With my fractured Spanish and a pathetic version of sign language, I miraculously conveyed I was there to see my friends.

With little emotion in her face, the small brown woman took me to a hospital room where I found Joan. When I entered her room and first saw her, I'm ashamed to say, I gasped from horror. She was emaciated, pale, and battered beyond belief. Partially healed cuts and brutal scrapes covered her face. Her cheeks and mouth were oddly sunken. Her left arm was in a poorly wrapped cast, as was her left leg. It was elevated by some type of crude hanging rig.

I rushed to her side as tears sprung involuntarily from my eyes. She appeared to be sleeping, but the moment I took her right hand, her eyes opened. Joan had trouble focusing as she was obviously on heavy medication. Once she recognized me, she sobbed so heavily her words were nearly unintelligible. I realised her sunken cheeks and lips were due to her teeth were missing. My senses were overwhelmed. Where's Trix? I'd asked, trying not to stare at the nearly unrecognizable Joan. She only sobbed harder. My guts turned into a boulder as my own tears flowed, because I feared to my marrow that what she was about to tell me I didn't want to know.

Through a translator and vague bits and drabs from Joan, I somehow pieced together the horrific details of The Cousins' misadventure. It seems the calamity had occurred shortly after their arrival in Cusco, on what would have been their initial sightseeing day. In search of the perfect shot with her new Pentax camera, Trix had ventured a little too far out onto a ledge overlooking the area. Without warning, she slipped on loose rock and lost her footing. Instinctively she reached out for Joan, who, at the last second, seeing what was happening, leapt to Trix, managing to catch her hand.

The authorities believed Joan got pulled over the edge with Trix. Joan remembered nothing of that part. They'd fallen over a hundred metres down the face of a sharp and jagged mountain rock to a narrow second ledge, then off it and down sixty more metres to a third ledge. If they had slid off it as well, they both would have plunged an additional three hundred metres to their certain deaths.

As it happened, Joan only barely survived the fall, but was left with broken limbs, a concussion and terrific lacerations and abrasions on her face and body. The medical professionals believe Trix most likely died upon impact on the second ledge when she landed on top of Joan, effectively trapping her. *It took three days before another tourist discovered them.*

Since first regaining consciousness in Lima, where she'd been evacuated first by bus, then by aeroplane, Joan was kept in a continuously sedated, near coma state. Her doctors had no choice. Whenever she came to, she would lose her mind over Trix, overwhelmed by the horror of being trapped beneath the dead body of her beloved for all those days. Joan's perpetual drugged state was why I never received a phone call or a telegram from her.

Other than their passports, there was no other contact information—emergency or otherwise. Authorities had gotten in touch with the Australian Embassy right away, but apparently the one thing Joan and Trix failed to do in their extensive preparation was list me as their next of kin in case of an emergency. The person at the embassy assured me they would eventually have found me. *Eventually?*

Yes, I was right livid. And, devastated. Our Trix was gone. Well, she was nearby, lying in the morgue somewhere in the basement of the local hospital awaiting final instructions, but she was gone. Dead. And, Joan? She was… well, devastated is not quite a big enough word for what Joan experienced. All I had to do was look at her and my heart broke for her each and every time. I'd never seen her or any other person in such a sorry state— physically, mentally or emotionally.

Three weeks later, when Joan got cleared to go home, the three of us returned to Australia: Trix in a crudely constructed pine coffin with Joan, grief-stricken, battered and broken. And me? I was more deeply disturbed and heartbroken to my core than I ever imagined possible.

The next couple years were terrible for Joan and for those of us who loved her and Trix. They had been inseparable and a tight unit unto themselves for nearly twenty years. I would sometimes tease them, calling them my two-headed monster; which, you must understand, *"monster"* was the exact opposite of what they were. The Cousins were two of the loveliest people I'd ever known. Unsurprisingly, without Trix, her life mate by her side, Joan was set adrift—lost in nearly every sense of the word.

Way back then, we didn't understand what was happening to her, what it was or that it even had a name. Now, I'm convinced Joan suffered from a crippling case of PTSD. The smallest things would set her off, sending her back to the moment of grabbing Trix's hand and their violent tumble over the side of the mountain. The havoc that would ensue with each flashback was frightening, and unsettling at best. Yes, those were awful, confusing times for her and us.

For at least a year before their fateful trip, with The Cousins' encouragement, I'd been making plans to leave the inn in order to explore the world. I still had lingering questions about my parents and myself I needed answered. Once I brought Joan back from South America, however, she depended upon me to care for her and run the inn. I couldn't leave her. If I'm being honest, she depended on me for everything.

I wasn't Trix, but I was an adequate substitute companion, I suppose, and partially filled a void. Trix had a gigantic personality, too big to ever replace, and I could not and never would seek to fill any of her roles in that special relationship. I truly felt no ill will against Joan having to postpone my plans in order to take care of her. I loved The Cousins dearly and would have done anything in the world for them. If delaying my plans by a few years, or the rest of my life, even, was what Joan needed, that's what I would do— willingly and without complaint.

The disaster left Joan with prominent scars on her arms and legs, but most vividly over her face. I honestly never knew she wore dentures until the disaster. They didn't survive the fall. As soon as we got back to Melbourne, we got them promptly replaced. She was so terribly self-conscious and, frankly, mortified without her teeth—she wouldn't even talk to me without holding her hand over her mouth. I wanted her to feel as much like her old self as much as possible; though, as it turned out, it wasn't possible. I finally had to remove all mirrors from Joan's sight, as looking at herself caused horrific flashbacks and debilitating depression.

Because her shattered leg and broken arm were both improperly set and allowed to heal that way, Joan relied upon a cane to assist with walking. Crutches, though recommended, were impossible for her. Going up or down the stairs was also quite the ordeal, effectively trapping her upstairs in her residence for extended periods of time. She had the means to afford the finest healthcare to repair both her arm, leg and even her face; but despite my pleading, Joan wouldn't hear of it. She'd had enough of hospitals and never wanted to step foot in another—ever. Of the two cousins, Joan was always the most stubborn. Her accident didn't lessen that trait—if anything, it only made her more resolute and intractable.

Doctors placed Joan on heavy doses of tranquilizers, which she had no hesitation using, too often more than she'd been prescribed. If she allowed herself out of a sedated state, she'd vividly relive her nightmare again and again. Making matters worse, in my opinion, despite my concern and vehement protestation, Joan insisted upon mixing her medications with alcohol—and heaps of it. Gin was her elixir of choice. I learned soon enough not to attempt to stifle her addiction lest the hell of all hells rained down on me. Truth is, I had gotten to my wits' end worrying over Joan. I couldn't make her do or not do whatever she was hell-bent on doing—or not doing. As much as I didn't want her to suffer, and tried whatever I could to ease her pain, she suffered greatly, every waking moment of her life. Each day left me wondering how long she could go on the way she was.

29

Joan

∞ ∞ ∞ ∞ ∞

Tending bar at the inn was no doubt the most enjoyable job I've ever had. It's tough for me to even refer to it as a job because I enjoyed it so much. Over the years I'd made many friends, rather, close acquaintances, and learned quite a lot about people, and even myself. The more I listened to customers' and friends' narratives, how they'd often share their most intimate details of their lives with me, the more it seemed as if I knew them, despite many being strangers to me. I'd been isolated the first sixteen years of my existence, so my customers' stories almost allowed me to relive my life through theirs—many times over. I looked at it as an extra benefit of my position.

I so loved Joan and Trix and felt quite close to them; but the few years I was with them, they had remained somewhat of a mystery to me. They rarely spoke of their younger years, or how or when they first got together—something I was dying to know. From the outside looking in, they had a vibe that said they had been a unit their entire lives. It was almost as if they were one. That dynamic between them had always intrigued me.

Until I met The Cousins, my parents had been my only measure of genuine love. Mam and Da obviously loved each other and were close, but their closeness paled in comparison to Joan and Trix's. Though they were in solidarity with most of their decisions, likes and dislikes, I never experienced the absolute "one person" sense from my parents as I did with the girls.

Interestingly, if Joan or Trix ever brought up the past, it was always with vague references. If I pressed them for more details, they'd quickly and politely divert the conversation to another direction, frustrating me to no end. In that way they reminded me so much of Mam and Da. I've always loved the story, the history of a person—fictional or otherwise—the finding out what makes a person tick, I suppose. After a while, though, I'd no choice but to accept them as they were—without history. I had no options in that regard. You cannot make people tell you what they are reluctant to disclose, and it became all too clear they chose not to tell. They had a story, for sure, but seemed determined to keep mum about it.

After Trix's demise, little by little, Joan began opening up to me. It was a slow, gruelling process, but as weeks, then months passed, it seemed missing Trix the way she did, Joan needed a way in which to hold on to their memories. Perhaps their history was fading for her. I can't say as I refrained from inquiring. Whatever the reason, Joan finally began talking to me. At first, it was dribs and drabs, usually when she was doped up on her meds. I often had a tough time piecing her stories together, and when I'd inquire later, she could not remember telling me, or she'd wave it off as "just the pills talking."

Joan experienced good days and terrible days, but in all honesty, all of her days were wretched, generally speaking. So much so, other people not normally privy to her everyday condition might consider her good days bad. Without Trix, and her body broken, scarred, and in constant pain, Joan's life had become relentlessly challenging and unbearably sad.

Trix and Joan had been what I consider a perfectly balanced couple. Trix was the joker, Joan was the serious, no nonsense part of them. Not to say Trix didn't have her serious moments, because she did; or, that Joan couldn't be funny, because even our serious Joan could set a filled room on their collective bums, roaring with laughter. It's just that with Trix and her dry, somewhat sarcastic wit gone, where once was a couple's dynamic and balance, only an unbalanced, deep void remained. Without her, Joan turned dark and morose. Melancholy. Withdrawn.

Nothing I could say could or would alter her state of being; and not for lack of trying, either. It was heartbreaking seeing her in such a miserable state; so, each day I gave my every effort to cheer her up, hoping to give her reason to live another turn of the Earth. Being the eternal optimist I am, I could not give up on her and I didn't. Despite overwhelming evidence to the contrary, I somehow believed everything would work out for Joan—someday.

Though her physical injuries from the Machu Picchu fall were long healed, Joan still endured non-stop pain, including mobility and self-esteem issues from her remaining scars. Though she was able to go downstairs, Joan spent most of her awake time in the en suite she and Trix had shared. Despite my heartfelt coaxing, she rarely agreed to come out of the bedroom for anything.

Before the tragedy, Joan was the most physically active of The Cousins, and despite her no-nonsense nature, between her and Trix, she was the most social one down in the pub. She was also quite attractive. One or two days a week, Joan would jog two, maybe three miles, and likely climbed up and down the stairs at least fifty times a day—often doing Trix's bidding. I won't claim

Trix was lazy, but she had a more laid back personality, preferring relaxing to physical activity.

Everything changed after the disaster. Because of Joan becoming a shut-in, I became a semi-recluse as well. When I wasn't working downstairs or asleep in my room, I would lie on Joan's bed with her, or sit in the overstuffed upholstered chair next to her and visit. Sometimes I'd read to her, or tell stories from the farm, but mostly we'd just stay quiet. I found it challenging for me to remain still for interminable periods, but I would endure anything for her. If she desired me to lie still with her for hours and hours every day, that's what I would do. It was more than an obligation I felt for Joan, despite feeling I owed her so much. No, it was the deep and abiding love I had for her that gave me the will to do all and everything she wanted me to do for her.

Somewhere around six months after we returned from South America, Joan experienced what I can comfortably report was a terrific day. She wasn't her old self, the Joan she was before losing Trix, but she was having the best day she'd had since our return. Though drugged up, which was her new norm, she wasn't groggy and disoriented as she often was when on her medications. We lay on her bed, quiet as usual, when, without warning, she began telling me her history. Initially, she spoke softly, haltingly, but clearly enough for me to understand her. I didn't have to prod or encourage her in the slightest—words and story just came out— and I, fascinated beyond all reason, listened with rapt attention.

Throughout the telling, there were extended pauses, but I think, more than anything, it was Joan struggling from time to time trying to climb out from her narcotic induced haze. I will tell you this: it was something completely unexpected. I cannot emphasize enough how greatly I was affected by what she shared with me. In fact, I was affected to the deepest part of me. To this day, when I think of Joan's story, which was partly Trix's as well, my heart literally aches. I've never shared this part of their history with anyone until now.

∞   ∞   ∞   ∞   ∞

On a day not unlike all others, we lay on Joan's bed on top of her cream-coloured chenille bedspread, with Pippa lying on the floor beside us, when completely out of the blue, Joan's soft, Australian-tinged voice interrupted the deep, unrelenting silence I'd become used to while lying with her.

"Trix and I... we were best mates..." she began, her voice drowsy and her words thick from the drugs. "Yeah. Right from the beginning."

"Yeah?" I responded, slightly startled. Though excited by the prospect of learning more about Trix and Joan, I slowly rolled onto my side, facing her.

"Yeah, from as far back as... She was three years older than me, y'know, but... from as early as... as *I* can remember, we were... *inseparable*. Yeah, yeah..." She sighed. "We lived on the same street, y'know, three, four houses away. Did you know? We're cousins—Trix's dad, Uncle Steffen, he was my mum's older brother."

"I am aware," I responded with sincerity, taken aback by her lucidity. "What was your mum's name?"

"Oh, erm... my mum? It's... it was erm... Loralei. Trix and her brother and sister called her, erm... Aunt Lori. My dad was Peter. And... there was Uncle Stef and Aunt Stell, Trix's mum and dad."

Joan got quiet again, but I dared not interrupt the rarity of the moment, forcing myself to wait and listen, hoping she would continue her train of thought.

"Earliest memory..." she finally said. "I... I remember... I'd wait, and... wait for Trix to come home from school every single day—that was before I... before I started school, y'see. Yeah... she'd get to her house... wasn't minutes 'til she showed up at ours, and... oh, Shiv... I'd be so happy. Ecstatic. Yeah... my earliest... memories are... of Trix. All of 'em." Joan stopped talking for a long while, her smile shaded with sadness, remembering.

"You both had siblings, yeah?" I asked, yearning for more.

"Oh, yeah, yeah. We both did. I have four... brothers—I'm the baby."

"Four brothers!" I exclaimed in a hushed voice. "That's..." I attempted to process the concept of having one sibling, let alone four. It seemed like a lot to me.

"Mmm hmm... Eight years older Leland is. Percy's got... erm... six years on me. Nick...? He's got four, I think... Yeah, four, and... Roger... mmm... he's two years more. Trix was in the middle. She had a baby sister and... Ben. He's three years older than Trix. Lucy's a year younger than me." Joan paused as she seemed to fade away for a spell, then came back to it.

"Yeah, we had brothers and sisters, but... y'know, we... we just didn't care about 'em. Not a bit." Joan shrugged. "We didn't. All we cared about was... us." Joan fiddled with the edge of her tee shirt. "We loved each other, Shiv. All the way back... to the beginning."

"Extraordinary," I whispered. I studied Joan's scarred face, still able to see the beautiful face I remembered—even though in reality it was gone, marred by jagged, ugly scars. Through it all, I could still see the love evident in her face when she spoke of Trix.

"Things were grand for quite a while. Oh, Shiv... I loved my child's life. It was... idyllic. Perfect, and Trix... but..."

Joan let her eyelids fall, sighing. In moments, a lone tear slipped from her eye and anemically rolled down her cheek.

"When I was... erm... ten... there was a kind of... terrific row... between our parents. It was a gigantic blowup. I'd never heard 'em argue... not like that, but... oh... that night... Mum called Uncle Stef... on the phone. She was yelling... really... loudly—shouting—but, I was up in my room... couldn't hear exactly.

"Not two minutes later... erm... Uncle Stef... he came pounding on our front door. Pounded so hard it rattled the windows... the walls. Scared me something... awful. Aunt Stell... she was with him. They were shouting... terrible. We all came out... to see what was... the commotion, but... my dad, he yelled at me and my brothers... to get back in our rooms.

"It was... awful. I felt sick, and... I didn't even understand... why? Yeah... I wasn't sure what happened, exactly; but suddenly, for no... bloody reason—none I understood... not—Trix and me? They wouldn't... we couldn't see each other. Not at all. Our families... we used to... every weekend, and holidays... be together.

"Trix and my dad... they loved art, so they... were... close; but after... the... row? Nothing. We were... in the midst of summer... and school vacation, so... we couldn't even meet each other at school. We... Trix and me? Well, we were... were... bloody well... devastated. I never cried so hard... or... so long in my life. I was... inconsolable. Trix, too... I heard."

"I can imagine. It sounds perfectly awful."

"Then..." Joan continued, almost as if I weren't there, "*then...* not too long after, Trix's family... went to America. I don't recall... how much later... sometime after Christmas, and before... school started back. I'm pretty sure about that, because I... went back to school by myself. I cried... every day because... because I missed Trix... so much.

"We were three grades apart, but we'd still... see each other... Then... a few months later, we went too—to The States, but... to a different one. We were... over a thousand miles apart! We ended up in... Colorado, and Trix and hers... California. Hollywood."

"Did you ever... get in touch, or...?"

"Hmmm...? Yeah, nah... We tried, Trix and me, writing... but our letters got... our mums got 'em. They'd ground us... I spent more time in my room than... anywhere... but... I didn't care. Without Trix... anywhere but my room... was misery. Then,

Trix... she hatched a grand idea. She was the smart one. Yeah... We used friends' addresses."

"How...?" I wondered how they'd communicate friends' addresses if they couldn't write or call.

Joan turned her head and looked at me inquisitively.

"If you couldn't write, or..."

"Oh... oh, right. Yeah, yeah... Trix... she knew my mum had her hair and nails done every month on the first Thursday afternoon... like clockwork. Always had. Don't remember her not. Didn't take long for her... to , y'know, continue her old... routine. Trix figured she would. Trix... she understood that about people." Joan fell silent for the longest while.

"So...?"

"Oh, right... sorry," Joan said, coming out of her trancelike state. "I just... yeah... so Trix called when I'd be home, but mum wouldn't be. The boys... they were always out. I was... the homebody. Trix gave me an address of a mate of hers... told me to find someone who... who she could send her letters to. Of course... we... we had to be careful what we wrote, so... yeah, yeah... tough, yeah, but at least we... could... communicate."

"Smart, that."

"Yeah."

"Did you ever find out what happened? What caused the... row?"

Joan sighed. After a long while, she nodded.

"Trix... She told me... erm... about four or five years after they split us up it was... erm... because of... her. Well, us... *me*, actually."

"You?" I breathed.

"Yeah, yeah... I'd made the... mistake... I said to my mum that erm... someday... when we grew up, Trix and me? We were gonna get... married... and live... happily... ever after."

Joan said nothing for perhaps a only minute or so, but to me, it felt like eons.

She finally began speaking again, but more quietly, "Our parents... they went quite rightly mad. Mum blamed Trix... 'cause she was older. Said Trix... couldn't come near me again. Called her an evil, incestuous... erm... paedophile."

I gasped.

"Yeah... That's the row."

"Why, you must have—" I had no words to express myself at that moment. I feared my heart might break in two for Joan, the little girl.

"Oh... when I discovered that... when Trix finally confessed... what had happened? What the row was all about? Shiv, it... it *gutted me*. Naturally, I... erm... yeah, I blamed myself."

"Oh, no... that's..."

"But, I did. Yeah, yeah, I did. For a long, long time... Years."

"I'm so sorry."

"I never stopped loving Trix—never, not for one moment—but... I'd get... I'd get... y'know, pashed... on other girls... at school, but... erm... *Always* kept my feelings... to myself. Never dated boys. Never wanted to. I got... asked out—a lot, but... I just... nah... didn't care for 'em... blokes.

"Trixie and me... we'd always planned on being together after I graduated... high school, but my dad insisted... I had to go to uni. He taught art history at... the University of... erm... Denver. They had a nursing programme there, and... I could go for nothing because of him, so... that's what I did. I became... erm... a... nurse.

"Why not? Yeah? Get an education... and a vocation for... erm... for free? Trix, she wasn't happy about it. She was in her... third year? at... at... UCLA and kept pretty busy. But... erm... we kept on writing. Sometimes... we'd talk. Not much, though, because... we didn't have much money, but...

"Four years later, I graduated from nursing college and ended up working at... Denver General... hospital. I wanted to go to Los

Angeles… and be with Trix, but…" Joan shut her eyes and just stopped speaking.

When it seemed as if Joan might not continue her story, I asked, "But…? What happened? Why didn't you?"

"Trix… she'd… erm… she met someone… a girl… in Los Angeles, and… erm… so…" Joan's eyes became moist. "She told me… best not… come."

"Oh, Joan… no… I'm *so* sorry…"

Joan shrugged. "It was inevitable, us being… apart for… so long—over ten years, yeah. My heart broke, but… yeah… well, it had been broken for… dunno, seems… forever. There was just a… a finality with us, I… y'know, I never expected we would end, so… I was…" Joan drew a long, deliberate breath before easing it out with a sigh. "Undone," she whispered.

"I didn't enjoy my job… at Denver General. Hated it, in fact. I loved it… nursing… I did, but I felt stuck. It was more about Denver than anything. The, erm, war in Korea was… ramping up, and a co-worker told me about… she had joined the… the Women's Army Corp to go there. Korea.

"I… I needed something big to… erm… I needed something different, so I joined, too. That was… 1950? It might have been '51. No… Ah, well, I don't remember. I served a year in-country— in Korea. It was… nothing like I expected it would be, but… it was an adventure, which… it's what I wanted. Couldn't complain. There was a part of me… when I first signed up… that… hoped I would die… while over there, but…"

I gasped softly.

"Quite obviously, I didn't, as I wasn't anywhere near combat. I knew of some girls… they died when their aircraft crashed, but I… erm… I never knew of any WACs perishing… not in Korea… from combat. In hindsight…"

She sighed. "When I completed my tour in Korea, they asked if I… would I sign up for another term. I said no straight away, so the Army shipped me back to the States. With another year left to serve, they assigned me to... erm... Walter Reed—the Army hospital in Washington... DC.

"I... I found it quite a... erm... depressing assignment. Each day proved more difficult... than the last. So many horribly... injured young blokes... permanently disfigured... crippled... physically and mentally... I... I wanted to call it... quits. But, erm... when I least expected it, with one foot out the door, I... I fell in love... with a... co-worker.

"Yeah, yeah. It was so much bigger than... crushes I'd had before... I thought... Dani... Danielle... I hoped there might be something there—for us both, y'know. Dani... she was a civilian... a clerk working in administration. She... she was..." Joan shut her eyes. "She was nice... actually... lovely, in fact. Pretty... and we got on famously... right off. We were besties... for... a while.

"One night after work, we... went out... much like many, many... nights before, and I... erm... I... I got to feeling... comfortable and... stupid. Alone for so long, I think... is the reason... Yeah, I completely... misread the situation. When I... I dropped Dani at her apartment... I said... *Ugh.* I told her... I said I had... feelings... for her. That I... I might have fallen... for her." Joan shook her head with disappointment.

"Yeah, yeah... I know. Stupid, stupid... mistake. I had... misjudged her... erm... her *character*. She physically... *recoiled*... and stormed from the car. 'Go fuck yourself... freak,' she screamed at me, and... slammed the car door... so hard it hurt my ears. Dani didn't talk to me... not at all... the whole next week.

"I'll admit... Shiv, it scared me. Scared me shitless. I thought she... y'know... she might say something to my... Captain, and... they'd send me to prison. So... rather than... erm... try to... mend things... between us? I... I kept my distance.

"Then... erm... I dunno... two weeks later? Three? I... we... Dani... she invited me out... with some friends. Her friends. Civilians... boys. Blokes. I said yes... stupid me... Thinking she'd forgiven me, y'know? And we'd go back to... just being friends, like... before. But... no. She erm... she..." Joan sighed. "She set me up. Plain and... simple. Evil... is what it was.

"They... I... erm... I got chockers, though... I know I'd barely drunk enough to get so thoroughly... but, yeah... I was pretty well maggot... before I even finished my first beer. Must've passed out, because... I only remember getting there... to the bar... drinking my beer, and then...

"I dunno... I... I came to in a strange... room, and... they... Dani's friends... they..." Joan swallowed hard, fighting tears that had welled, threatening to spill with a vengeance.

She pulled in a deep breath and looked directly into my eyes, her ice-blue, tear-filled eyes piercing mine, but didn't speak for... I can't say, but it was a while. I had the good sense to wait quietly as I felt in my bones she was about to drop a bomb. I wasn't wrong.

"They... they had their way with me. They... *raped* me... Shiv. All of 'em. I think... Dani... too."

A gasp fought to burst from my lips, but I held it in so as not to disturb Joan's story. Horrified, I waited in agonizing silence as my stomach churned.

"There were... erm... f-five. Ones that I... already had their turn... razzed on about... how... much... how much better they'd done than... the one on me." Joan's voice got quiet. "She... she was there, too. Holding a bottle... Even though I... I was in a fog... at that point... I heard her. *Cheering*... cheering them on. Sick..." Joan choked back a sob.

"I... erm... I... I... heard them all... laughing... her especially... Them saying... *'all you need is a good fucking... dyke... or several—you need some good hard... cock... to cure you... of your... your... disgusting... sickness.'* It was as if... as if I were... trapped... in a nightmare.

"When I... when I realised I wasn't dreaming... that what was happening was real... what they'd been doing to me? I... I went right crazy, Siobhán. I did... I did my ever lovin' best... trying to escape, to get... to get the one off me, but... oh, no... they weren't havin' it. The others, they... they held me down... but... I still fought.

"Then... as if... raping... wasn't.... The one on me... hit me... with his fist—in my face. Hard. I almost passed out from the pain... maybe I did for a second. Truth is, I dunno... I can't... erm... really remember, but... When I came to... I knew... I knew... if I didn't fight to... free myself... they would... kill me. So... I fought even harder." Joan didn't speak as tears spilled down her cheeks.

Dumbstruck and sick to my stomach, I fought back my own tears, but I was losing the battle.

"Next I knew... I woke up in hospital. Dunno know how... how long I'd been there, but... I was... in a bad way—inside... and out. They did... terrible..." she whispered, "terrible... wicked things... to me..."

"Oh, Joan..."

"Yeah, yeah... First thing... after my head cleared a bit, I had a nurse call Trix. I couldn't talk—they'd broke my jaw... knocked out my front teeth... shattered my... erm... eye-socket. All the surgeries on my face... they... got done while I was... erm... unconscious.

"And, Trix? God love her, she... I dunno know how she managed, but... She... got to my side by the very next day. Must've... I dunno, got on a plane... in Los Angeles straight away and was... there... right there... with me. Never left. She never... left. Not for two weeks... not ever."

"Wow," I breathed as my own tears rolled down my cheeks.

"Yeah. I tried to... to press charges, but..." Joan shook her head. "I wouldn't... couldn't... go through it again. Talking to the police... it started to... It was as if they were back on me again, but... somehow they, the police, made it... as if it... it was all *my* fault. No. No. I couldn't do it.

"The day they released me... from hospital, Trix and me... we went direct to my... erm... commander, and I resigned... my commission. That afternoon… Trix, she got us on a train and took me home with her. I… I couldn't fly because… of how… they said… the pressure wasn't good for… my face, so… we took a train. We've been… *we were*… together… ever since… until…" Joan stifled a sob.

"Did she know everything that happened?"

Joan shook her head. "Nah… She knew some… not all—but, after we left DC, she never mentioned it, any of it, and I… I never did, neither. We just… we didn't need to, Shiv." Joan stared at me, taking me in for what seemed like an hour but was probably only minutes—seconds, perhaps. She studied me as if my face were a portal to the past, and I let her. Finally, ever so softly, she once again began to speak.

"I've told no one else… what happened… only you, Siobhán. And Trix, natch, but… not everything. No, I couldn't tell her… not everything. It would have… *ruined* her. She already felt… to blame —I couldn't… Still… Trix took care of me, and… erm… put me back… together.

"She was… my rock, my hero… my lover… bestie… soulmate… my… family… my *everything*. Always. Since we were kids, Trix really was… she was… the love… of my life, Shiv." Joan fell silent, then whispered, "I… I miss… her." Joan closed her eyes again. "We didn't… have enough… time. Not enough…"

I reached over and took Joan's hand. We'd never before been physical in our friendship, but I didn't give it a second thought as I reached out for her. She grabbed onto mine with an energy I can only describe as desperate for human contact. And then, she wept. Softly at first, then full-on, heart-wrenching sobbing followed. I gently pulled her into my arms and held her close to me.

My own tears fell unnoticed onto her tee shirt. She stayed there in my arms, weeping until she fell asleep. As she sobbed into my chest, I experienced a deep sense and level of heartbreak I'd never known before or since. It's hard to describe as it was wholly different from how I felt about Mam and Da passing, or Trix, even.

I experienced something similar listening to Fionn's story about his family's massacre, but not with the magnitude I had for Joan.

The ignorance and evil entwined in The Cousins' story crushed me. I was quite well read, particularly in world history. Because of that, I'd learned a bit about the wicked things people have done to each other throughout time—as such, I was not naïve to the potential of evil acts by human beings. I suppose the stark reality of it, the proximity of it to someone I loved with all my heart, was what hit me the hardest.

Until the day I die, I will never forget The Cousins—two of the most dear, kind and loving people I've ever known. Had they not taken me in and cared for me as if I were family, I cannot say who I'd be today. What I can say is this: I would have most certainly been a lesser human being if not for them.

30

Not Trudi

∞ ∞ ∞ ∞ ∞

In the spring, not quite two years after we'd lost Trix, an extraordinary thing happened to me. I'd been downstairs in the pub taking advantage of the quiet time, trying to get a few things done before customers started coming in.

Joan, as usual, was up in her room, knocked out from her after-brekky medications. Pippa had taken to staying with Joan each day after brekky and until she woke up some time in the mid-afternoon. Until Pippa came downstairs to alert me that Joan was up and needed me, I was on my own. I really didn't mind Pippa staying with Joan. I actually thought it incredibly sweet for my precious pup to take it upon herself to watch after Joan while I worked downstairs.

I recall it being a Thursday when the extraordinary thing happened, because Thursday mornings were typically slow for both the pub and the inn. It was when I preferred taking care of mundane tasks such as inventory and restocking. Not expecting any customers until noon, and thoroughly absorbed in my task, hunkered down behind the bar, a male voice startled me, causing me to lose my balance for a moment.

"Excuse me," he said. "Erm… s'it too early for…?"

As I regained my balance, I silently chastised myself for not locking the entrance door after I'd fetched the morning papers.

"Ya lookin' for a drink, lad?" I asked without looking up over the counter.

With a chuckled, the voice replied, "Well, I'm not here to fuck spiders, mate, so… yeah."

Amused, I stopped counting bottles and raised myself up to peer over the bench top. A young man, possibly in his early twenties, hands jammed deep into his tan trouser pockets, stood right at the edge of the bench. The second our eyes met, he reeled back and exclaimed with great elation, "Holy Dooley! *Trudi Johansen-Arvesen!* Whoa! I can't believe it! What in God's name are you doing here, mate?"

I stood up, and with a tilt of my head responded, "Come again?"

"Wha… what? Trudi! C'mon, it's… me. *Tom!*" He paused, flushed with excitement as he waited in earnest for me to recognize him. When I didn't, he continued with urgency.

"Tom Dix," he insisted, puzzled. He shook his head. "What the…?"

I scrutinized him, noting his casual, though neat attire, and nicely barbered blond hair. He had what I would consider an honest face.

"I'm sorry, Mr., *erm*, Dix, is it? I… I-I'm not…" I squinted, confused. "*My* name is Siobhán. O'Shea. It's not… I'm not your…" I scrunched my face as I looked into bright, sparkling baby blue eyes framed by bushy dark blond eyebrows. "… your Trudi… or whoever you think I'm… supposed to be. Do I, *erm*… Have we met?"

The youthful-looking man had an obvious look of disbelief all over his face. He continued staring at me.

"Mr. Dix? *Mr. Dix?*" he exclaimed. "Trude… you winding me up, now? Ah! You are! You're… wait… wait… Ahhh… ha!" he laughed, clapping his hands together. "You got me, Trude. Good one. *Good* one." He pointed at me as he chuckled heartily. "Whew! You had me going for a… Right. Right. So. What're ya doin' way over here in the Cabbage Patch?"

I studied the man's face, clean-shaven with a hint of pink on his cheeks, but no matter how I tried, I could not place him. I'm normally pretty good with faces. Not so much with names, but if I've seen you once, I'll not likely forget you. I was certain we'd not met before; yet, there he was, insistent we were not only acquaintances, but *mates.*

"One," I began with a smirk, "I live here, and have for… well, several years now. Two, I believe I'd have to actually know you for us to be mates, yeah? But there's the dig… *mate.* I don't—know you." I half-shrugged.

"The hell you don't, Trudi," he scoffed, perturbed. "We lived two doors apart all through school. You and Mimi, you've been best friends since… well, I can't remember when you weren't. Inseparable, you were."

"Mimi?"

"Mimi? Yeah. *Mimi.* My little sister? Your bestie?" He scoffed again, full on annoyed. "Stop tryin' to have a go with me, Trude. C'mon, now… out with it. What ya doin' over here? I haven't seen you since… well, since I left for uni. That's been, what? Five… six years now?"

Exasperated, I leaned in, putting both hands on the bench top. "What do I need to say to convince ya? I am not acquainted with *erm*… your sister, Mm-Mimi. And, I have certainly never made your acquaintance, Mister… erm… *Tom*. Never met ya. Ever. First I've ever seen ya. Fair dinkum." Somewhat amused by the odd situation, I smiled warmly, seeing he found my truth difficult to accept. "So. What can I get for ya?" I asked with an understanding grin. "Y'look like you need a bevvie, mate."

He stared at me for the longest time, befuddled. Finally, he dragged the stool from the bench, making a soft scrapping sound on the wood floor with it as he did, and sat down. "Erm… gimme a…" He hesitated for a beat, then looked at the wristwatch on his left wrist. "Half past ten? Ah, what the hell. I came in for a fizzy, but… gimme a Brownie. Please."

I grabbed a brown bottle of beer from the metal cooler, popped the top off with an opener and slid it over to him. "Wanna glass?" I asked, knowing with certainty he'd say no.

"Yeah, nah," he said as he snatched the bottle by its neck. In mere seconds, he'd guzzled half the beer. He set it firmly on the counter, wiping his lips with the back of his hand. His eyes squinted while studying my face. If I'm honest, his focused attention directly on me gave me the Willies. To avoid further disquieting scrutiny, I crouched back down and resumed my task at hand: counting and putting overstock away.

"It's right uncanny is what it is," I heard Tom say, more to himself than me.

I stood up again. "What's that?"

"You. You could be… I mean, uh, you're just… you could be… Hell, you and Trudi? You could right well be doppelgängers."

"Doppel…?"

"Doppelgängers. Y'know… doubles. *Identical twins.*"

"Really," I answered more as a statement than a question.

"*Really*," he insisted. "No kidding. You look and sound exactly like Trudi. Like I said, it's right… queer."

"Huh."

He nodded with bewilderment. "Stuffed, I'll be…" he muttered to himself.

"Where're you from?" I asked, continuing to work.

"Perth. Well, originally. In Sydney now. Since uni. I work in the financial district... international finance, actually." He took another long drink of his beer. "I'm down visiting my mum's parents. Just for a few days before I fly over to Perth to see Mum and Dad. I see 'em every three, four months, but I come down here once a month to check in on the Grands for Mum—they're gettin' on... y'know. Mum can't make it over too often, so I..." He shrugged.

"Sorry to hear."

"No, yeah, it's nice. Granny and Grandad... they're all right. I'd come see 'em even if Mum didn't need me to."

I nodded. A lengthy, frightfully awkward pause followed my acknowledgement as we each searched for something to say. Finally, I spoke.

"So, erm, this erm... my... my doppel...?" I furrowed my brow and leaned my elbows on the edge of my side of the counter.

"Gänger. *Doppelgänger.*"

"Right, my doppelgänger..." I'd never heard the word doppelgänger said, but I'd read it somewhere along the way. It sounded more peculiar out loud than it ever did in my head, making me grin. *Doppelgänger.* The fact I might actually have one aroused my interest. "She... she lived in Perth, then?" I asked.

"Yeah, yeah. Still in Perth, far as I'm aware. Well, erm, if you're *honestly* not her, like you've not got amnesia or takin' the piss..."

I shook my head. "Nope. Neither." I grinned mischievously. "But... would I even realise?"

"Eh?"

"If I had amnesia. Would I actually realise it if I did?" I teased. "I mean... is that something I'd be aware of? I'm not sure..."

"Oh. Ha. Well... huh... I guess," he shrugged with a lazy grin. "Yeah, I... dunno," he replied sincerely. "Probably... no."

"So y'know... I don't have it. I'm quite right in the head," I snickered. "So... you're pretty sure she's still there. In Perth," I stated.

"Yeah, yeah. Last I knew, yeah."

"Huh."

"You should..." Tom began, still staring at me, but stopped himself.

"Hmm...?"

"Ever been to Perth?"

"Me? Oh, no. Never. Nope. Never."

"Y'should go. Go and meet your body double. I promise, Siobhán, it'll be... like looking in a mirror."

I scoffed, though a slight tingle ran down my spine.

Tom shook his head. "No, no, I mean it," he insisted. "You'll be right... *gobsmacked*. Fair dinkum."

"Gobsmacked, eh? That's, erm, pretty... serious." I grinned. "I dunno... it's a far way to Perth, and I... y'know, I have... obligations..." I mumbled, thinking of Joan who depended on me for almost everything.

"I'm flying over in two days. You could... erm... come with me."

My eyes opened wide as I reeled back slightly.

"No, no..." he began, clearly concerned I'd taken his meaning wrong. "I mean... ugh... My intentions are..." He sighed. "Listen, I know Trudi, where she lives. I'd introduce ya. Get the two of yous together."

I continued to examine Tom's face for truth, concerned he might be attempting to con me.

"I'm on the level, Siobhán. If not this trip... I get to Perth every quarter or thereabouts. I drive down first for the Grands, then fly out from here."

I raised my shoulders with a noncommittal shrug.

"Think about it, yeah? Here." He pulled a white business card from his shirt pocket. "That's my office number." He picked up a pen I'd been using. "Y'mind?" he asked.

I shrugged.

He turned the card over and swiftly wrote on it with quick and precise printing. "Here's my home number. If you change your mind, give me a bell, eh? Really. I'll give Trudi a tingle when I go over this time, and… erm…"

I nodded as I took his card, studying it. *Sydney Group Ltd. Thomas L. Dix, Financial Analyst, International Division.* "Yeah…"

"Yeah?"

"Yeah, sure. Let me, erm… I'll give it a think."

"Sweet. Cheers," he said; lifting his bottle, then drained the remaining contents down his throat. He set the empty bottle on the counter. As he stood up to leave he beamed a bright smile at me. "What do I owe ya… Doppelgänger?"

I smiled back and waved my hand as if swatting him away. "My shout, Mr. Dix," I answered, then winked, a quirky habit I'd picked up from Fionn and The Cousins.

"Thanks, mate," Tom said as he turned. He walked towards the door, shaking his head. "*Ooroo,*" he said over his shoulder. I watched with only mild interest as he exited the front door, then I got back to work.

31

All Gone

∞ ∞ ∞ ∞ ∞

On the morning of November 12th, 1973, The Cousins' saga came to a sad, but not unexpected conclusion. Though, as much as one expects something bad to come, when it finally does, it can still knock you down.

I'd gone upstairs to awaken Joan, Pippa as always right with me. I'd brought up Joan's brekky, along with her morning meds, same as I did every morning. I announced myself as I entered her room, setting her tray on a footstool. I called out her name, but she failed to answer me; which in itself wasn't unusual, but there was an odd and unfamiliar stillness about her. I approached her bed with hesitance.

I stood at the edge of the bed and stared down at Joan for the longest time, hoping with all hope what I feared was not true. Even before I checked her pulse, instinctively, I knew what I'd find. It was over. She hadn't moved an iota the entire time I'd been standing there. Pippa's soft whimper confirmed what I suspected. Indeed, there on her nightstand were an empty bottle of barbiturates and a nearly empty bottle of gin. With her skin already cool to the touch, I knew there was no reviving her. Despite knowing Joan's torment had finally come to a merciful end, my heart broke into a million pieces—again.

Not knowing what else to do, I laid down on the bed beside my dear departed friend, and was joined immediately by Pippa. I held Pippa close to me while I cried tears of grief and joy into her fur. Yes, I experienced both things. Deeply. I missed Joan already. She'd been so unhappy and right miserable since losing Trix; but selfishly, I still wanted her there with me.

After Trix, all I ever desired for Joan was that by some miracle she might find some measure of happiness. I was content she'd found the peace she sought and deserved, but I hated how she found it. Trying to reconcile my contradicting feelings didn't come easily. I loved her. I loved them both, but with Trix gone, Joan and I had gotten much closer. She also got all the love I had for them both. They were my family. With both departed, I could no longer dismiss my own feelings for Joan's benefit. My beloved cousin aunties were dead and gone, and once again I was alone.

A few days after Joan's well-attended funeral—one that was beautifully planned by Joan herself—I received an unscheduled visit from The Cousins' solicitor. It surprised me beyond comprehension to learn they'd left everything they owned, what amounted to a considerable amount of wealth, to me. Touched to my soul, I'd no idea they thought so much of me to want to do that. I'd never gotten around to telling them about my financial situation. Not that I didn't try many times over; but in the end, I thought it best not to disturb our perfect dynamic. Somehow, though, I find it comforting to think it mightn't have made a difference if they had known.

For the next many months I continued to run the establishment as I had since The Cousins' ill-fated trip to Peru. In a way, I felt a deep responsibility to them to do so. They loved the place, and it loved them—so it seemed the proper thing to do in their memory. I did all right, managing to make a nice profit each month; but, truth be told, my heart wasn't in it, and hadn't been since Peru. As time went on, I found I could no longer bear to carry on living and working in The Cousins' space without them. Their absence had created a vast emptiness I didn't know how to fill.

Prior to their trip to South America, I'd been making my own plans to travel and discover the world first-hand. Their demise had placed a pause on my plans. I didn't mind while Joan was alive, but at a certain point after her death I decided I needed to move on.

I considered signing everything I'd inherited over to their siblings, but knowing how they'd ostracized Joan and Trix about their relationship and how Hugo favoured the girls over their siblings, I ultimately nixed that harebrained idea. Instead, after much deliberation, I donated not quite half of the Brown House to a local artists' collective The Cousins loved and supported. I'd allow the collective to operate the inn while I maintained a majority holding. I claimed The Cousins' flat for my own. I couldn't let the Brown House go completely, but the collective would allow me the freedom I so desperately desired.

To The Cousins' siblings, I divvied up a portion of their cash holdings so as to avoid any hard feelings and quash the contentious lawsuit that had been brewing in the background. I know it wasn't Joan and Trix's wish, but I felt certain they'd approve if they'd had the opportunity to hear my reasoning to keep the peace. The remainder of cash I set aside as an emergency fund for the inn. The few residential properties they owned in America and Australia, I donated to local women's charities. I knew The Cousins would approve of my decision. After I signed the legal papers, I bid adieu to a place I considered my home for several years, and left in search of my next adventures.

Part Four

One In A Million

∞ ∞ ∞ ∞ ∞

The year 1974 proved to be the best and worst year I've lived thus far. You might ask how the same year could be both, but it was—in spades. Oh, to be sure, I've had years I could say were worse or better, but none that were both, and nearly equally so.

For eleven years, according to my best calculations, Pippa was my constant companion. My shadow. I moved, she moved. I stopped, she stopped. We'd been that way since the beginning, for so long I gave it little thought. I might even have taken Pippa's constant and certain presence for granted. Still, I loved knowing she was with me always. One day she was there—always, and then… she wasn't. Pippa leaving me wasn't a dramatic leaving on its face, but it was abrupt, unexpected and heartbreaking all in one.

In early January of that year, I woke up expecting our morning ritual of greeting each other with playing and kisses. Instead, Pippa remained still. With Dolly under her jaw, she remained on the floor, asleep.

"Pippa! C'mon, PipPip!" I urged. "Wake up, my girl! Up, up Pippa BlueBlack'nWhite O'Shea! Rise and shine, Dolly Doll." Despite my urging, Pippa didn't move. Not a muscle. I caught my breath the second I realised she wasn't breathing. Horrified, I gently nudged her body, but she felt strange, not like my Pippa at all. I gently shook her, and she seemed... not alive.

I don't know quite how to explain it, but her fur, her body, she... seemed foreign to me. Her temperature was wrong, and as I mentioned, her fur was odd and unusual; well, I may as well say it, it appeared lifeless. Dead. Yes, it appeared dead because for some inexplicable reason my lovely pup had left this world, and me— without warning. Once I realised she'd gone, I'll admit it, I went out of my mind.

Losing Trix, then Joan... then Pippa; honestly, how I managed keeping it as together as I did is a mystery to me. As my heart shattered into a million pieces, I temporarily lost myself, and the rest of the day was an absolute weeping blur.

The next morning, Fionn came to offer me comfort and pay his respects to Pippa. Pippa loved Fionn, and he loved her as well. We cried together over our loss. Then, Fionn drove us out to the farm where he helped me bury Pippa with her beloved Dolly.

We buried them both next to Mam and Da. Initially, I considered cremation, keeping Pippa's remains with me forever, but I could not bear the idea of my sweet girl being torched down to ashes. Was it better than being buried? Who's to say? Neither choice was my preference, but burial, I suppose, seemed less... horrific. If not for Fionn, I cannot imagine how I'd have managed. I've been sad over losing loved ones in my life, but losing Pippa... that loss left me bereft for a long, long time. In fact, I'm not sure the loss ever left.

After we laid Pippa and Dolly to rest, Fionn returned to the house. I stayed behind, wailing unfettered on the ground where I remained grieving until long after nightfall. I finally dragged myself into the house, utterly drained. Knackered to the core. I'm amazed I could even walk back to the house without falling into a sobbing heap. It wasn't even ninety metres, but it felt like a long, arduous trek. Sad, empty and heart-wrenching days lay ahead.

Pippa's sudden absence shattered my world. I suspect it was the last straw for my emotional state. In the days, weeks and months after her death, it was like a part of me had gone missing—as if I'd had a limb removed. And, what I didn't expect was that I felt scared for the first time in quite a while. It was the most curious experience. Through all I'd lived through, with Pippa by my side, I'd never been afraid of... well, anything. Except for The Attic and the mirror; but even then, I knew Pip would protect me against actual peril.

Without my Pippa with me, an irrational sense of vulnerability consumed me. Yes, I felt sad, excruciatingly so, and unprotected. I will confess, I've never shed so many tears over any of the humans I've lost as I did for Pippa. Other than Fionn, I had no one left who I loved or who loved me back with such unwavering devotion as my Pippa.

It's been well over forty years since I lost Pippa, and I still miss her. There are still times I'll look down to the ground expecting her to be there at my heel, her beautiful and soulful blue eyes looking up at me with devoted adoration. Each time it happens, I'm genuinely surprised she's no longer there. I've had several dogs since, but not one has touched my heart like my Pippa BlueBlack'nWhite O'Shea. She was one in a million. Whenever I visit Australia, I still visit Mam, Da and my darling Pippa. No matter how many years have passed, the loss has not lessened. It hasn't, but through the years I've learned how to contain it and how to live without my dearest love and best friend.

33

Doppelgänger

∞ ∞ ∞ ∞ ∞

Once I'd sorted my inheritance from Joan and Trix, I had no reason to remain in Melbourne—aside from Fionn, that is. Without the inn to run, I'd not much to do. Fionn and I had often discussed my future, and each time he encouraged me to explore the world. I had the means to do so, he'd mercilessly remind me; and with Joan, Trix, and Pippa gone, and with the Brown House managed, I was free to roam to my heart's content.

It had been nearly a year from when Tom Dix stopped at the inn and insisted I had a doppelgänger living in Perth, but the probability of it never left my mind. Could it be possible? Each and every day I wondered about her, my alleged doppelgänger, Trudi, but I never called Tom. I'd kept his card, but as I remained busy taking care of Joan and the inn, it would have been futile to even entertain the possibility of travelling to Perth. I couldn't leave her —or the inn.

However, once I was unencumbered by the inn and caregiving duties, I seriously began considering a trip west. Tom Dix saying it would be like seeing myself in a mirror stuck with me, niggling at the outer edges of my psyche. I remembered all too vividly what seeing my face in a mirror for the first time was like. The shock alone nearly did me in. Did I really want to experience *that* again? No, I conceded, not really. But then, on a dare from Fionn, I broke down and called Tom Dix at his office. He was excited to hear from me. I immediately made plans to fly with him from Melbourne to the other side of Australia the following month.

When I'd first met Tom, I'd been behind the bar with him on the other side. It wasn't until we met at the airport in Melbourne when I realised he was considerably shorter than I. I would be generous saying he was much taller than a hundred and sixty-five centimetres, or five feet, five inches. Though short in stature, his build was not in the least slight. He had what one might describe as a wrestler's body. Broad and muscular, stocky, with not an ounce of fat on him.

I considered him good looking in a wholesome, but not particularly a handsome way—more like a kind of ordinary boy-next-door way. I liked him as a person, and nothing more. His voice had a pleasant tenor timbre, until he became excited. Then it pitched considerably higher. It amused me greatly whenever his voice spiked, though I did my best to hide my mirth so as not to offend him. Tom Dix was much too nice to offend on purpose.

Travelling by air didn't make me nervous, but travelling with a man I still considered a stranger did. My trip to South America to rescue Joan had immunized me to any worries about flying. The harrowing flights I endured to rescue The Cousins will remain in my memory banks until I die. Nothing short of a nosedive into the ocean or a fiery crash into the side of a mountain could ever be worse than those.

As it happened, the flight to Perth was so uneventful, it surprised me when the pilot announced our landing. Tom and I chatted most of the flight, though to be fair, he did more than his share of the talking. He did so love to go on and on about international affairs and finance. Not that I minded at all as I'm a bit of a curious person and love learning new things.

I learned loads about Tom's view of the world, politics, finance and even religion on our way to meet Trudi. As for myself, Tom didn't learn much. One, I rarely talk about myself; and two, from working as a barkeep, I've found people are happiest when other people listen to what they have to say. By the time we landed, Tom seemed pretty happy.

Fionn had insisted upon making all my travel arrangements to ensure my safety. Tom had generously offered to let me stay with him at his parent' house, but Fionn wouldn't have it. Instead, he arranged for me to stay at a lovely bed-and-breakfast owned by a friend of a friend near where my alleged doppelgänger lived.

The next morning, after sharing breakfast with some other B&B guests, Tom arrived to take me to meet my "twin." Until we parked in front of her house, I'd not been nervous at all. Not one iota. But the moment I exited Tom's car, my insides quivered. I couldn't understand why I was having such a visceral response, but my body felt queer.

"You ready, Siobhán?" Tom asked as he rounded the car to me.

"Yeah, yeah… sure," I muttered.

"C'mon, then." He took me by the elbow, gently escorting me to the entrance of a modest inner-city home in an area Tom called Hyde Park. "Siobhán," he asked somewhat incredulously, "are you shaking?"

"Me? Nah…" I lied, shaking my head.

At the front door, Tom didn't bother to knock. Instead, he opened it as if he lived there and walked right through. "Hiya, Trude!" he called out. "Trudi! It's Tom! We're here!"

As if on cue, a woman rounded the corner from another room in the house. Upon seeing each other, we both audibly gasped, reeling backwards. For me, it was as if I were looking at myself dressed in someone else's clothes with a different hairstyle. For Trudi, I imagine her experience was the same. We stood gawking at each other for what seemed an eternity, speechless, marveling at our incredible likeness.

Finally, clearing his throat, Tom said, "So, erm, uh… Trudi, this is Siobhán. Siobhán, Trudi…"

Not one of us said a word as Trudi and I continued staring at each other.

"I told you, didn't I?" Tom prodded with obvious glee, smiling ear-to-ear. "Doppelgängers!"

We could not tear our eyes from each other.

"Right," Tom said, nervously. "Yeah, so… I'm gonna run some errands, yeah?" He waited for a reply but got nothing. "It's safe to leave you two alone?" he asked with a chuckle. "You'll not kill each other? Eh?"

Both of us turned to Tom and in unison, said, "No!" surprising us all.

Tom laughed. "Righto. Be back in the arvo, yeah?"

"Yeah," we answered again in unison, giggling as we did.

∞   ∞   ∞   ∞   ∞

"It's… it's uncanny, isn't it?" Trudi finally whispered. "I…"

"Yes," I replied, also whispering. "It's like… looking at myself," I marveled.

"Well, hey," Trudi said, motioning for me to enter. "Come on through and sit. You want some tea? Coffee… beer? No, wait… it's half-past nine," she said, giggling nervously.

"Coffee's good," I answered, following her into a bright sitting room with modern furnishings.

"So, Siobhán, erm... where are you from? When were you born? How...?" Trudi rattled off questions as she brought a tray with coffee accoutrements into the room. I watched her place the tray on a small table in front of the sofa where I sat.

"*Erm...*" I squirmed. "... the countryside... near Dunkeld. And... I... I don't know," I admitted sheepishly. "Not exactly."

"Not exactly... what?"

"I, erm... when I was born. My... my parents didn't believe in birthdays, so... I... I don't actually know. Never did."

"Fair dinkum?" she asked, her astonishment visible on her face.

"Fair dinkum." I nodded.

"Why, that's..." Trudi stared at me, dumbfounded. "That's just... cracked... isn't it?"

I shrugged. "I... I didn't wonder growing up because, well... I... I didn't know any better, did I? Mam and Da were the only people I'd ever seen until I... *erm*... 'til I moved to Melbourne. But, yeah... I'm finding it's... yeah, apparently it's fairly odd."

"What do you mean? They were the only ones...?" Obviously confused, Trudi cocked her head to the side. "I'm sorry, I... I don't really... understand."

I paused, contemplating how much I should tell the stranger who was a perfect, though oddly dressed, rendering of me.

"How old are you?" she asked.

"Dunno," I shrugged. "Best I can figure, maybe... twenty? Older? Younger? I just can't say. Not for sure. I have a bit of an idea, but..."

"Fascinating."

I immediately noticed a slight change in Trudi. Her breathing had become heavier, and something seemed to have altered in her body. It was so subtle it's something I just cannot describe, but no doubt I was witnessing a metamorphosis of sorts.

Trudi cleared her throat. "Look… I don't want to pry, Siobhán, but… erm… why did you only know your parents?"

"Oh…" I sighed. "It's a long story, but—"

"I'd love to hear it," she interrupted, urging me to go on, perhaps a little too eagerly.

"Really?"

Trudi nodded solemnly, then practically whispered, "Really."

I took a contemplative sip of coffee, then told her about myself. Although I had my suspicions of what might have happened to me, I couldn't be sure. In telling my story I tried to protect my parents best as I could; but, as I heard my own story out loud, I realised it didn't sound good at all. Even in my telling to Fionn, I'd left certain aspects of it out because even in my head it sounded farfetched. Strange. I watched Trudi as I told her about my extraordinary life, and at one point her facial expression changed, and it wasn't subtle —not in the least.

"What is it?" I asked.

Her eyes filled with tears as she attempted to speak. Her dramatic reaction to my story puzzled me, leaving me wondering what had triggered her emotions.

"Siobhán, I… I… you… you might…" she caught a sob. "I know this may sound… I dunno, but… I think you're my… my… sister! *My identical twin sister.*"

"Well, yeah," I replied, cocking my head quizzically. "I believe we've established we look enough alike to be twins, but…"

"No, no," Trudi interrupted emphatically, shaking her head as she wiped tears from her face. "I mean, my *birth* twin. Siobhán… I had… I *have* an identical twin sister. Her name was… *is* Hilde."

I gasped softly.

"We were born December twenty-first, nineteen fifty-three. Hilde's older by three minutes, thirty-three seconds."

"But… I… what…?"

"Hilde… erm… somebody stole her from our pram when we were not quite two months old. From in front of this very house."

"*No...*" I whispered as my insides churned.

"Yeah. Mum... we... we were off for our daily walk up to the store. She'd forgotten her pocketbook in the house and ran back inside to get it. Not away even a minute. When she came out... Hilde was... gone. Next day, Mama and Papa got a crudely written ransom note asking for money, but even though they met all the demands, no one ever came for it, or... and... and our Hilde never... she... never came back.

"My parents... were heartbroken. I only ever knew them as sad, but I never understood why. I often wondered, but never dared ask. They were older. Mama had us in her early early forties, and Papa was fifteen years older. I wondered sometimes if they regretted having me was why they were so sad. When I was twelve, they both died—seven and a half months apart. Papa went first from a heart attack. Mama followed with a massive stroke. Both should have survived, according to the doctors, but...

"Now? I'm convinced they were completely heartbroken over losing Hilde and never got over it. After they died, my aunts, uncles and grandparents told me of happier times, but I never ever remember either of them laughing. Ever. Smiles were rare and were always, *always* shaded with sadness.

"Left an orphan, I moved in with my Aunt Jo, erm... Josephine, and Uncle Remi until I turned eighteen. That's when my Aunt Jo finally told me the truth about my stolen twin sister. She told me everything, and it... it rocked me. Eviscerated me, like... Yeah. I... I'd always felt... I don't know... incomplete? Or... unduly alone my *entire* life. Aunt Jo said Mama and Papa didn't tell me because they didn't want to make me feel bad, or sad, or..." Trudi sighed. "But, I instantly understood why I'd felt the way I did all my life."

While Trudi told me her... *our* story, I must have stopped breathing. I became lightheaded until I finally took a deep breath. "Wow," I said, exhaling hard.

"Yeah… yeah… Anyway, Mama and Papa left the house and everything to me, so when I came of age, I just came back home."

I shook my head. "I'm so sorry, Trudi. I cannot imagine—"

Trudi interrupted. "I think… Siobhán, I… you… you might be my long-lost sister."

"What?" I asked, only partly shocked because I had come to the same conclusion.

"I really do. It makes sense, doesn't it? I mean, *look at us.* This is not a mere coincidence. This is… *cosmic!* And, how your parents raised you? Odd, yeah?"

"Yeah… odd," I muttered. I had to agree with her. Things like us don't just happen.

Dreamlike is how I would describe the rest of my visit with Trudi. All my life I, too, had felt odd, different, alone—despite Mam and Da—and as it turned out, it seemed I may have had a legitimate reason for my feelings. Not hardly in this world two months, I'd likely been separated from an actual part of me. I realised sitting there with Trudi, I'd felt more in harmony with the world, I suppose, that day than I ever had.

At the end of the visit, we agreed to get genetic testing. Back then, it wasn't as easy to learn what we can now from testing, but at least we'd have confirmation whether we were even related to each other. If we were, we would need no further proof. As it stood, that we looked and sounded exactly alike was probably evidence enough. Though our accents had slight differences, as was our vocabulary and regional slang, the tone and timbre of our voices were identical—as were we. We were both left-handed. Trudi's family photos and memorabilia had gone into storage when she redesigned the house, but she promised she'd retrieve them in time for our next visit.

The time I spent with Trudi fascinated me to no end. I learned quite a lot about my presumed identical twin that day. Trudi had been an honor student throughout school, graduating from university with honors. She earned degrees in both architecture and art history. She'd just recently started working for a firm specializing in custom residential properties in Perth, though her future plans included a graduate degree in architectural design. She'd already redesigned and remodeled her house, which was grand. She had a boyfriend, Trevor, she felt certain she would someday marry.

Her grandparents had all passed, but she had two aunts and three uncles with their respective spouses still living. Only widowed Aunt Jo still lived nearby, with the rest of her siblings and their families scattered to the four corners of the earth.

Still reeling from my visit with Trudi, when I left Perth, I didn't return to Melbourne. Instead, I set off for Ireland to meet with the private detective Fionn had found. The detective couldn't speak nor read The Cant, but he had the connections we needed to find Quinn. Though Fionn urged me to not get my hopes too high, when I boarded the jet for Ireland, the prospect of what I might find there excited me. I'd given Trudi the information about where I'd be staying so when the results of our tests came back she could contact me.

Six weeks later, still looking for Mam's sister, Quinn, I received a phone call in my hotel room in Dublin. It was Trudi, excited to share the grand news—*we were sisters!* It's funny, but when first presented with the possibility I might have an exact twin, I thought I understood shock. But, when the DNA results of our sisterhood came back positive, it was more like a bombshell, or a meteor crashing onto my head, than shock. So many emotions I'd tamped down in case it turned out to be nothing burst through the surface like a geyser.

After Trudi shared the results, she continued talking to me, but I honestly recall little of what she said other than that she'd sent a copy of our tests, my original birth certificate and pictures of our family to me in Ireland.

Our family.

With so much to process, rather than shut down, my mind seemed to enter a hyper state. After all my years in the dark, wondering, I finally had a birthdate, *and* a name—Gunhild Evy Johansen-Arvesen. My sister's full name was Gjertrud Eli Johansen-Arvesen. I had actual biological parents, Grethe Johansen-Arvesen and Erik Arvesen from Trondheim, Norway. I had aunts, uncles and cousins. I was twenty-one years old, from Perth, and... an identical twin. What's more, I wasn't Irish, but full-blooded Norwegian! Before hanging up the phone, I promised Trudi I'd be back for a visit as soon as I finished up in Ireland. I was excited to see her again knowing the truth of us.

A week later, I received the package from Trudi. I will confess, I wept an ocean of tears as I combed through the photos, seeing my actual parents for the first time, photos of Trudi as a baby and a growing child. That could have been, no... *should have been*, my life. Though I loved Mam and Da as the only parents I knew, in fact, they had robbed me of the authentic life that was mine. Not to mention what they did to my biological sister, my mother and father, and the rest of my family—the torture of losing and not knowing what had happened to their wee darling girl all that time.

Despite the new and unsettling discovery of my origins, I still wanted to and needed to find Quinn, but couldn't wait to see my sister again. *My twin sister...* my mind boggled.

34

Fallon O'Toole

∞ ∞ ∞ ∞ ∞

A little while after Joan died, I wondered again about Mam's sister, Quinn. Then, after Pippa's unexpected departure, my attention to Mam and Quinn and my maternal family ties resumed in earnest. I still had Mam's letters; but after several years, could not decipher them. I'd left a forwarding address in Dunkeld should Quinn write again, but as I had received nothing in years, I enlisted the advice of Fionn. If there was anything to be done, he would know.

Indeed, when I showed the letters to Fionn, he guessed the unintelligible words might be a thing he called The Cant, also known as Gammon, a Traveler language. Travelers were an Irish group, he explained, who, like their name indicated, travelled around the countryside. Some were grifters, others were tinkers and tradesmen looking for work wherever they found it; and, they had their own language. As far as Fionn was aware, typically, it wasn't a written language.

Fionn proposed the possibility my parents might have been Irish Travelers. Or Gypsies. His understanding was that most of them were illiterate. In fact, it surprised him to learn Mam was able to read and write at all. He also suggested the possibility Quinn and Mam somehow translated their spoken language onto paper, which would explain why neither of us were able to make heads or tails of it.

Sitting in a cafe across town, I watched Fionn study one of Mam's letters, keeping quiet while he pondered.

"Hmmm…" he uttered softly. "I think, darling… there's only one thing left to do."

I leaned in, intrigued. "That is…?"

Fionn pulled his gaze up from the letter as he laid it on the table. He raised an eyebrow as he looked directly at me. "We'll hire a private detective, maybe even get lucky to find one who knows the Cant—but who can also read it."

I didn't respond right away, as I mulled over my response. Finally, "Is there… such a person?"

Fionn laughed. "Yes, Siobhán… well, I hope so, anyway. I have some contacts in Europe. Let me reach out to them and see what we can see. I'll tell you now, unless it's by some miracle, you'll never find Quinn any other way. Not on your own, you won't. It won't be cheap, but…" he laughed again, "I suspect you'll manage it alright. Yeah?"

I nodded, smiling. "Yeah."

∞ ∞ ∞ ∞ ∞

After several months of waiting, searching and then working in Ireland with the private detective Fionn had hired for me, Rory Dolan, I finally met Mam's sister, Quinn. She'd been living in Dublin, not as Quinn, but as Fallon O'Toole—just one of many roadblocks we ran into trying to locate her. The most prevalent roadblock was that no one who we suspected might know her would share any information with Rory. I pestered him mercilessly, hoping he'd divulge how he finally broke through the wall of silence, me being the curious type. But no matter how I tried, Rory remained tight-lipped on the subject. He'd just laugh and say it was a proprietary trick of the trade he'd prefer not to divulge. Given that he'd found Quinn, in the end, I really didn't care how he got it done, just that he did.

Rory met with her first, explaining we weren't looking to harm her, nor did we have any legal motivations. Apparently, strangers hunting her down made her skittish. Funny that. Rory assured her her niece, me, only wanted to learn more about her mam, and wanted nothing else. After days of consideration, Quinn, rather Fallon, agreed to meet with me. She worked the mid-shift at an apparel factory, but suggested we meet at Sheehan's, a pub on Chatham Street, at ten the next morning. It seems Fallon was friends with Sheehan's manager, who agreed to let us meet before the pub opened.

The impending meeting had me nervous, and worried sick about what I might learn about Mam and Da. I had a deep sense of foreboding I couldn't shake. Because of my anxiety, I hardly slept the night before. As I left to meet Fallon the next morning, I found Rory waiting for me outside my hotel. I'd told him I wanted to meet with Fallon on my own; but despite my protestations, he insisted upon accompanying me. I'm pretty certain Fionn had a little something to do with Rory's hovering. I finally consented under the condition he would keep his distance, and stay in the background. I insisted on meeting Fallon one-on-one and refused to budge. Reluctantly, Rory agreed to my terms.

The moment I spotted Quinn entering the pub, there was no doubt I'd found Mam's sister. Though older, with a bold streak of white like Mam's through her long, slightly wavy medium brown hair, Fallon looked to be two, perhaps three inches taller than Mam had been, with a bit more meat on her bones. A lump caught in my throat when I first saw her, surprising me as I fought back tears. She seemed surprised by me and my emotional response to her.

"Y'must be Siobhán," she said to me with a smile, displaying a familiar gap in her front teeth. She noticed Rory lurking well behind me.

"Dat your bodyguard standin' over dere?" she asked with a chuckle. Her Irish accent instantly reminded me of Mam and Da. It'd been donkey's years since I'd heard authentic Irish unmolested by Australian. Mine had disappeared years earlier, but the silent h's and dropped gs were almost music to my ears.

I nodded with a shrug.

She called out to the bartender, preparing for his day. "Oi, Mick!"

"Oi, Fallon," he replied with a distracted smile. "De usual?"

"Aye, mate. Black stuff 'n uisce beathe." She turned to me, "Whatcha 'avin', girl?"

I stammered, "The-the-the… same?"

Fallon laughed. "Y'sure 'bout dat?"

I nodded, not sure at all.

"Make it two, Micky." Fallon took off her grey wool coat and threw it onto the booth bench. "G'on 'n si'down. I need de Jacks. I'll pick up our drinks on me way back."

Fallon left me and headed to the public restroom on the farside of the pub. I took off my green corduroy jacket, tossed it onto the seat, then slid into the booth opposite Fallon's deposited coat. While I waited, as is my habit, I took in my surroundings. Several minutes later I saw her at the bar conversing with Jack the Bartender while he prepared our drinks.

It seemed to me the pub had been around for at least several decades, with a sense of worn warmth I found right inviting. Though dissimilar in many ways to The Brown House Inn, it still felt oddly familiar to me. I soaked in every detail. Within minutes,

Fallon interrupted my visual survey as she arrived at our table expertly holding two pints of Guinness and two shot glasses filled to the top with Irish whiskey.

"'Ere y'go, love," Fallon said with a smile in her voice. She raised her glass to me. "Sláinte." Still standing, she put the small glass up to her lips and tossed her head back, consuming the whiskey in one swift gulp, followed by a long pull on her Guinness. "Ahhh… Mam's nectar," she purred, her Irish thick as ever as she gracefully slid into the booth.

I followed her lead, self-consciously muttering the Irish toast back to her. I slowly poured the liquor into my mouth and down my throat, instantly appreciating the warmth of the whiskey as it oozed through my body, its resultant courage a bonus.

Fallon stared at me for what seemed like forever, and I wordlessly let her, not feeling self-conscious in the least. At last, she asked me what had brought me all the way to Ireland from Down Under to seek her out.

I asked her if she knew about Mam. *Kellen.*

"Y'd know more'n me. She need sumtin'? Dat why she sent ya?"

My stomach clenched. *She didn't know.* She'd never gotten my letter.

"*Erm…* Mam… *Kellen…* and *erm…* Eoin… my da… they, uh…" I stopped. I couldn't think how to tell her. She stared at me, waiting, completely unsuspecting.

"Yeah?"

"They-they-they… they d-d-ied. They're dead," I blurted.

In an instant, the colour drained from Fallon's face leaving her light complexion so pale it was nearly translucent. "Dead?" she whispered. "Yer not takin' a piss…?"

"I'm not," I whispered back. "I-I'm… so… so… sorry. I… I-I-I sent you a letter, but… They…" I drew in a deep breath, dreading this part of our meeting. "It was flu… probably. Maybe. 1967."

"Nineteen… 1967? Why, dat's… dat's…"

"Yeah, a long time since now," I admitted with regret.

Fallon collapsed back into the booth seat. "Why I stopped 'earin' from 'er…"

I nodded. I pulled Fallon's letters to Mam from my bag. "I found these, but… I didn't understand them—still don't, so I… I wrote you at this address," I said, pointing to the return address on one of the envelopes, "but… I never heard back."

Fallon pulled out a box of Dunhill cigarettes. She offered one to me.

"N-no… no, thank you," I replied.

"Y'mind?" she asked.

"N-n-n-no."

Fallon quickly lit up, fighting back tears as she did. Her hands shook a little while lighting the cigarette, then, once lit, with the cigarette held between her lips, she pulled smoke deeply into her lungs. She blew the smoke to the side so as not to blow it in my face, closing her eyes as she did. "'ow d'ya not get it," she asked, her eyes still closed.

"Huh?"

"D'plague. Erm… flu, y'said?"

"Oh… But… but I-I-I did… get it. After they passed… though. I-I-I… I thought I… I might die, too. I was… can't believe I didn't… actually."

Fallon opened her eyes and set her gaze directly on me. She had dark green eyes, not blue like Mam's. They glimmered brightly with tears on the verge of spilling.

"Dey get buried proper?" she asked, her voice quiet and slightly hoarse.

I nodded. "Y-y-y-yes. I… did. I… buried 'em myself."

"You?" she asked, reeling back with surprise. "On yer own?"

I nodded again.

Fallon's eyes squinted as she continued to stare at my face. "But y'wouldn't've been more'n…" I recognized her attempting the math in her head.

"I think I was thirteen?"

She fell quiet for a long time.

"Well," she answered, finally. "Dey raised y'right, at least."

I had so many questions for Fallon, but I'd feared our first meeting wasn't the right time to seek answers from her. Until her last comment, I'd been paralysed with indecision.

"W-w-what do you m-mean? You said 'at least?'" I asked. "What…?"

Fallon shook her head with a sigh, then took another drag from her cigarette. "Whatcha know 'bout… yer… mam 'n yer da?"

"Actually, erm… not much."

"*Hmph.*"

"I… I'm not… I wasn't… I-I know I wasn't… theirs," I mumbled. "I-I-I… I know that. I-I-I know what they did… where they got me."

"Oh… y'do, do ya?" Fallon asked, incredulous and seemingly wary at the same time.

"Mmm hmm. They stole me… from my real family in Perth."

"Naw, how…? How wouldya…?"

"I… erm… Just a-a f-f-ew months ago, I-I-I met my sister. My *identical twin* sister. She told me everything—well, at least a-a-as much as she knows."

Astonished, Fallon exclaimed, "Yer a twin?"

I nodded. "I am. Identical."

"Shite…" Fallon's shoulders sagged as she sighed heavily. "Well, naw… dat's sum kinda fucked fuckery, 'tis."

"It is. But…"

"Aye?"

"Quinn… erm, I mean, *Fallon*… Sorry."

"Eh, 's all right." Fallon waved her hand in the air as if to dismiss my error.

"Well, I… I have so many questions, I-I-I… I know nothing about them. I only just learned their names after… they… erm… departed. I just… I didn't know they weren't my real mam and da, but... I didn't know any different. I thought they w-w-were mine, 'n I loved them. Now, I-I-I just... I..."

"I'll tell ya all about 'em, lass, but... Gonna need a lot more Black stuff," Fallon said, then downed the rest of her Guinness. "Y'all right?" she asked as she slid out of the booth. "Need a top-up?"

"I-I... I don't... no..." I muttered, looking at my nearly full pint, then watched Fallon as she walked to the bar. She was different from how she was before I told her about Mam. Her posture had deflated some, and she'd lost the lightness in her step. I didn't even know her, yet my heart ached for her. I looked across the pub to see Rory still waiting and watching from another booth. I nodded to acknowledge him. He nodded back in reply.

35

Kellen and Eoin

∞ ∞ ∞ ∞ ∞

"Where t'start…" Fallon murmured as she lit another cigarette.

"Please tell me everything… well, I mean… a-a-anything you can tell me… about them."

Fallon nodded as she contemplated, taking a long, deep drag as she did. She settled back into the booth seat. She seemed smaller. Her strong Irish dialect hadn't lessened at all, but the more she spoke, the more familiar it became.

"Well, den, I s'pose it started when Eoin first come into d'family. He were a wee babby, not more'n two, tree weeks old. Me? I were… dunno, mebbe tree… four year when we got 'im?"

"Erm… when you got him?"

"Eoin... he were an outsider—not one o' us. His mammy? She were Gypsy—Romani—'n his da, 'e were a regul'r Irish lad. Eoin's granda kilt Eoin's da fer spoilin' his wee girl. Not more'n fourteen, she were. We 'appened upon d'Gyps on d'road, 'n... Eoin's granda, 'e told us what Eoin's da did. Didna want Eoin. D'granda left Eoin wid us—traded 'im fer two horses. Dat's how he come t'us."

Stunned, I gasped softly.

"Aye. 'Tis true. Eoin, naw, he were a good lad, but always 'd'otter one.' Never part o' us. 'Tis a pity, really. He tried sumtin' terrible t'be... y'know, one o' us, 'n 'e were grand wit d'horses, but..." she shrugged, "half Gyp, 'im," then pulled on her cigarette.

She must have seen in my face that what she said puzzled me.

"*Romani* blood, 'im—e'd *never* be us." She shrugged. "Not 'is fault, but... 's our way. Kellen, naw, she got born a wee bit after Eoin come. D'two of 'em come up togedder—always togedder. Peas 'n a pod, dem two." She held up her index and middle finger pressed together. "Like dis. When dey was wee," she shrugged, "no one paid 'em no mind, see? But den... dey begun t'change, 'n me da, Kellen's 'n mine, he wouldna have 'em spendin' time togedder like dey did. Him, me da, 'e knew what were 'appenin' 'tween 'em 'fore anyone.

"We was a big clan, Siobhán... mmmm... six, mebbe seven families all togedder? But Da, 'e said no more, 'n 'e banished Eoin from d'family. Trew him right out t'd'cold. Couldn't've been more'n... twelve? Tirteen? 'im, Eoin? Trown out like he were nuttin', but... 'e never left. Nah. 'e lived in d'woods or just outta sight o' where we was d'whole time. Kellen 'n 'im? Dey snuck around fer 'bout a year after d'banishment. I knew 'e never left, but not me da nor me mam. Den? No surprise, Kellen, she come up d'pole."

I shook my head. I didn't understand.

"Preggers. Not even fifteen. Da, oh, 'e were outta 'is mind, and so were me mam. Da swore e'd skin Eoin alive if 'e ever saw 'im

again—'n 'e woulda done, but… d'babby… it didna take—Kellen
lost it halfways trew. Shoulda been it, but nah. Not six monts later
it were, she were up d'pole again. I never seen me da so mad in all
me life. Liked t'scare me t'death is what 'e did.

"Ah, but Kellen, she lost dat one, too. Dat one lasted nigh unto
six monts. Had t'bury it. Still, couldna keep dem two apart. Not
too long 'til she were in d'family way again." Fallon shook her
head, mournfully. "Aye. Da, 'e said dat were d'last straw, 'e did.
Kicked Kellen 'erself clean out d'family. It were a holy show, it
were. Called 'er names—names I canna repeat, 'n banished 'er fer
life. Da swore Eoin, 'e were a dead man if 'e ever got near our
Kellen again.

"Now, me da, 'e 'ad people most ev'rywhere who'd do
whatever 'e wanted if 'e asked 'em. Ev'ryone knew 'e meant it.
Scared shiteless, Kellen 'n Eoin legged it to Glasgow, but den… she
lost dat babby, too. 'Fore dey left, I told 'er t'post letters t'd'postal
office in Galway. Dat way, least I'd know dey was still alive. Den, fer
a long time—'ad t'be more'n a year—I heard nuttin'. I tought dey
was dead, dat Da'd got 'em after all. Not 'til I got a letter from
Australia did I know… dey wasn't dead."

Fallon half grinned. She picked up the letters. "We never got
no schoolin'—wasn't nowhere long enough; 'n it's our way—'ers 'n
mine—keepin' outsiders from knowin'. Yeah," she smiled. "We got
our own way o' talkin' 'tween us."

"The Cant?" I asked.

Fallon shrugged and waved her hand as if to dismiss my
question. "Nah, not d'Cant. Dat's what some call it. Sum, dey call
it Gammon. Aul ting, too. But, me 'n Kellen…" She waved her
hand again. "We 'ad our very own. We didna read nor write, but
what we knew were from otters in d'family—'n dey didna know
much, neidder.

"From dat letter I knew dey was alive. Dat's it… 'n I were glad
fer it. From den on, we'd write, best we could, few times a year. She
got better at it… d'writin'… better 'n me. Tree, four pages she'd

write—sumtimes more." She stared at her cigarette. "Always tought I'd see 'er again. Never tought she'd…" She shook her head with a sigh, then murmured, "Ah… well."

I considered what Fallon told me, with my burning question on the tip of my tongue, but couldn't bring myself to utter the words.

She squinted at me, knowingly.

"What's dat troublin' ya, girl?" she asked. "C'mon… spid it out. Ya got sumtin' on yer mind."

I nodded and pulled a deep breath to steel my nerves, then asked, "Did you… did they tell you about Patrick Mottorshaw? Me?"

"Oh, shite…" Fallon said under her breath. She looked at me, not saying anything for the longest time. "Aye," she whispered, finally. She slowly turned the box of cigarettes in her fingers. "Dey found 'im in Ad'laide 'n 'e… 'e took 'em in. 'e needed 'elp at 'is gaff, 'n dey needed t'hide out from me Da. Patrick, 'e were a good aul fella."

"What about me? Did they…"

"Ah, nah… dey didna. Well, naw… Kellen didna say d'ting dey did, but… d'minute I laid me eyes on ya, I…" she pulled a deep drag on her waning cigarette. With a sigh, she said, blowing the smoke into the air. "I figured what dey done. Kellen said she'd *got* a babby… never said she *had* a babby. All dem miscarriages… I guess I knew, but… I never asked." She shrugged.

"Did…" I hesitated because I was afraid to ask the question I wasn't sure I wanted answered. "Did Mam and Da… did they…" I paused.

"Did dey…?" Fallon leaned forwards.

"I was… *erm*… wondering…" I sighed. "Did they… k-k-k-kill him? P-P-Patrick?"

My question startled Fallon, causing her to lean away from me.

"*Kill 'im?* Y'tink dey *kilt* 'im?"

I shrugged. "Maybe... I dunno..." Her reaction took me by surprise, instantly filling me with shame for asking, and doubt for even thinking it.

She clicked her tongue, shaking her head. "Nah, lass. Far as I could tell, 'e went... ar mire. Mental. Den, one day, 'e just legged it. Dey searched fer days 'til Eoin found 'im—far 'way from d'gaff, dead." Fallon pulled a final drag from her cigarette, then ground it out into the glass ashtray as she quickly blew the smoke from her lungs. "Dey loved 'im like a da, Siobhán. Broke deir hearts 'e went like dat, tinkin' bad tings 'bout 'em 'n all."

I breathed a deep sigh of relief. Mam and Da weren't cold-hearted killers after all.

"Thank you," I whispered.

Fallon remained with me at the pub rather than report for her shift at work. We talked until tea time. Rather, Fallon did most of the talking and I listened. Rory must have decided Fallon was no threat to me as he'd left sometime after noon. One minute he was there, and the next time I looked over in his direction, he'd gone.

In my time with her, I learned that Fallon's husband, Seamus Ó Dubhghaill, had died in a pub brawl with a rival family only four years after they married. They never had children. Heartbroken over losing him, soon after his death she left the family and set off on her own. Staying with the family, she said, was a constant reminder of all she'd lost. Seamus was the love of her life and irreplaceable. She blamed the family and their senseless feuds.

Fallon and Seamus had always wanted something different, but could never leave because of the hold the family had on them. After she lost Seamus, in order to leave the family, Fallon had to actually run away. Changing her name, she fled to Dublin and never looked back, which is why Rory had such a difficult time locating her.

Soon, she secured a job at the dress factory where a co-worker and friend offered to teach her to read and write better. She began moonlighting as a seamstress, making and designing tailored clothing for more well-off residents of Dublin. Fallon felt certain she could leave the factory within a year and work only for herself. When she told me that bit of news, I could see her whole being almost swell with pride.

I learned about Fallon's other siblings besides Mam—five older brothers, two younger brothers, a younger sister, and two older sisters. Three additional siblings had died before they were a year old. It's an understatement to say it stunned me. Had the three younger ones lived, that would have been fifteen children! Growing up as an only child, I couldn't imagine what that might be like. I also learned that including Fallon, only four of the fifteen were still living—as far as she knew, anyway. That, too, escaped my comprehension, and left me feeling somber.

After that day, we only saw each other a few more times, usually meeting for tea. I wanted to stay in Ireland longer, to get to know her even better; but, unexpectedly, I had to leave. I liked Fallon well enough, and could have even grown to love her—but as a friend, not an aunt. After all, because Mam and Da had stolen me, Fallon and I weren't even rellies. I was, for all intents and purposes, an outsider just like Da had been.

At least I got to know a little more about the people who raised me, who pretended to be my proper mam and da. I've tried my best not to hate them for what they did to me and my birth family, and I think I've been successful in doing so. I have no ill will towards them—only regret.

I Hardly Knew Ye

∞ ∞ ∞ ∞ ∞

It had taken three months to find Mam's sister Quinn before I could get back to Perth. Once I'd found her, I wanted us to spend more time together, mostly in order to learn about Mam and Da. Of course, my desire had been dampened after learning they weren't my proper mam and da; but, still, they were all I knew. It was impossible to trade my true life experiences with something I never had.

After talking with Quinn, I more fully understood why Mam and Da would resort to stealing me, and their assumed justification for doing so as well. At the time, I found it difficult to forgive them for that, but I believe with my heart they didn't take me for evil reasons. When all is said and done, Mam and Da gave me a wonderful childhood, filled with love and adventure. I cannot say I am who I am solely because of how they raised me, but they certainly laid the foundation upon which I built the rest of my life.

As fate would have it, I had to cut my visit with Quinn short and leave Ireland far sooner than planned. I'd received a cable from Trudi's Aunt Jo asking me to contact her ASAP. Once Trudi and I confirmed we were sisters, all the rellies had begun calling me, especially the aunts and uncles—one right after the other. They were quite lovely people, each crying with joy I'd been found. Funny, I'd never really felt lost... or had I?

I spoke to my many cousins as well. I can just imagine what their phone bills were, as our calls were quite lengthy. I heard from Aunt Jo in Perth, Aunt Ann and Uncle Fritz in Hong Kong; Aunt Signy and Uncle Henry in Oslo, Norway, Aunt Frida and Uncle Mikal in New York City, and Aunt Nora and Uncle Bertram in Bern, Switzerland. Aunt Josephine, the widow, phoned me most often. What a surreal experience, I'd think, to speak to strangers I'd never met who said they loved me, were convinced they knew me, and who insisted upon calling me Hilde. Only Trudi called me Siobhán. Trudi and I spoke at least once a week, and sometimes twice. We couldn't seem to get enough of each other.

Days before receiving Aunt Jo's urgent message, I'd had a terrible, disturbing dream. When I awoke from it, startled, and drenched with sweat, I remembered nothing of it, only that it startled me... well, I actually can't say precisely how it left me. I suppose *incomplete* is the best I can describe. I couldn't seem to shake it, and the feeling stayed with me until I received the cable from Aunt Jo. Intrigued by the urgency evident in her communique, I decided to call her before calling Trudi. I'd planned on calling my twin to tell her the latest of what I'd learned from Quinn. I wanted to stay and find out even more, but wanted to reassure Trudi I'd be back in Australia soon. My desire to spend time with my sister had eclipsed my commitment to learning more about Mam.

Shortly after speaking with Aunt Jo, an ocean of tears followed. Between her own woeful sobs, Aunt Jo informed me that Trudi, my long lost identical twin sister, had been killed in an auto accident with a co-worker only days before.

In that moment, before Aunt Jo finished telling me, time stopped for me. Even though it's impossible for it to have done so, I want to say time literally stopped. My brain stopped working, and I almost felt like an apparition—there, but not.

"*How? How did this terrible thing happen?*" I asked, nearly incoherent as I sobbed into the phone.

It seems a commercial truck travelling the opposite way on the highway had lost control from a blown tyre, came across the road and hit Trudi's friend's car head on. The authorities are fairly certain they all died instantly. How they could be so sure, I can't say, but for the sake of my sanity, I needed to believe them. Just the possibility of my twin suffering even for a second was too much for me to bear.

In a flash of time, it was as if the very air I breathed had been violently ripped from my lungs—directly followed by the violent shredding of my heart. Woefully unprepared for the onslaught of emotions for a person I'd only met face-to-face once before, incapacity engulfed me. In short order, I understood my terrible dream wasn't a dream at all. No, it was a most dreadful premonition, or worse. Perhaps what I experienced was the very moment Trudi died—the same instant a part of me died as well.

The next time I saw my sister was also the last time—at her funeral. I'd only just begun getting to know her, but even so, we had created a deep connection. Not only that, but she was me in so many ways. As I looked down at her, lying so serenely in her coffin, it was as if I were saying goodbye to myself. It was both disturbing and incomprehensible to me. Yes, it was more than surreal. I've never experienced such an overwhelming sense of bereavement and loss in my life before or since.

While at the funeral, I finally met my aunts, uncles, and cousins in the flesh for the first time. And, Trevor, Trudi's boyfriend. Poor, lost and bereft, Trevor. From each of them, I sensed they found me, myself—the spitting image of Trudi—quite disturbing and comforting at the same time. For me, the entire experience, start to finish, overwhelmed me. I didn't mind meeting them, and I wanted to; but on that day, the only person I yearned to see and get to know better, and form a lifelong bond with, lie dead in a fancy box. I was angry, gutted, and utterly lost. Robbed—*again*. I hardly knew Trudi, but... fact is, I suppose I knew her better than anyone else I'd ever known. Truth is, I loved her.

After the service, they buried her next to our parents. Later, I learned she had recently changed her will, making me the beneficiary of her house and most of her belongings. You could have knocked me over with a soft breeze. The family had also advocated giving the remainder of Trudi's belongings to me as well —familial heirlooms and the like as I had been deprived of my family all those years prior. I protested, but they insisted, it being the right thing to do, they said. I was incapable of speaking because of me blubbering my face off; but in time, I told them how much what they did for me touched me—more than I ever hoped to express.

I still own Trudi's house, and everything in it is exactly the same as it was when we first met since we were separated as infants. I have the house cleaned and maintained regularly; and when I have the opportunity to travel to Australia, I divide my time between the inn, the farm and Trudi's. While at hers, I'll spend hours and hours studying our family photographs. It hurts to do so, deeper than I can express, but it connects me to a family of strangers in a way I'd never known with Mam and Da.

I've never called the house mine, because I consider it my sister's. Little has changed over the years, as I've left it be, so it sits as a shrine of sorts to my dear departed twin. I suppose it keeps her 'alive' for me. For that brief moment when I enter the home, and I relive the exact moment we first laid eyes on each other, I'm reminded why I leave it as it was. The moment is fleeting, but significant. When I leave this world, I'll leave Trudi's house to our cousins, the last of our biological family, who may do as they wish with it. No family members live in Perth now, but when I'm gone, they can use it as a holiday house, rent it, sell it, or do whatever they choose with it, as it will no longer matter to me.

After I met Trudi and found out about who I really was, I gave great consideration to assuming my birth identity as Gunhild Evy Johansen-Arvesen. After Trudi was killed, though, I just couldn't do it. It was almost as if Gunhild Evy Johansen-Arvesen, or Hilde as my birth family called me, died along with her identical twin. Or, perhaps she died the day she was stolen.

To this day, if one of my relatives calls me Hilde, or I happen to see my birth name among Trudi's things at the house in Perth, it's as if she, Hilde, is another person. As if they're speaking to someone other than me. Well, I suppose, you might say, she *was* another person. I was only Hilde for less than two months before Mam and Da took me and made me Siobhán. Who Hilde might have been had her life not been stolen is impossible to say. Trudi was the closest I ever got to finding out.

It's all so difficult to comprehend, though I have spent decades trying. These days, I no longer bother. I've learned I can't change anything that's happened and have come to accept the popular adage—it is what it is.

Epilogue

Trudi's premature departure from my life and this world left me unmoored and excruciatingly alone. When I signed half of the inn over to its new owners, though our regular patrons kept their gathering place, and despite me claiming The Cousins' flat for my own, I still felt as if I'd lost my home. My chosen family—Trix, Joan, Darwins, my sister… even Fionn—were all gone. Fionn hadn't passed, of course, but he'd relocated to America, on the other side of the globe.

Yes, while I'd gone searching for Quinn in Ireland, after hinting at a change of scenery for a long while, in my absence, Fionn had immigrated to America. Fionn surprised me when he returned my call from California instead of Melbourne, breaking the news of his big move to me then. Somehow, despite his long-time desire to go to America, I'd had it in my head he'd wait in Melbourne for my return.

I'll admit it, his news crushed me. I didn't let on to Fionn in so many words, but he knew. I could just tell. We were familiar enough with each other to sense when something was off. Still, he never mentioned it, nor did I.

For the next four years I knocked about, visiting Hong Kong, South Africa, Europe, Scandinavia, the United Kingdom, and New Zealand. On one occasion I returned to Ireland, in hopes of reconnecting with Quinn, but she had apparently moved on—disappeared. I couldn't find her again. Truth is, I didn't make a herculean effort to search for her, figuring she didn't want to get found—by me or anyone else.

And, to be honest, I was almost half glad for her vanishing. Aside from being my mam-in-name-only's sister, she wasn't anything to me. Not to seem cold, but I'd learned what I needed to from her when we'd met on my first trip. Beyond that, I had no genuine reason or desire to find her or even to see her again.

All those years I roamed about aimlessly, trying to... well, I suppose I was in search of something, though for what I didn't know. I suppose I hoped I'd know it when I found it. Or, perhaps my travels were more about avoiding that something than finding it. Maybe a bit of both. Hard to tell. Whatever the reason, I had a strange feeling if I stopped moving, just like a shark, I might die if I did, so... I kept moving.

Often, I'd travel on cruise ships, one of my preferred modes of transportation. Sometimes I'd book fare as a passenger, other times I'd sign on as a member of the crew. Once I even stowed away! The time I stowed away I'd hoped for a grand adventure; but as it happened, I spent more time hiding in the cargo area than anywhere else. It was an adventure of sorts, but overall, it was a miserable experience, and not one of my most brilliant ideas.

Trains were my next favourite mode of transportation, though having learned my lesson as a stowaway, my excursions were always as a passenger. Train or ship, it didn't matter—I favoured them both equally. They each offered adventure, beautiful scenery and grand comfort. Or, I'd rent a car and drive; but I never took buses if avoidable.

The rugged life wasn't for me, as I'd lived quite enough of it on the farm. And, after my experience in South America travelling for days on a miserably hot, antiquated buses, that was it for me. I shied away from flying whenever possible, reserving it for the transport of last resort. If I couldn't cruise, take a train or drive, I would fly, but with great reluctance. Again, my experience with South American travel soured me on buses; and particularly, anything with wings.

I yearned to experience life in as many ways possible, which I suspect drove my penchant for travel. But I committed to roaming as an observer, not a participant. Whether it was a conscious decision, I cannot say. Nonetheless, I took everything in, quietly, as if a bodach. All the while, I did my best to ignore the emptiness that seemed to have engulfed the whole of me. I purposefully avoided making friends, choosing to isolate myself, isolation being a state I could handle, because, well, I understood it. I truly believed isolation would shield me from hurt.

The people I'd grown to love and consider my family over the previous five or so years had all gone, either permanently or were so far away it sometimes seemed they may as well have been gone forever, and it hurt. Immensely. To keep the pain at bay I kept moving, remaining unavailable, unattached. Since living an isolated life on the farm, it was somewhat easy for me to survive alone; though, in truth, there were times the loneliness threatened to engulf me.

In effect, I lived a nomad's life, never staying in one place longer than a month or two at the most. If I found myself on the verge of making a meaningful human connection, without a second thought I'd pack up and move on, leaving the possibility of feeling something, anything, behind. In the deepest part of me, I wasn't willing to take the chance of being hurt again—certainly not then, and hopefully, not for a long time. Another heartbreak would surely kill me.

I travelled light, with only three changes of clothes, which I'd wear until I tired of them. Less to carry, less to launder. After four to six months, I'd toss them and buy a whole new wardrobe—of no more and no less than three outfits.

Of all the places I visited, I favoured the United Kingdom most. I have a certain affinity to England, specifically. I thought Norway might be my most-preferred locale given my newfound heritage, but something about the UK spoke to me like nowhere else. I'd spend a few months in Europe, only to find myself drawn back across The Channel again to England. Partly, I'll confess, because it was the one place I'd allowed myself to connect with another human.

It's a story I wouldn't mind telling you today, but at this time, I cannot. I swore on my life I would keep that relationship to myself unless and until I were the last of us standing. We're both still alive, thank goodness, so it's mum for now. Even though the unique connection I'd made there eventually evaporated, England remained my number one travel destination.

When I needed funds to continue my wandering, I'd contact Fionn through his message service. He'd then promptly procure whatever I might need, wiring it to wherever I was at the time. I called it my mad money. Years before, I'd heard Trix use the phrase "mad money" and concluded it must be money to have fun with and go "mad" with it, and so I adopted the phrase.

It wasn't until years and years later I learned it was actually money women took with them on a date, just in case they quarreled with their date and needed car fare home. There are other versions that have popped up over the years, but honestly, I prefer mine. I rarely needed much spending money as I am naturally frugal, despite not needing to be.

From time to time, I'd allow myself to splurge on a fancy hotel and live the high life for a tick; but, before I knew it, I'd ache for simplicity, ending up staying in simple pensions again. I have a talent for stretching my operating funds quite far.

When I could actually speak to Fionn, even if it was just for a few minutes, it thrilled me, making me ever so happy. He'd typically sound a million miles away depending on the quality of our connection, but I didn't mind. I missed him terribly.

Whenever we spoke I was reminded of what I'd had at the inn. We'd been a family—Fionn, Trix, Joan, Pippa, Darwins and me. Them and, of course, Trudi, my biological identical twin sister who I only knew but for a minute. Sometimes, though, no matter how much I longed hearing it, just the sound of Fionn's voice would cut me to the marrow, reminding me of how much my chosen family meant to me and all I'd lost.

By mid-December of '78, weary of my nomadic lifestyle, I'd left a message with Fionn's service, asking him to please ring me back. As ever, I wanted his voice in my ear again, but I was also in need of funds to get to my next destination. I'd been in Zurich nearly two months and itched to move on. Problem was, I didn't know where to go next, and almost didn't care. Constant moving about had lost its zeal for me.

It seemed I'd been everywhere in Europe and Scandinavia I ever cared to visit. The Orient interested me somewhat, but not enough to ever return. South Africa wasn't my cup of tea; and, anyway, I'd been there already. The USSR was out of the question, and the Middle East held zero interest for me. I needed to get going again, but... to where?

Sitting on the edge of my queen-sized feather bed, I gazed contemplatively out of my window. As I took in the snow-covered hotel grounds, deliberating my next destination, the state of the world, and whatever other random thoughts happened to pop into my head, the hotel room phone rang, startling me from my near-meditative state.

I gingerly picked up the off-white handset and placed the receiver against my ear. "Hello?" I asked, likely sounding as lethargic as I felt.

"Shiv!" Fionn answered. "Darling! It's you!"

"Fionny!" I exclaimed, perking right up. "G'day, mate!"

"I was just thinking of you when I picked up your message," he replied, a smile apparent in his voice.

"Fair dinkum?" I answered, my own smile commandeering every muscle in my face.

"Fair dinkum! You're in Switzerland," he added with certainty.

"Yep. Zurich. How d'you...?"

"The number."

"Oh... right, right."

"And, The Atlantis Hotel, too, yeah? Ooooh la la... that's swanky, Jillaroo," he chided.

"I know, I know," I admitted, somewhat embarrassed at my extravagance. "I wanted to see how the richies live. It's not that thrilling, y'know. I'm told there're several famous people staying here, but..." I shrugged. "I don't know who they are—not that I'd care if I did, but... Ugh, Fionn! I'm right bored, mate," I whinged.

"Ah... *Tsk tsk*... are ya now," he teased. "*Poooor* bub."

"I am. So bloody sick of snow, Fionny," I sighed, looking out on what I described as a white wonderland, though I was no longer impressed by its stunning beauty. "It's fekkin' everywhere."

"Yeah, yeah... can't imagine, poor thing," he chuckled softly.

"Huh. Wait a sec... where're you?" I asked, hearing unfamiliar sounds coming from his end of the line. Was it static, or...?

"Ah..." Fionn chortled. "My weekend house."

I groaned. "Nah... mate... Is that the ocean I hear?" I asked, about to turn envious at the sounds of crashing waves and the promise of sunshine as I stared at the endless white blanket of snow outside.

"Righto, mate. Malibu. Workin' on my goldie brown suntan as we speak."

"But... erm... wait... I thought... erm, I thought your house was in L.A.."

"It is, love. I've still got the place in Brentwood, but," he chuckled, "I wanted a little beach getaway. Y'know, when the rat race and city life get to be too much," he said with a jovial laugh.

I laughed. "Ah, it sounds grand, Fionn."

"It is. So... You need some dough, love?"

"Yeah, yeah... Not the only reason I called, y'know..." I began, somewhat defensively.

"Oh, no..." Fionn jabbed, his tone dripping with friendly sarcasm.

I giggled. "Nah, yeah... I do miss ya, mate. And, yep... I need money—it's time to move on."

"I figured."

"But, erm... Fionn?"

"Yeah?"

"I've got no idea where to go. Feel like I've been everywhere I ever wanted to go." I sighed. "Much as I hate to say... it might be time to go back."

"Melbourne?"

"Yep... maybe Perth. Dunno..." I answered without enthusiasm. "But to what? You're not there. There's... nothing ... no one for me..." my voice cracked as I tried unsuccessfully to hide my emotions.

Neither of us said anything for several moments while I composed myself.

"Well, love," Fionn said, finally, "I really was thinkin' about you today."

"Yeah?"

"Yeah, because... I think you should come here."

"America?"

"Yeah, Los Angeles. L.A. It's grand, Shiv. You haven't been over yet. It's time, mate."

"Los Angeles, eh?"

"I think you'd like it. Stay with me—long as ya like."

"Yeah?"

"Yeah... I do miss your lovely face."

I laughed out loud. "Not just my face, now, but my *lovely* face, yeah?"

"All right..." he chuckled. "Might've exaggerated a bit."

"Too right!"

"C'mon, love. I've got loads to tell ya, but... let's just say I daren't say on the phone."

"Okay," I answered with hesitance, somewhat perplexed, questioning.

"And..."

"And?"

"Lukey's here."

"Your Lucas? How...? I thought...?"

"Like I said, darling, heaps to tell you. Come see us, love."

I let the telephone line go silent as I mulled over Fionn's offer for a tick. He was right, I'd never been to America. Though, unlike most everyone I'd ever known, I never had a burning desire to visit. I did miss Fionn terribly, and if he enjoyed it enough to buy two houses and leave Australia for good, perhaps it was worth giving it a squizz. If I didn't like it, I decided, I could always leave.

"Okay... Sure. Yeah, I'll do it!" I exclaimed.

"Right on. You will *love* it here."

"All right... I'm gonna trust you, yeah?"

"Natch."

"So, okay, tell me what I need to know. I'll book the next flight out. Hate flying," I muttered as an aside.

Knowing me as he did, Fionn chuckled softly. I could just see him in my mind's eye, with that annoying, knowing smirk of his.

"Siobhán, darling," he began, "start packing. Let me take care of your travel over. Yeah? I'll wire your itinerary over to your hotel as soon as I get you sorted."

"What? Oh, no, no, Fionn... I can't let you—"

"Shush. Call it your birthday prezzie," Fionn interrupted. "Hey?"

"My...? *Ahhh...* right." Startled at first, as I'd been every year by the novel concept of having an *actual* birthday, not the made up one The Cousins gave me, and on a specific date, no less. The idea of having a real one had also thrilled me a bit. Still, each birthday since learning who I really was and when I'd been born, there'd been a sense of melancholy that nibbled around the edges of the thrilling part. I never got to spend even one birthday with my twin sister, Trudi—my birth mate, which left me with an underlying sadness that permeated my soul and never seemed to go away.

"You got me, mate," I sighed. "All right. Get me out of here. I'm done with the white stuff."

"Aye," Fionn replied. "Now, go on and pack, darling. I'll arrange everything. Can't wait to see you, love. Pick you up at LAX in a few days, yeah?"

"Yeah! Erm... LAX?"

"The airport—Los Angeles International, love."

"Oh! Haha," I chuckled. "I'm excited! Cheers, Fionn!"

"Cheers!"

Three days later, on December 21ˢᵗ—my twenty-fifth birthday to be exact—I boarded a luxurious private jet headed for America. It surprised me to find myself as the only passenger on the flight, somewhat easing my flying anxiety, but not entirely. Being up in skies is unnatural and potentially deadly, in my opinion, anyway. The entire flight, both legs of it, the flight crew treated me like royalty. Fionn really knew how to travel in style.

With a two-hour layover at London Heathrow, I landed at Los Angeles International nearly eighteen hours after departing Switzerland. Not having slept a single minute of the trip, I exited the jet bone-tired. Thankfully, I didn't have to look for Fionn as he stood right there, waiting for me with arms open as I disembarked and entered the waiting area. A younger, slightly taller man stood next to Fionn, smiling. It was his son, Lucas, looking as what I imagined Fionn must have looked thirty years before. With his handsome son looking on, Fionn and I hugged, thrilled to pieces to see each other for the first time in four years. Breathing in the familiar aroma of Fionn's earthy cologne and him, I almost melted with relief into his strong, tan arms as I began the next chapter of my strange, but extraordinary life.

To be continued…

Translations

1 Stone = 14 Lbs = 6.35 Kilograms
Metre = 3.281 Feet
Kilometre = 1.609 km = 1 mile
1 Litre = .2642 gal. 1 Litre = .2642 gal.
1 Stone = 14 Lbs = 6.35 Kilograms

Ar mire—Crazy
Bench—Counter, countertop
Black stuff 'n uisce beathe—*Oozy Beetha*
—Guinness and whiskey
Bodach—*Bo-datch*—Ghost or apparition
Chockers—Drunk
Chook, Chooks, Chookies—Hens, chickens
Ciotóg—*Ki-toyg*—Left-hander
Cobber—Friend
Da—Father
Dada—Daddy
Distillate—Diesel fuel
Dunny—Outdoor toilet
Eoin—*Owen*
Fair Dinkum—Truth or speaking truth
Fionn—*Fee-un*
Fizzy—Soft drink
Gaff—House
Jillaroo—Female farmhand
Joie de vivre—*Sha-de-viv*—Fr. Joy of life
Jumper—Sweater
Kilometre = 1.609 km = 1 mile
Knackered—Tired
Loo—Bathroom

Mam—*Mahm*—Mom

Mammy—*Mahmmy*—Mommy

Mashed—Drunk

Metre = 3.281 Feet

Ooroo—Good-bye

Pash—Strong feelings of liking of loving someone or something

Pension—*Pens-ee-on*—European boarding house

Pork Chop—Acting silly or stupid

Quinn Róisín Mahoney Ó Dubhghaill—Quinn *Rosheen* Mahoney O *Du-gall*

Rellies—Relatives

Ripper—Great

Root—Sex

Rotten—Drunk

Siobhán Aoife—*Shivawn Effie*

Sláinte —*Slanch-eh*—Cheers

Snog—Kiss and cuddle, pasionate kissing.

Squizz—A look

Starkers—Naked

Stickybeak—A Gossip

Suss Up—Sizing up

Tea—Dinner

Wanker—Ridiculous person

Whacked—Exhausted

Yoke—Thing

Australia

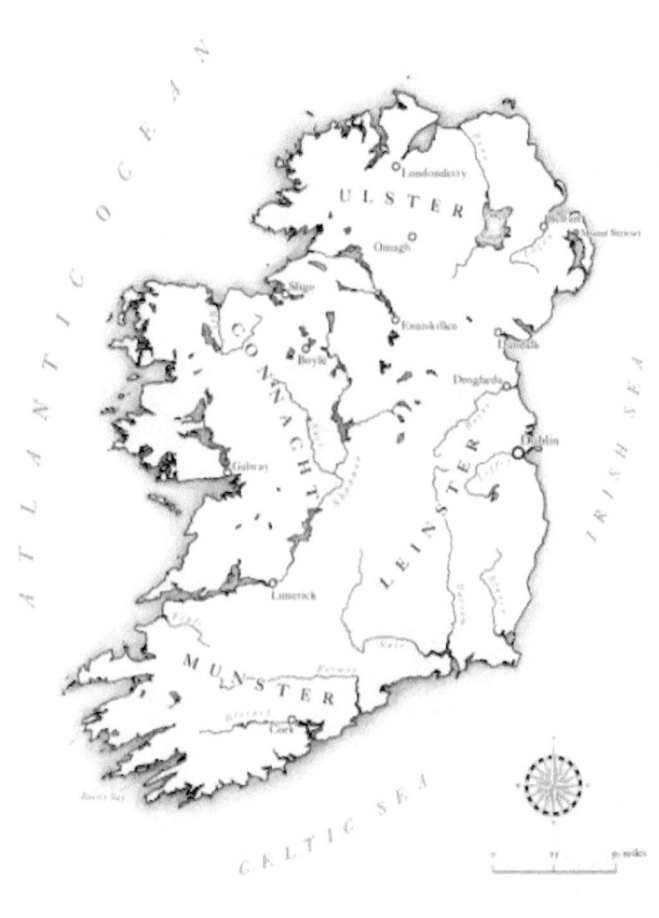

ATLANTIC OCEAN

ULSTER

Londonderry

Belfast Mount Stewart

Omagh

Sligo

Enniskillen

Donegala

CONNACHT

Boyle

Drogheda

Dublin

Galway

IRISH SEA

LEINSTER

Limerick

MUNSTER

Cork

Bantry Bay

CELTIC SEA

My Dear Reader:

Thank you so much for reading my novel, "Nom de Plume—An Extraordinary Life—Vol 1."

If you enjoyed reading Nom de Plume, I invite you to please leave a positive comment on your favorite social media sites, as well as on the website where you purchased it. By doing so, you may help other readers who need help deciding whether to purchase. It will also help increase my book's exposure, which is always so appreciated.

Thank you!

Stay tuned... there's much more to come!

XO Djuna Shellam

P.S. You can now find me on:
　　MeWe.com/i/djunashellam;
　　Patreon.com/djunashellam;
　　Amazon.com/author/djunashellam;
　　Magnhild.com/djuna-shellam;
　　Instagram.com/thedjunashellam;
　　Goodreads.com/djuna-shellam; and,
　　Facebook.com/DjunaShellamAuthor

The Incredible Transformations of

ALICE HOLLYWOOD

The Em Suite—Book 1
A Novel by Djuna Shellam
Copyright 2020 Djuna Shellam
Magnhild Press
All Rights Reserved

Alice Hollywell, the young spitfire from Hollywood, and her best friend, the poor little rich girl Em Martin from nearby Bel Air, CA, are stationed on a remote military base in West Texas in the mid-1970s.

Worldly Alice "Hollywood" Hollywell is notorious for changing "teams" without notice. Em is shy and seemingly sheltered and has a secret. Despite their differences, their friendship blossoms into something they never imagined. The arrest of their friend Whitey and rumors about an investigation into his friends and associates creates a frightening environment, complicating everything.

On base, and particularly within their inner circle, the atmosphere is rife with suspicion and fear. Alice and Em realize the military is a very dangerous place for them, and quickly find themselves in the middle of a rabid witch-hunt. Decisions are made with disastrous consequences.

Alice Hollywood is a bonafide page-turner. Leading the reader down a road of what's next and through myriad subplots, this multi-dimensional story and its equally dimensional characters are a reader's delight. Once you start reading, you won't want to stop, even when you read the last line. But don't worry, because there's much more to come! *Alice Hollywood* is Book One of *The Em Suite Series.*

The Incredible Transformations of Alice Hollywood isn't just a love story. It's history, intrigue, the human condition; drama, comedy, and everything in-between.

Violence, Harsh Language, Adult Situations

Available in Trade Paperback and Digital Formats

Mackenna on the Edge

The Em Suite—Book 2
A Novel by Djuna Shellam
Copyright 2020 Djuna Shellam
Magnhild Press
All Rights Reserved

In this sequel/prequel to *The Incredible Transformations of Alice Hollywood*, nearly twenty years have passed since a fiery crash changed Em Martin's life. Now living in Los Angeles, and known professionally as Mackenna, a recent life-altering tragedy has her in an emotional tailspin. Memories and regrets previously buried and ignored have been churned up.

In a desperate effort to stop her downward spiral into melancholy, Mackenna turns to her writing for emotional support; as well as a vehicle for getting to the root cause of her current mental and emotional frailty. While culling through her life for clues, the Southland is rocked by a devastating earthquake, further complicating Mackenna's difficult self-exploration. Enter Eve, an earthquake refugee and an uncomfortable reminder of a past Mackenna has spent many years trying to ignore—and forget.

A delicate dance of avoidance ensues until a devastating secret is exposed, driving Mackenna to the edge of disaster. Will Eve be the last straw, and push Mackenna over the edge? Or will she be the one to save Mackenna from the lower depths?

In a departure from her first novel, *Alice Hollywood*, Djuna Shellam takes us back and forth in time in a seamless fashion to tell the story in a story.

Strong Language, Adult Situations

Available in Trade Paperback and Digital Formats

Prairie Fire

The Em Suite—Book 3
A Novel by Djuna Shellam
Copyright 2020 Djuna Shellam
Magnhild Press
All Rights Reserved

Angry, debilitated, and depressed, Em would rather just give up and die than get better, but Dot Baverstock has other plans for her. Enter Prairie Vaughn, aka 'Wonder Woman.'

In the third installment of The Em Suite Series, we meet Prairie, the red-headed physical therapist—a female Casanova—who takes on the monumental task of bringing an unwilling Em back to health. Set in Highland Park, Bel Air, and Palm Springs, California between 1976 and 1996, the story deftly travels back and forth in time.

Secrets, drama, heartbreak, and passion offer a similar page-turning and satisfying experience readers have found in *The Incredible Transformations of Alice Hollywood* and *Mackenna on the Edge*. Djuna Shellam has once again created characters you will love to love, intertwined with an entertaining and addicting story. Don't be surprised if you find yourself laughing out loud, spontaneously crying, and maybe even standing in the shower with the cold water on full blast. It's just how Djuna Shellam rolls.

Strong Language, Adult Situations

Available in Trade Paperback and Digital Formats

Dot in the Weeds

The Em Suite—Book 4
A Novel by Djuna Shellam
Copyright 2020 Djuna Shellam
Magnhild Press
All Rights Reserved

Much beloved and fan-favorite Dot Baverstock is back in this fourth installment of The Em Suite—but not in a way you'd ever expect.

Dot has a deep, dark secret they've been keeping for years. When she suffers a traumatic fall, she makes the difficult and daring decision to expose herself to her extended family.

Em and Eve rush out to the Palm Springs desert to the rescue. Along for the ride is Prairie.

Dot's secret—the "Big Mystery" and the true reason the family is needed—is revealed soon after their arrival. It appears far more will be needed from them than caretaking, while also putting them in peril. There's no question. They love Dot. They'll do anything for her—even if it means breaking the law or putting their lives in jeopardy.

Love, tragedy, humor, heartbreak; adventure, mystery, and danger all deliciously intertwine in this fun, yet heart-tugging installment of The Em Suite.

Violence, Harsh Language, Adult Situations

Available in Trade Paperback and Digital Formats

A Woman Like Eve

The Em Suite—Book 5
A Novel by Djuna Shellam

Picking up where we left off in *Dot in the Weeds*… you're not going to want to miss this installment!

Available late 2021.

About The Author

Author of The Em Suite Series and Nom de Plume An Extraordinary Life Vol 1, *Djuna Shellam* was raised on a farm in the countryside of Victoria, Australia. On her own since approximately the age of fourteen, Shellam has traveled the world, picking up interesting experiences along the way. She now resides in North Idaho—until the travel bug bites her once again. She currently has four novels published with Magnhild Press (The Em Suite) and is working on the fifth, which is scheduled for publication sometime in November 2020 (barring the arrival of an Earth-destroying meteor, zombies or, aliens from outer space).

www.DjunaShellam.com

Portrait by Kristina Kauffman
https://www.facebook.com/KauffmanArts/